Women's Work

KARI AGUILA

Cover design by Jessie W. Chandler

ISBN: 0991165004

ISBN-13: 978-0-9911650-0-1

To David Thibodeau, for all his years of writing.

Women's Work

~ One ~

SHE MOVES QUIETLY, mindful of her footfalls, to avoid the broken sections of blacktop. It has become her habit to walk cautiously, even in such well-used areas. Recent reports of raiders have made everyone wary of traveling alone. The woman listens for what might be coming around the next curve, or what might be hiding in the rubble of the burned-out buildings on both sides of her. The only sounds she hears are the rhythmic shush of her thin canvas pants and the subtle breeze rippling through the overgrown grass.

She stops to adjust the straps of her heavy backpack, arching her long spine, her thick blond braid lying heavily over her shoulder. Noticing Queen Anne's lace growing through a wide crack in the road, she stoops to study the deceptively delicate-looking white heads. "Pull it up by the root and it will smell like carrots," a long-ago friend had said. A smile flickers over her face with the memory of the man, dead now for twelve years. He'd been teaching a class at the college the day of the missile strikes.

Grasping a small bunch of stems, she pulls them out of the ground, the tangle of hairy roots sprinkling fresh dirt onto her tattered shoes. She breathes in the scent before choosing two of the largest and best-formed flowers. Sliding the long knife from its sheath on her belt, she holds the stems near their base and quickly cuts off the blooms. Still crouching low to the ground, she visually surveys the broken landscape and listens to the wind. Sure she is alone, she stands and continues along the road.

As she walks, a large earthen mound comes into view, and she veers toward it onto a small dirt path. From this distance, she sees a red fox digging among a pile of bricks and rubble. Its tiny paws claw and scratch, stopping from time to time so its nose can poke and sniff the ground. Catching her scent, the animal's head jerks up. Its black, beady eyes stare at her, its body suddenly frozen. It turns and scurries away, disappearing into the grass.

A marker, held high by scrap wood found after the end of the Last War, leans slightly to the right at the top of the mound. Several branches of a dogwood tree are twined together to form the large circle at the top. A straight weave of branches bisects the circle, a reminder of the balance they hoped to create, and the new peace between men and women. Though hundreds of millions died during that terrible time a decade ago, the majority of corpses didn't get the luxury of a burial. The dozens resting here were the lucky ones who died close to the end of the war, the ones who had family left behind to collect their scattered remains. Few people visit the mound anymore.

A recently covered grave swells from the ground to the left of the mound, and flowers in various stages of decay are scattered over the fresh dirt. She was there on the spring day they buried the man, and had helped the other women prepare him for his grave. They had wrapped him in long strips of cloth and prayed for his soul before they shoveled dirt onto his body. After the burial, they held the hand of the one who had killed him and cried with her for what she had done.

Today, as the sun climbs higher into the clear sky, she stands upwind of the grave and says, "May his mother find peace" as she tosses the white flowers to the ground. Her eyes wander over the small markers that have been pounded into the dirt. Noting the names of people she once knew, she struggles to recall their faces. A few of the names stand out—Carlos Merced, Patricia Jergins, Lila Bertrand. They had been found in their homes, dead from starvation during the second winter after the war. Pulling her eyes away from the graves, she exhales loudly, looks around her, then follows the path back to the main road.

After a quarter mile, she reaches the edge of a sandy bluff and looks down to the water below. A fishing boat is anchored about two hundred yards offshore, bobbing gently in the breeze. Several other boats list to the side in the shallow water along the shore, abandoned and wrecked. She follows a switchback path down to the beach and crouches in the long grass behind the berm before going out onto the sand. She listens to the wind, and her eyes sparkle as she looks intently around the area from her hiding place. Satisfied that she is safe, and ready to begin the market, she emerges and walks out to the water's edge.

Within minutes, another woman emerges from the grass, her long legs easily navigating the rocks and driftwood. Though several years older than the first woman, she is just as tall and thin, and they greet each other with warm smiles and a strong embrace.

"Peace to you, and good morning, Iris," the younger woman says to the new arrival as they pull away from each other.

Iris removes the long bow from her shoulder and sets it gently onto the sand before replying. "Peace to you, Kate. It's good to see you again." Her salt-and-pepper hair sticks out in several wild wisps, seemingly untamed by the bun twisted at the back of her head.

Kate looks her friend over. "Is everything okay? I heard you were sick last week. I was worried."

"No need to worry," says Iris. "I'm fine."

"Anything serious?"

"No, it was just a cold, but I was taken care of. Two of my younger grandchildren doted over me for three days. We had tea parties, and they braided my hair more times than I care to remember, but it was sweet to watch them play mommy for a while." Iris unbuckles her heavy backpack and lowers it to the sand before bending her long body from side to side in a stretch.

Kate squeezes her friend's arm affectionately. "Did you get the food we sent along with Patrice? If we lived closer to each other, I could have brought it myself."

"I got the food," Iris says, nodding.

"Did you get four containers? We sent four."

"I got all four." Iris's chin drops slightly as her eyes narrow. "Look, I know what you're thinking, but Patrice isn't going to steal food from me."

"No, of course not. I wasn't saying—"

"Yeah, but you were thinking it. Kate, that was almost three years ago. And she didn't steal food. She thought she was protecting us from him when she hid it."

Kate glances down at the sand, quickly trying to think of a

way to back out of her accusation. "I know," she says. "And she was right. That man took a lot of our supplies." She smiles at her friend. "I'm just glad you're feeling better."

"I am. Thanks." Iris looks sideways at her and repeats an idea she has spoken of before. "Though I do wish you lived inside the neighborhood instead of out by the river, so far from everyone."

Kate smiles, then looks to the water, squinting as the morning sun sparkles on the surface.

During the next ten minutes, twenty-seven other women arrive through the grass to join Kate and Iris. "Peace to you, and good morning," they say as they gather along the beach. Comfortable together at this weekly meeting, the women talk easily, catching up on news. "How are your children? Is your mother well? Isn't Sarah's birthday this month?"

Kate waves toward the boat anchored in the water, and watches as the captain emerges from the cabin, waving in response. The squeak of ropes passing through metal pulleys carries across the water as a rowboat descends from the side of the larger fishing boat. Within moments, the rowboat slides onto the shore, with several women bending to help pull it halfway onto the sand.

A small woman leaps out of the rowboat and begins to unfold a large sheet of blue plastic. Her curly black hair is cut short, and a wide-brimmed hat shadows much of her dark face while she works to ready the area for the market. At twenty-one, Rhia is one of the youngest women at the market. She learned to fish and to sail from her father when she was only a child during the Last War. Kate often wonders if Rhia's father is still on the fishing boat with her, hiding down in the cabin while the trading takes place.

With a quick shake, the plastic flutters up and flattens

before drifting down onto the sand. Rhia works quickly to unload her boat, setting out twenty-four freshly killed large fish and nearly forty small ones. Then she dumps out a bucket, dropping a dozen small cloth bags onto the sheet, each one tied closed with string. They are filled with salt that she has spent the week desiccating, boiling pot after pot of seawater over driftwood fires along the shore.

Kate and Iris squat to examine the fish lined up on the tarp. The salmon, some over twenty inches long, were caught on their way back to the rivers of their birth to spawn. Strong and meaty on their homeward journey, they will be filleted and dried on racks in the late summer sun.

"This one must be nearly twenty-five pounds," Iris says, lifting the largest fish with both hands. The coho's sides shine silver, with black spots speckling its back and the upper lobe of its tailfin. "He's a beauty."

Two other women step to the side of the boat, and together they pull out a large wooden crate. As they set it on the beach, a crowd gathers around and women begin to paw through a collection of tattered books—*How to Raise Chickens*, *The Urban Farmer*, *Edible Plants of the Pacific Northwest*, *The Household Plumber*, and several others. Finally, Rhia turns to the women with a bright smile, and says, "Peace to you, and good morning. It was a good week for fishing."

The women on the beach have unloaded the contents of their backpacks into neat rows, many taking out jars of carefully preserved fruits and vegetables. An abundance of golden peaches and ruby plums have been prepared during the past weeks. The children have been busy climbing the heavily laden trees to pick the ripe fruit, working in the sun to gather the harvest, avoiding any waste. The older children teach the younger how to choose the best fruit, how to pack them into the baskets and onto the carts, and how to pull the carts around the bomb craters full of broken brick and glass back to mothers waiting to process another batch at home. Late summer is a busy time, but the neighborhood is thankful for the produce during the long, dark winter months.

In addition to precious glass jars of preserved goods, the women have fresh foods packed in homemade boxes and bins. Small containers full of blackberries; large containers of beets, fava beans, and kale; and bunches of carrots, zucchini, and onions are on display. Women lucky enough to tend goats pull jars and jugs of milk out of their packs. The family gardens produce more than enough fresh food during the height of the season, so the women have learned to preserve, learned to share. They were forced to revive this nearly forgotten art of growing food. It had been a choice between that or starving.

After setting out the items she has brought to trade, Kate lifts her backpack and pulls it closer to Rhia. She takes a lightweight cloth bag and a neatly folded square of fabric from the front pocket. Tied inside the bag are green leaves of spinach, kale, and dandelion, mixed with brilliant orange and yellow calendula and nasturtium blossoms. With a smile, she passes the salad to Rhia. "Here you go," she says. "This should get you through the next few days."

"Thank you, Kate."

"I also brought some corn bread for the women in Bellwether. You'll see them Friday, right?"

"Right," Rhia says, taking the small fabric square. "Oh, and one of the children in Campbell sent this down for your neighborhood." Rhia reaches into her pocket and pulls out a small figure carved out of wood. She hands it to Kate with a smile. "I'm sure you'll find someone who'll love it."

Iris moves to the center of the group to officially begin

the market. She raises her hands, and the women become quiet. "Welcome, friends! As the summer comes to a close, we are grateful for the food we have here today. A couple of reminders before we begin: On the first of September we have the Remember Gathering. I hope to see you all in the neighborhood center that day at seven a.m. It's hard to believe it's been fourteen years since the start of the Last War, and we are happy to know it has been ten since the end of it." The women nod, and Kate thinks of the terror of those days. The memories of the sounds, sights, and smells of the fires are still fresh in her mind after all this time.

"Patrice will need some help setting up the tables and chairs that morning, so if you are able to send one of your children to the center, please talk to her today about that. Also, keep in mind that next month it will be time to plant the winter wheat, so Kate is going to need your older kids to help in the field for a couple days." At this, Iris turns to Rhia with a smile and then continues. "Does anyone have anything else to add?"

Rhia steps forward. "Well, there are a couple of things this week. I was in Campbell a few days ago." She pauses and adjusts her heavy belt. "They've had an incident with a man." The women all take an involuntary step closer to hear what Rhia will say next. "Apparently, one of the older men living in their neighborhood has been causing trouble lately. Nothing big—just talking about being ignored, and trying to get the younger men to agree with him."

"Ignored?" Iris asks. "His wife is welcome to speak at the meetings, just like we all are. Why does he feel ignored?"

"Well, I don't know," Rhia answers. "But there's more. You remember that they had raiders pass through there about a year ago? They killed a woman and took her son away before anyone knew what was going on." The women nod. Some look down at the sand. "Well, last week the old man said that he doesn't think it was raiders at all. He thinks that the son killed his mother and ran off."

A murmur stirs through the crowd, and Kate hears a gruff voice say, "What a shit." "That's not possible," one of the women says, shaking her head. "Our boys would never do that. Nonviolence is one of the main tenets of the Habits of Humanity. I talk about it every week in school."

"Sarah," Iris asks the woman, "you know the teachers in Campbell. Their children learn the same things we teach ours, right?"

"More or less," Sarah replies. "Certainly the seven Habits are the foundation, just like they are here. And someone would have known if the boy was having that sort of trouble. Someone would have helped him."

"Rhia, what are they going to do?" Iris asks, her brow furrowed.

"They're having a meeting about it this week. I'll be able to tell you more next time." Rhia crosses her arms in front of her chest. "I also have some news from Rhineder. When I was there last week, they waved me away from the market. Javiela stood on the beach and shouted to me that several of the little ones there have chicken pox."

A small woman near the back of the group raises her hand, and Rhia calls on her. "Patrice?"

The woman pushes past several people, only the top of her gray head visible as she weaves through the crowd. When she gets to the front, her large blue eyes shine over the scowl on her lips. She juts her angular chin forward, and Kate can see the long, straight scar that cuts its way across the right side of her neck, ropy and as thick as twine. In a gravelly voice, she asks, "Did they ask for any help?"

"No, they said they were doing all right. Just a long couple of weeks for those families." Rhia replies. "So, I—"

"Next time ask them if they need some help," Patrice says. "*You* can't do anything, because you got those useless shots, but the older women here had chicken pox already. We could help."

"Okay. I'll ask next time." Rhia says. She pauses, waiting for Patrice to respond. Some of the women shuffle their feet. Finally, Rhia says, "Sorry."

Iris steps next to Patrice. "Thank you for passing that along, Rhia. Hopefully, everything will be better by the next time you land there." She looks around to the crowd of women and asks, "Anybody else have news?" When no one speaks up, Iris says, "Well then, let's begin the market."

The next half hour is a happy one, with the women sharing stories of their week while they trade food and talk about the future. Most of the women see each other in passing throughout the week but have little time to talk with so much work to be done around their homes and families. Kate enjoys the camaraderie of the market, but she is ready to begin the walk back to her home and her children by the time it is over. The women reload their backpacks with a fresh assortment of food and begin to walk toward the tall grass of the bluff.

Rhia folds her plastic sheet and places her bartered goods into the rowboat, saying good-bye to her friends. She looks up suddenly, and calls out, "Hey, Kate!"

"Yes?"

"I keep forgetting to tell you: I got to talk to the captain of the boat that does the run north of here. She has a book we might want to borrow. Something like *Medicinal Plants of North America.*"

Kate looks to Iris, who has moved closer, and lifts one

finger. "One second, Iris." Turning back to Rhia, she says, "That would be great. Can you get it?"

"I hope to see her next week. I'll ask. It sounds like there's some good information in there. She said if you grind up dried dandelion root, it tastes like coffee."

"Does it have caffeine in it?" Iris asks, stepping close to Kate.

"I don't think so. Just tastes like it."

"Then what's the point?" A smile breaks across Iris's face, and the three women laugh.

"Thanks, Rhia. Happy fishing." Kate buckles the strap of her own backpack snugly around her chest, then moves with Iris to the path along the edge of the cliff. They will begin their walk home together along a common road until Kate veers off onto the small path that leads to her home by the river.

~ Two ~

KATE WAKES UP to the soft clucking of chickens as the first light shines through the rippled plastic of the bedroom window. Her thirteen-year-old twin daughters, Margaret and Laura, and her ten-year-old son, Jonah, are still sleeping quietly on the mattresses near her, and she listens to their deep breathing before stretching and slipping out from under the covers. As the first one to wake in the morning, she always tries to be quiet, to let her children sleep a few more precious minutes in the crowded room. She softly steps into the hall, selects her clothes from the shelves, and goes to the bathroom to change.

Her eyes still half-closed, Kate hikes up her long T-shirt and sits on the toilet. A minute later, she picks up the small bowl on the windowsill and dips it into a large trough of water next to her. With her left hand and the water, she washes between her legs, then stands placing the bowl back on the sill.

A bucket lies submerged in the trough. Kate lifts it up, then pours the water quickly into the toilet, flushing the waste away with a quiet gurgling sound. The broken sewer lines are a tangle of buried leaks, but most of the waste remains underground. She and the kids have learned to avoid the area east of here, where the smell gets strong during the wettest time of the year.

Kate washes her hands with rough soap at the sink, then looks up into the cracked mirror on the wall. She tilts her head slightly to the side and looks at the fine lines in the corners of her eyes. The white creases are highlighted by the tan on her skin from a long summer working in the gardens. With a yawn, she picks up the worn toothbrush from the cup at the edge of the sink and pops open the top of a small container next to it. She dips the toothbrush into a mixture of crushed peppermint and sea salt, and begins brushing.

Birds are chittering in the tree outside the small bathroom window, and the rooster crows. Kate pauses to listen to them and sighs.

The bomb that fell nearby had destroyed half of their house, but the rubble was cleared long ago, what was left of the second floor was dismantled, and new walls were built to close the gaping holes left behind. The house is now a small but sturdy structure.

Of the twelve other houses on their street, nine were completely obliterated, and three were as badly damaged as theirs. The Schumers, an elderly couple who lived five houses away, somehow survived the blast. Kate and the girls had done their best to care for them in the years after, but their spirits seemed as broken as their house. Eventually, the Schumers could not bear the depth of their losses, and hung themselves from a tree in the yard. Kate always told her daughters that caring for the old people had been the right thing to do, and she hated the part deep inside her that was glad the burden of them was gone.

When dressed, Kate makes her way to the cluttered kitchen. A long rope spans the length of the room, with several shirts and pants hanging to dry. Other clothes are soaking in the dented white washing machine tucked into a corner, its lid gone. A dark-brown dresser with several of the knobs missing leans awkwardly against one wall, one of its feet broken long ago. On the counter, a wooden box holding mismatched utensils is pushed in next to a metal mesh drying rack. Six golden cakes of rough rebatched soap have been drying there for two weeks, hardening with time.

Kate kneels in front of the stove and opens the door. With a thick metal poker, she knocks the ashes off the bank of warm coals Jonah had gathered together and covered the night before to keep the fire alive. Bending close to the opening, Kate gently blows on the coals, sending small sparks flashing before her eyes. She selects several small dry sticks from the nearby crate and places them inside the stove, blows again, and watches as the fire crackles and spreads.

Rising to her feet, Kate turns to the two large dogs watching her from their beds near the rear entrance. Kiko and Ruby wag their tails as she smiles at them, the soft thump against their overstuffed beds sounding loud in the stillness of the morning. "Good morning, pups," she says. They stand and stretch, then prance after her as she walks into the front room. As soon as she opens the door, they bound out to the yard.

When she gets back to the kitchen, Margaret is padding quietly into the room to join her. She is nearly as tall as her mother but bears little resemblance. Her dark-brown shoulder-length hair is tucked behind her ears, framing her light-brown face. Some people say they can see a bit of Kate in the way that Margaret smiles, but, like Laura and Jonah, her large eyes and wide nose are from her father's Filipino side.

"Good morning, Mom."

Kate kisses her daughter on the cheek. "Good morning, Mags. Did you sleep okay?"

"I did." Margaret lifts the heavy black pot from the drying rack and fills it with water from the sink. The pump hums as it kicks on. The water sloshes in the pot as she sets it onto the thick metal stove top. She opens the cookstove door and tosses in several more sticks to fuel the fire.

Working alongside her daughter, Kate flips the switch at the front of the stove, and a fan begins to swirl the red-and-orange flames inside the combustion chamber. Margaret turns one of the baffles to allow the heat up to the stove top, where the pot of water begins to bubble. As the fire heats up, compressed air is pumped into a chamber above the stove. They hear the soft vibration of the magnets and coils that produce the electricity the family uses throughout the day.

The new government made it a top priority to supply households with these cookstoves after it became obvious that the rebuilding of the nation's infrastructure would take decades. Most homes now have some combination of solar and thermoelectric power, although several houses that are close together often still share one unit. Since one of the causes of the Last War was a global inequality in the distribution of electricity and fuel, the new government has been keen on making homes as efficient and self-sufficient as possible.

Kate was thrilled the day she got her cookstove-and-refrigerator combination. Like most people, her family had nearly starved during the first two years after the war, when no one had electricity or enough food. Jonah had been born into a dark and hungry world. Kate could recall the nights of his futile nursing, when she could hardly produce enough milk for the tiny baby crying in her arms. Having electricity allowed the family the luxury of fresh water pumped into their home, refrigeration for their food, and light through the dark depths of winter.

"Morning," Laura says as she walks into the kitchen. Her elbows jut forward as she pulls her long brown hair back into a tight ponytail.

"Good morning, honey," Kate says as she steps close to Laura. For a moment, her hand rubs the girl's back, and then she moves to the cupboards to pull down mugs for the morning tea. The house begins to fill with the sounds of the family as their day begins.

"Laura, feed the chickens while you're out there getting eggs," Margaret says.

"I know."

"And bring in a bunch of peppermint. We're almost out."

Laura stops and glares at her sister. "I said, I know." She slips her shoes on at the back door and swings it wide to leave.

"Don't bang the door," Kate says a moment too late.

"Morning, Mom. Morning, Mags." Jonah says with a groggy smile as he shuffles in from the hall. He picks up two small bowls near the sink and heads out the kitchen door to collect fresh berries for breakfast. At ten years old, his long, lanky body seems out of proportion, making him a bit awkward and off-balance, and he bumps the bowls into the doorframe as he leaves. Kate notices that he has forgotten to put on shoes again.

"Jonah, your shoes!" she hollers. "There could still be broken glass out there." But the door has already swung shut.

"He's okay," Margaret says.

"He won't be okay if he cuts his foot again. I don't know," Kate mumbles with a small smile. "I have to remind him about everything lately. Sometimes I just don't know what's going on in his head."

"You could ask one of the other moms in the neighborhood what they think. Maybe they've had the same thing with their sons."

"Hmm," Kate says, busying herself with breakfast preparations.

Just thinking about turning to another family for help with her son makes Kate's heart ache a little. She's done a good job putting aside the pain of losing David, and she prides herself in what she has accomplished for her family. A memory of her husband suddenly glows bright in her mind. Kate can almost see him leaning on the edge of the kitchen counter, and she imagines what he would say if he were here now. Probably something about being patient, and Jonah finding his path in this life.

For a fleeting moment, she thinks it would be nice to have a man in the house to do the cooking and cleaning, the way some of the other women do. She knows if David were still alive, Jonah might not seem so alone and she might have a better understanding of him. Maybe she wouldn't feel so lonely, either.

Then she remembers what the men did before the women rose up. She remembers the restrictions they put on women, the rules they enforced, their viciousness and cruelty.

Their aggression grew slowly over several years, starting with local rules about the health care women could have and the clothes women could wear. Next came national laws making birth control illegal without written approval from one's husband. Slowly, women were removed from political positions. It was all done through legal votes and elections, though the money for those political campaigns flowed hard and fast from male-dominated corporations. Soon, women were barred from the military, under the notion that they were, by nature, less aggressive than men, weaker than men, not cruel enough to do what is required during battle.

The men had all the power, and they had used it to manipulate the weak, consolidate the wealth, and destroy the environment. And the men used their power to keep their power.

When the Traditionalist Party swept the elections in 2034, the new rules were implemented quickly. Laws with deceptive names, like the Family Focus Act and the Beauty of Motherhood Act, were passed to keep women at home. Videos of smiling families saturated their screens, the women in heavy clothing with children around, all of them looking up to the strong and handsome husbands.

Kate remembers the day she realized the Equality Movement wouldn't be able to stop the tide of oppression. She had written a letter to her sister in Illinois. Knowing that electronic communication was monitored, she had used paper, even writing her husband's name on the return label and her nephew's name on the address to make it less likely to draw attention. But the postman refused to deliver it. He had opened it and read it on his walk to the next house on the street. Deciding the content was too offensive, he brought it back to Kate's front door and knocked loudly. When she answered, he said, "You should thank me for returning this to you instead of turning it in." She hadn't heard from her sister since. Kate didn't even know if Sofia and her family were still alive.

Some politicians later claimed that the men who ruled the country had been distracted by the small groups of people who continued to fight for equal rights, and that's why they didn't see the global war coming. Kate thought it was more likely that the men simply became lost in their world of arrogance and couldn't believe the other countries would ever find the strength and conviction to fight back. Either way, it was the men of the world who created the storm that almost destroyed them all. Arguing about energy and money, religion and power, they pulled everyone down into the Last War and kept them there for nearly four years.

During that time, even good men like her husband had to stop arguing for women's rights, because suddenly just staying alive became so difficult. At least David was around to help at first. Then, three years into the war, there was a shortage of soldiers, and he was taken away.

Kate didn't know she was pregnant when they heard the truck rumbling down the street that morning. Heavily armed men in gray fatigues leaped from the truck and walked to what was left of their house. David met them in the front yard, refusing to go before they could say a word.

"You have no business in this neighborhood!" he shouted to the men. "The draft is over here. The law clearly states that at least twenty-five percent of a region must be men. I'm not leaving my family."

One soldier stood in front of David, menacingly close with his gun held in his arms. Without emotion he said, "The laws have changed. It's your duty to go."

"I have two children and a wife to take care of! Who will protect them if you take all the men from our neighborhood?"

"Just get in the truck," the soldier said.

Another gray soldier walked to the porch, where Kate and the girls were standing. Margaret and Laura were crying and whimpering. The soldier waved an arm in the air, as if to shoo them back into the house. "Get those kids inside!" he yelled at

Kate. She held the girls close to her but did not move.

David was still arguing. "You must know this war is wrong! There'd be plenty of energy for us all, if we just learned how to use it. How many more lives must you destroy before you see this?"

"Just get in the fucking truck!" the soldier yelled in David's face.

The soldier closest to Kate looked back to the others and started to say something. He didn't notice Margaret break away from Kate and run toward her father. As he waved his arms again, he hit Margaret on the side of her head. She screamed and Kate erupted. "Get away from my daughter! Get away from us!"

The soldier's initial remorse quickly turned to anger. "Then do what I tell you, and get the fuck in the house!"

David was pleading with the other soldier now, and the children were screeching in Kate's arms. The passenger door of the truck opened, and another soldier stepped down into the yard, carrying a heavy gun. Without a word, he slammed the butt of the weapon into David's nose. Red blood spurted from his face as he crumpled to the ground in a heap. He tried to push himself onto his knees, but the soldier kicked him hard in the side, sending him down to the ground again. Lying flat, David turned his head to look at his family.

The girls screamed even louder, and Kate tried to turn their faces away from the sight, holding them tightly to her chest, wishing she could pull her own eyes away. Two soldiers dragged David by his arms to the back of the truck, where they heaved him into the tarp-covered bed. The soldier near the porch began to walk toward the truck, pausing before he got in to look back at Kate with disgust. The truck's engine revved, and the gray men drove away.

Later, after she had managed to calm the girls and they were sleeping on their mattress in the cellar, Kate went back out to the front yard. She walked to the place where her husband had lain and saw the dried pool of his blood where his broken face had hit the ground. Long streaks of dark red showed the path along which they had dragged him through the dirt. Her legs buckled beneath her, and she collapsed to the ground, sobbing.

No, Kate would not allow a man in her house after the atrocities they had carried out. They had burned and bombed and raped their way across the planet, proving over and over how cruel they could be. She knew she could figure out how to help Jonah, and she knew the women of the neighborhood would help. She still had ten years before Jonah would have to decide whether he wanted to stay with her at home, or leave to marry someone in the neighborhood. Either way, Kate had plenty of time left to guide him.

~

The family sits down together for a warm breakfast of pumpkin pancakes, scrambled eggs, fresh raspberries, and wedges of dried apple. Between mouthfuls, Margaret says, "I thought I heard a deer in the garden again last night."

"I heard that, too, honey," Kate says. "I've been noticing a few of the vegetables missing the last couple weeks. Whatever it is must be bigger than a rabbit, because a whole zucchini is gone, not just nibbles."

"They always take the best ones, you know?" adds Jonah. "I was watching this tomato for a couple days, just waiting for it to get really red, and then, wham! The next morning it's gone."

"Could we raise the fence?" asks Margaret.

Kate rubs her eyes with the palms of her hands and yawns

before answering. "We can look around for more fence material, I suppose, but I thought it was high enough. Let's check today to see if there's a hole in it someplace where they're getting through."

"Can I have more eggs, please?" Jonah says as he tosses a handful of raspberries into his mouth. "And another pancake?"

"Jonah, you had two already," Laura says with a smile. She picks up her chipped ceramic mug and takes a drink of the goat milk Kate brought from the market this week. "You're a pig!"

"I am not! I'm just hungry."

"If he was a pig," Margaret laughs, "he wouldn't be so skinny. JoJo, I think you should eat all the pancakes. You look like you need them."

Jonah snuffles and snorts, and then bends his arms and wiggles his shoulders.

"You're like a pig-monkey!" Margaret says.

They all laugh, until Laura starts to cough, half choking on her milk. "Don't let it come out your nose," Jonah shouts, leaping up from his chair to pat Laura on the back.

"Okay, okay." Kate smiles. "Finish up your breakfast so we can check the fence before Sarah gets here," She picks up her empty plate and starts for the kitchen. "Jonah, did you finish your lesson last night?"

"Yep. We're learning about the geography and culture of India." Jonah's eyes light up as he turns toward his mother. "Did you know the women in India were the first to protest against the bad men?"

"I did," Kate says, stopping in the doorway and looking back at her son. "They really started the peace."

"Those women must have been really strong to fight off men," Jonah says, picking up his plate and following his mom to the kitchen.

"Not strong, really," Kate replies. "Sometimes it takes more than physical strength to win a battle. I think they were brave and smart, but most of all, they realized they could work together. Women weren't allowed in the military, so there were a lot more women than men by that time in the war. And they had been living under the fear of violence from men for long enough, I suppose. You can only oppress a group for so long before it rises up against you."

"But why?" Jonah asks. "I mean, I don't understand why women would have let men oppress them at all."

Kate furrows her brow and takes a deep breath before answering. "Well, for a long time we didn't have any choice. Men were bigger and stronger. Women were just supposed to have babies, cook, and clean. It went on like that for thousands of years. Millions." With a soft clunk, she sets her plate in the sink. "There was a time when it was more equal in this country, but even then, it wasn't really equal. Not really." She shrugs. "I guess when the whole world thinks that way, it's almost impossible to escape it."

"So," Jonah says slowly. "When most of the men were dead, women saw their chance to take over."

"Not exactly," Kate says, turning to look at her son. "The point wasn't to take over. It was to fix things. The men were the ones making the war. The men were the ones destroying the planet. They had been telling us for years that women were not the same as men. We just finally realized they were right."

Looking across the room at Jonah, she sees a skinny boy full of light and goodness. She cannot connect him with the men who perpetrated vicious rapes and slaughters during the Last War.

Kate sees so much of David in Jonah—more so each

passing year. His dark-brown hair parts to the same side that her husband's did. His round dark eyes stare back at her. In the moments after he was born, she felt like she could have fallen into those dark eyes. It felt like looking over the edge of a ship into the depths of the ocean at midnight.

She glances down at her feet before continuing. "Men did so many terrible things during that war. After three years of it, women finally understood that it was up to them to broker the peace. To fix it."

The protests began peacefully with marches in the bombed-out city streets. Rumors of the women's uprising spread slowly across the globe, passed around by the broken and battered people desperate for any hope. In February of that year, bombs dropped onto three hundred women and children marching peacefully in London, and women worldwide united against the men. After that massacre, women knew it would take more than protests and slogans to stop the horror of the war, that they must first fight before they could make peace.

They had run out of options. They were forced to pick up the guns and bombs that they had struggled to stop. They were forced to become warriors, justified by the idea that together they would be able to do a better job than the men had done. They painted SISTER, DAUGHTER, or MOTHER in red across the front of their shirts and banners, so that the men would see this as they charged over hills or around corners—hesitating long enough for the women to shoot. By then, most of these men were too old or too young to be soldiers, and had been taken against their will from their homes and families. Enough of these men were happy to lay down their guns, rather than shoot back.

Because the number of women was many times larger

than the number of men after years of war, the conflict was over by the following September and the new government was elected that December. It had simply been a matter of standing up and taking control.

"And that's why the women are in charge of making all the rules now?" Jonah asks.

"When the war was over, we worked together with the men to barter the peace agreement and design the new laws." Kate takes Jonah's breakfast plate and sets it in the kitchen sink. Censoring the details for his sake, she says, "Men were happy to have us take care of it. Honestly, most people were so tired of fighting they were willing to agree to just about anything under the promise of peace. And, keeping men closer to home, helping with the housework and the children, helps them remember why that peace is so important."

She leans over to put her arm around her son, giving him a quick squeeze. "When you're done with the dishes, come on out and check the traps, okay?" Kate walks to the kitchen door, stoops to pull on her shoes, and wraps the heavy belt that carries her sheathed knife around her waist.

Jonah says, "My dad wasn't like that though, right?"

Kate's hand rests on the doorknob, and her shoulders slump. "No," she says, turning back to her son. "Your dad was one of the good guys. And you know what, Jonah?"

"What?"

"You're one of the good guys, too."

Jonah smiles, then turns back to the sink to wash the dishes.

~ Three ~

PUSHING THE KITCHEN DOOR OPEN, Kate moves
into the flood of late summer sunlight that streams across the
large garden. She steps down from the small back porch that
runs the length of the house onto a thick mulch of
decomposing leaves and plant litter. Following the winding
path through the vegetables, Kate visually inspects the plants,
noting which areas will need weeding and watering today. The
tops of the onions, beets, kale, and carrots are tall and green.
The long prickly vines of the pumpkins wind their tendrils
among the dry cornstalks, pumping energy into the small green
globes. They won't begin to turn orange for another month or
so. Green beans climb bamboo teepees, holding tight to the
strings that crisscross between the sturdy poles. The bamboo
was harvested from once-ornamental trees that were planted
decades ago by a man who lived nearby, back when gardening
was mostly for show.

Looping back toward the side of the garden, Kate reaches
down to pluck a sprig of peppermint from the cluster of herbs

near the fence and puts it into her mouth. Her leg brushes past the rough lavender bush on her left, sending its subtle scent into the morning air. Some of the thyme, fennel, oregano, and chive has gone to seed here, but most of it hangs in dry bunches from her dining room ceiling.

They built the fence around the garden with whatever they could find in the rubble of the destroyed homes around them, piecing together scraps of wood and wire. Once the structure was built, it didn't take long for the grapes, raspberries, blackberries, and nasturtium to tangle their way up the fence, providing sturdy protection from the deer that live in the forests nearby. But the recent theft of vegetables and fruit from the garden meant that something was getting through, and Kate intended to stop it.

When Kate reaches the tall gate at the side of the garden, she slides open the lock. The gate squeaks loudly as she pushes it, the parts of the metal hinges scraping against each other. Walking along the outside of the fence, she looks for holes as she circles around to the back of the garden. A long shed stands here, and Kate has to squeeze sideways through the narrow alley between it and the fence to check this area. Finding nothing out of the ordinary, she walks to the front of the shed. She inspects the outside to see if any animals have been burrowing under the floor but finds no evidence of this.

Unlocking the heavy padlock, Kate swings the shed door open and peers inside. Nothing scurries away. She doesn't see any feces or shredded sacks—only the empty canvas bags, sheets, metal storage bins, and harvesting tools that are kept inside. In one corner, her long gloves and stitched-together overalls hang on a hook with the mesh hat she uses as protection from the bees. Whatever has been raiding the garden, at least it hasn't set up a home in here, she thinks.

Kate leaves the shed, clicks the padlock closed, and continues her inspection of the garden fence. The thick tangle of raspberry bushes is near the corner farthest from the house. Red, ripe fruit hangs heavy on the long stems, and she picks several berries, popping them in her mouth. When she tugs one berry that's not quite ripe enough, she feels the whole bush sway, and a nearby patch of dirt catches her attention.

It is difficult to see behind the thorny bushes, but Kate notices that the dirt below them has been disturbed. It is easier than it should be to push a part of the raspberry bush aside, and Kate knows she has found the spot she was looking for. A section of the fence is loose. A few boards have come free from the post, and the green vines tangled around the fence have been pulled with them. The damage meant that an animal's nose or paw could open up a small section of the fence, and it would swing back into place once the animal had gone through. A lovely swinging door for a little thief, thinks Kate. She'll have to get some string from the house to repair this corner.

Jonah walks toward her, beaming. He is cradling a large brown rabbit in his arms, holding tight to its long ears to keep it from struggling in his grasp. "He was in one of the traps."

"Nice work! Put him in the box by the front of the house, and I'll take care of him in a bit. I found the hole in the fence," Kate says.

"I'll fix it!" Jonah says. "Just show me where the hole is." He runs off with the rabbit in his arms.

Minutes later, he has returned, and Kate shows him the damaged part of the fence, instructing him to use thick twine to mend it. Satisfied that he understands, she heads back into the house. Margaret and Laura have finished their chores and are already working on their lessons.

"Peace to you, Sarah! When did you get here?" Kate asks the young woman sitting with her daughters at the table.

"Peace to you, too. I just got here." Sarah is one of several women who volunteer their time to teach the children of the neighborhood. Most of the kids who live in the center of the neighborhood meet together at a school for lessons twice each week, but since Kate and her family live farther out, near the river, Kate can only afford time to bring her children in once a week. Sarah is kind enough to come to them on Fridays to make up the difference.

She walks thirty minutes through craters and rubble caused by a heavy missile strike during the Last War. The small college that had existed between Kate's house and the rest of the town had been active in researching green-energy alternatives, which made it a target for utter annihilation. The military forces dropped more than a dozen missiles along a line encompassing the college and the surrounding streets, creating a swath of destruction which made the journey to the river nearly impossible. When they let loose the incendiary devices within the town the following day, hundreds of people died, unable to flee to the safety of the water. During the years since the war, the women have worked to make paths through the rubble, but the walk is still treacherous and slow.

Kate sits down at the table next to Sarah. "How is the baby?"

"He's beautiful. He'll be two in October already," Sarah says, smiling.

"Is he talking much yet?" Kate asks.

"He says a few things. He's good at Mama, Daddy, Sissy, and he calls my mom GaGa," Sarah says. "I think as the fourth child, he doesn't need to say much. His big sisters do all the talking for him."

"I remember how that goes," Kate says. Sarah was young during the war, barely eighteen at the end of it. She and her husband had been friends since they were children, and it didn't take them long to marry once the neighborhood settled down. Kate knew Eric to be a good man, always gentle and kind to Sarah and their children.

"Girls, I'm going out front, and Jonah's fixing the fence in back. Let me know if you need anything." Kate opens a closet near the front door and takes out a short-handled ax. Then, calling over her shoulder as she swings the door open, she adds, "And make sure Sarah gets something to eat."

Kate whistles once sharply, and the two dogs come running to the porch. "Head in, you two." She closes the door behind her and walks to the box where the rabbit is waiting. She swings open the top, pulls him out by his ears, and tucks him firmly under her left arm. She carries him to the edge of the forest, about fifty yards from the house, and sets the rabbit on top of a thick stump. Holding the furry body tightly, she raises the ax above her head and brings the blade down with all her strength onto the rabbit's neck. The head is severed completely. She turns him so his back legs dangle off the edge of the stump and firmly strokes down his belly with her hand, expressing his bladder into the grass.

With three quick chops, the rabbit's front feet, back feet, and tail are removed. Kate pulls the knife from her belt and lays the dead rabbit on his back across the stump, exposing his furry white belly. She pulls the skin above his rib cage up away from his body and makes a horizontal slice there. Then, turning the blade so the sharp edge is up, she slices through the soft fur in a vertical line down to the bottom of his belly. She moves with skill, careful not to go too deep into the body cavity, careful not to nick any part of the intestines or stomach.

It is a surgery she has performed on rabbits many times since the war.

Once the animal is sliced open, Kate lifts him by his shoulders and gives him a quick shake. As he hangs from her left hand, she reaches into the opening with two fingers of her right hand and gives the guts a quick, firm downward tug. The internal organs slide out in a slippery mass onto the ground next to the stump.

It is easy to skin him when he is this fresh. Kate only has to tug at the light-brown fur around the rabbit's open belly and it pulls away from the muscle. She removes the skin around his middle, then, holding onto the rabbit's exposed back with one hand and the fur with the other, gives a quick yank to pop his back legs out. She flips him upside down and pulls the entire pelt off his front legs. She tosses what looks like an inside-out sweater onto the ground and sets the naked animal on the stump.

Bending to the ground, she picks up the head, feet, and tail with one hand and the guts in the other. She walks several feet into the forest and tosses them all into the underbrush, the sticky insides plopping onto the ground with a slurping sound. The mess will be a feast for the wild dogs that roam the area at night. Kate picks up the rabbit's meaty body, his pelt, and the ax, and walks back toward the house. She washes the ax and her knife at the spigot on the side of the house and dries them on the legs of her pants. She hangs the soft brown pelt on the rail of the front porch. Finally, she thoroughly rinses the carcass and goes inside to put the ax away. She carries the rabbit into the kitchen and sets it in a pot on the counter.

"But don't you think the Native Americans could tell the English were dangerous?" Laura has her hands on the table, leaning toward Sarah as she speaks. "They came with guns and cannons. The Natives should have known it wasn't going to end well."

"At first, it was only a few people, though," Margaret says. "And they probably didn't seem dangerous, since they were starving and freezing to death all winter."

Kate is pleased to overhear her daughters questioning Sarah. They are growing into strong, intelligent young women, she thinks.

"I think the native people are always wary when a strange group shows up on their land," Sarah says. "You could wonder the same thing about any indigenous group that had a conquering force show up. Maybe it comes down to a question of what you believe about the human heart. Laura, when you meet someone new, do you assume they are good or bad?"

Kate stands quietly at the kitchen counter, waiting for her daughter's answer.

"It depends what they look like," Laura says.

"What?" Margaret laughs. "That's ridiculous."

"No, not that way. I mean, you can just tell sometimes when you see someone. Sometimes, you just know."

Margaret's laugh fades. "Well, around here, there's no one new to meet anyway."

Kate washes her hands and dries them on the front of her pants. Turning toward the dining room, she calls out. "Margaret, I put the rabbit in here. Can you start it when you're done with your lesson, please?"

"Okay, Mom."

Heading to the garden, Kate lightly treads down the small back-porch steps and once again pushes through the tall, squeaky gate. She rounds back to the shed and checks Jonah's progress on the fence. He is nearly finished, and she kneels down beside him to inspect his work. "This looks great.

Thanks!"

"Mom, can I help you with the rabbit?" Jonah asks.

"It's already done, honey. Besides, Sarah is with your sisters, and she'll be ready for your lesson soon."

"Isn't there anything else I can do outside to help you?"

"Not right now. Anyway, you're getting old enough to do more of the inside chores."

Jonah's face falls a bit. "I'll just weed until Sarah's ready, okay?"

"Sure, that would be helpful." Kate understands Jonah's desire to help her outside. He never shies away from outdoor work, however difficult, but he struggles to concentrate on his indoor household tasks, especially his weekly lessons. Sarah is a good teacher, though, and knows what to do when he begins to fidget. She often allows him the freedom to move around the room as they discuss concepts, and even takes him for walks around the yard when it might help to illustrate a point.

Confident that Jonah can complete the patch of the fence without her, Kate walks across the yard. Passing close to the small grove of young apple, plum, and pear trees, she bends her neck a little to peer at the three battered dressers nestled between the trunks. The deep hum of the bees housed there drones lazily in the dappled morning sun. It hadn't taken them long to find them once she modified the drawers and built the wooden frames. Involuntarily, her hand flutters to her neck with the memory of the painful stings there during those first months learning about the hives.

Veering toward the river, Kate notices the first leaves turning gold in the distant trees along the hillside behind the fields, and is thankful for these last few weeks of summer. Her mind ticks through the list of work that needs to be done during the next month before the cooler weather sets in. The soil of her fields will need to be turned and fertilized. The acre that held the peas and beans will be planted with winter wheat, and the second acre will be left fallow until the spring.

Kate nears the wooden dam that was built across the river with help from people in the neighborhood. There hasn't been rain for weeks around here, and only a small trickle of water cascades over the top of the dam this morning. Behind it, a small, quiet pool of water glistens in the sun. Kate sees water striders floating on the surface and smiles, secretly wishing she could be so lazy on such a fine day.

Tall metal plates have been inserted into both corners of the dam, and shallow trenches in the dirt behind the plates lead away from the river. Straddling the trench on this side of the dam, Kate grasps a metal wheel perched on top of a thick screw. As she turns the wheel, the metal weir below her begins to rise, allowing a stream of water into the trench. When the weir is fully raised, she follows the flow of water for several feet along the irrigation ditch that leads back to her garden. Watching the quick bubbling water fill the ditch, she knows it will make its way to her garden to sink into the soil and nourish her plants.

Kate turns back to the river, walks downstream, and crosses a small wooden bridge to the other side. Here are her two acres of land, painstakingly cleared of weeds and rubble after the Last War, which grow the field crops that help feed the neighborhood. The south acre, which grew the peas and beans this summer, is full of wilting vines, recently stripped of their bounty and beginning to brown. Kate and the children will have to begin the process of turning the dead plants into the ground this week. They will till the soil again before leveling it and sowing the seeds for the winter wheat next month.

The north acre is full of the golden stubble of the recently harvested summer wheat. This field she will leave fallow until the spring, at which time she will prepare it for the rotation of peas and beans that will fix the nitrogen in the soil. They'll turn the chickens onto this field during the winter, allowing them to peck for bugs and drop their waste. Kate walks through the scratchy, dry field, picking up occasional rocks and tossing them far into the hilly forest surrounding her land.

With help from her neighbors, Kate's large summer crop was harvested two weeks ago. She had picked several handfuls of wheat a few days earlier, pinching them in her hand and crunching them in her mouth before deciding it was time to summon her friends.

On harvesting day, the stone-sharpened scythes they had fashioned from salvaged fan blades sliced through the stalks of summer wheat. Children followed behind with twine to bundle the shocks and stack them to dry in the field. Other families worked in the field of peas and beans, backs bent to the sun, filling bags they would carry to Kate's house. Mothers lined up in the kitchen to process their loads. One dumped the fresh vegetables into large pots of boiling water. One scooped them out after two minutes and transferred them to pots of cold water. Another hauled the cool beans and peas back outside.

Dozens of faded bedsheets were brought from the women's homes and stretched across Kate's yard, their corners held fast by sharpened sticks pressed into the ground. Once blanched, the peas and beans were scattered across these sheets and left to dry under the hot summer sun.

Each family was willing to do this hard work for the reward it offered. It had taken them several years to learn the process of growing, harvesting, and storing the food. Tears of anger and frustration had spilled over these fields during the first years after the war. They had waited too long to plant or to harvest, and hundreds of pounds of food were lost to rot or rain. By trial and error, and the eventual circulation of books between the neighborhoods, they had finally learned to read the signs in the crops and in the weather. This year's harvest was the largest yet, and the women talked about trying to clear another acre sometime soon.

Five days later the neighbors were back, shoveling the peas and beans into bags of all shapes and sizes, then laying the dried wheat stalks onto the now-empty sheets. With old baseball bats, heavy sticks, and broom handles, they threshed the wheat, knocking the crispy kernels out of their stalks. Women held the edges of the sheets and tossed the kernels into the air, allowing the breeze to whisk away the chaff. Smiles stretched their dirt-streaked faces as they sang songs of gratitude and songs of remembrance.

Our love is like the morning sun
Our life is like the morning rain
Hold on, Hold on
Spring will come again
Hold tight to the hope of the new spring
day
Hold tight to the promise of the sun's
bright rays . . .

The following day, the sluice gate was opened in the dam, allowing water to flow down to the water wheel at the edge of the river. Children poured sacks of wheat into hoppers positioned above two large round stones. A hole in the center of the top stone caught the wheat and as the wheel slowly spun, gears turned, the flat stones ground together, and the small mill churned out flour. Children filled thirty-pound sacks and hauled them to mothers waiting with modified grocery carts and baby strollers to push the loads home. The wheat from these two acres provides the thirty-three families in the neighborhood with enough flour for a loaf of bread each week, plus a little extra for biscuits or an occasional pie. The wheat fields meant their families would thrive throughout the year. The wheat fields meant life.

Kate's family fed everyone soup and bread when the work was done. The children played games and ran through the fields of stubble and vines. The exhausted women laughed and talked and sang songs they remembered from their childhood. And at the end of the day, as the sun began to dip toward the west, the neighbors left Kate's home with heavy loads, which would last them through the coming months.

Being in charge of the field crops is a great responsibility, and Kate is respected for the food she is able to provide to the other women, but few people would trade places with her. A remote field of wheat and a working mill, even one as small as Kate's, could draw the attention of raiders passing through the area. They would steal whatever they could carry on their backs and in their carts, and they would burn the rest out of hate. They might take the children with them, or they might slaughter them alongside her.

Near the far edge of the field, Kate pauses before making her way back to the bridge. The morning sun is climbing higher and now shines above the tall trees. Kate puts her hands on her hips and tilts her chin up to the sky, soaking in the warmth on her face. Her eyes close, and an unwelcome memory bubbles up through her body, penetrating her mind.

It is a memory of David, long before the war. They had been dating for over a year, and had snuck out to the river for a picnic on a warm summer day.

"Don't worry," David said. "You can apply for another advanced work permit in six months." He was lying next to where she sat on the rock, propped up on one elbow as he watched frustration wrinkle her brow.

"Yeah, but I don't know if I can handle data entry for six more months." Kate threw a rock into the river, then wrapped her arms around her knees, curling into a ball. "I was only eight credits short of my electrical engineering degree. You'd think they would let me do more than that."

"We'll try again in six months."

Kate noticed how David had said "we," and turned to him. She watched as he bit into a triangle of watermelon, and a dribble of its juice ran down his chin. Smiling, she leaned over to wipe it away with the back of her arm. He laughed and took hold of her hand, pulling her down to him. She remembers the way the sun felt on her face that day, warm and comfortable, as he kissed her.

Today in the field of stubble, Kate struggles to bury that memory and a thousand others she shared with David. There was no use in letting herself continue to feel that sadness and loss. She takes a deep breath and then tilts her chin back down, opening her eyes. Standing in front of her, near the edge of the forest, is a man. He is watching her.

~ Four ~

A HUNDRED THOUGHTS fly through Kate's head as she tries to process the sight of the bedraggled man standing alone by the trees. He isn't moving. He knows he has been caught. Unlike Iris and some of the other women, Kate does not carry a bow and arrows, so she cannot defend herself from this distance. The knife on her belt will help if he tries to attack her, but what if he has a knife of his own? Then the idea that he is not alone occurs to Kate, and she is truly terrified. What if this man is with a group of raiders, and the others have already gotten to her house?

Kate turns and begins to run through field, the beat of her pulse pounding in her head. She sprints to the bridge without looking back. Her feet thud loudly on the wood as she crosses the bridge, then she leaps over the irrigation ditch. She can see her house and the garden fence. No one is outside.

Kate pulls the knife from her belt as she flings open the garden gate and bursts through the back door. Sarah and the three children sit at the table, working on their lessons. They all stop what they're doing and look toward the kitchen when the door bangs open.

"Everyone in the cellar," Kate says, running into the dining room. "Right now."

Seeing the knife in Kate's hand and the fear in her eyes, Sarah quickly stands and says, "Come on. Let's go." Sarah follows Kate into the kitchen, tugging on Jonah's and Laura's arms.

During the war, Kate and David dug into the dirt of the crawl space below the house and installed heavy cinder blocks and sheets of metal to create the eight- by ten-foot cellar under the kitchen. A sliding metal door below the kitchen floorboards can be locked from inside. Several small pipes lead under the ground and up to the surface, acting as air vents. Originally designed to be a bomb shelter, this room was what saved them during the raid that destroyed the houses around them. Now it was used primarily as a food cellar, with enough preserved goods to last through the winter. Even if raiders attacked the house and took everything above, Kate and her children would be able to hide out below until the men left.

Trembling, Kate grips the black metal handle and lifts up the wooden hatch. One by one, she ushers her children down the ladder into the small space below. Turning to Sarah, she says, "You, too."

"First, tell me what's going on," Sarah says.

"I saw a man," Kate says with a shaky voice.

"Where?" Sarah moves to the kitchen window and looks out over the yard.

"We need to get in!"

"I don't see anyone. Where was he?"

Kate's shoulders slump, and she exhales loudly at her friend's delay. She looks down into the dark cellar, smiles weakly at her three children, and says to them, "Slide the metal door closed." Without another word, she closes the wooden hatch. "Across the river, behind the field, over by the forest." Kate hurries toward Sarah and looks over her shoulder through the window. "He was just standing there."

"Did he hurt you?"

"No. He didn't come near me, but he could be with a group." Kate still holds the knife and begins to move through the house, looking out each window, checking their surroundings. "We need to get into the cellar."

"But you only saw one?" Sarah walks in a different direction, peering through windows as well.

"Outside, pups," Kate quietly says to the dogs. Kiko and Ruby are following her. Their ears had perked up the moment she burst into the room, as if they sensed the tension in her. If someone is out there, the dogs will know it before we do, Kate thinks. She opens the front door, and they push out into the front yard, their backs arched and their tails low.

A few minutes later, Sarah comes into the front room. "Anything?"

"No. I let the dogs out. They're circling the house, but they haven't barked at all."

Sarah strides to the front door and picks up her quiver and bow. She begins to turn the knob when Kate says, "Wait! Don't go out. What if they're out there?"

"The dogs would have barked. And you have good visibility here. He can't sneak up on us." Sarah is young and, though she remembers the war, she still carries the confidence of youth. "I'll just go look around."

Kate knows she is right. They cannot wait here, frightened and weak; they must be proactive to protect themselves. They will see a raid coming from any direction and have enough time to barricade themselves in the cellar with the children.

"Bring your knife, too," Kate says, and hands her the heavy belt Sarah took off when she arrived.

Kate moves to the front window to watch as Sarah cranes her neck to look around the yard from the safety of the porch, then slowly walks down the steps and disappears around the side of the house. Kate keeps moving from room to room, looking out the windows, watching for any signs of attack. Several minutes later, Sarah comes back inside.

"I didn't see anything. I left the dogs out."

A soft scratching noise comes from the kitchen, and Kate turns to see Margaret slowly lifting the wooden hatch in the kitchen floor. "Mom?" Margaret whispers.

Kate turns to her and reaches out with the hand not holding her knife. "It's okay. You can come out. Come here by me."

Sarah says, "I'll take another look in a few minutes."

"Good idea." Kate's adrenaline is starting to subside, and she puts the knife back into the sheath in her belt. "Maybe it was just one man. But that's so unusual."

Sarah continues to stand near the door, but she, too, has relaxed a little. "I don't know. There have been rumors about an increase in raids lately, but we've seen no evidence of them. The last man seen around here was the one in the spring. "

"And the ones in Campbell last year. Do you doubt that there are raiders around here?" Kate asks in disbelief. "There have been stories about them for the last six years."

"Sometimes I wonder if the stories from the Carriers are a little exaggerated," Sarah says. "They only pass through every couple months. Seems like the tales get taller the more often they're told. I'm sure their ride across the region can be fraught with danger, and I know it's an arduous job. But I also think it must be a little dull just carrying supplies around all that time. They seem to really love to talk when they come to a neighborhood."

"Out here, I don't have the luxury of not believing those stories," says Kate firmly. She turns to her children, who have emerged from the cellar. "I saw a man out there today, and we need to be on the lookout."

"Where did you see him, Mom?" Jonah asks. Kate notices that he is holding his body taut, his hands clenched into fists by his side. She puts her arm around him and pulls him close, then begins to gently rub his shoulder.

"He was across the river, at the far end of the north field. He was just standing there." The girls have moved close to their mom now, too, and Kate tries to calm them and reassure them by slowing her own breathing and relaxing her own stance.

"Should we go out to find him?" asks Jonah.

"No, honey. I don't want any of you to go out there right now."

"But what if he tries to come into the house?"

"Kiko and Ruby will bark if they see him, and we can hide in the cellar." The more she thinks it through, the more convinced Kate becomes. Here in the house they are relatively safe. They have worked hard to make sure of it. "Sarah, you keep watch and I'll go out with the dogs this time."

"Sure." Looking at the children, she says, "It's okay. Your mom is right. It was probably just one man, and he's probably halfway to the next neighborhood by now. Wouldn't *you* run away if you saw your mom standing there with her big knife?" She is trying to lighten the mood, and the girls give her weak smiles, but Jonah still hasn't calmed down. "Come sit down at the table. You can work on your lessons."

"Mom, I think I should go out with you," Jonah says.

"No."

"But if he's out there, I can help you look. You always tell me I'm good at finding things, and—"

"No, honey. Not this time. I need you to stay with Sarah now." Proud of his bravery, Kate leans close to him so she can whisper into his ear. "I need you to stay here in case I call you. You have good ears, and you'll hear me if I shout. I need you to be here to help your sisters."

Jonah agrees, though it's clear he's not entirely satisfied.

The children all sit back down at the table, and Kate whispers to Sarah, "I'll holler if I see anything." Kate kisses each of the kids on the top of their heads before pivoting toward the front door. She does not look back as she leaves. She does not want them to see the fear building again in her eyes.

Outside, the dogs lope around the yard, sniffing at the grass and the few small bushes that are scattered around the area. They stop from time to time to look up toward the forest or the fields, to take in a scent or to analyze a sound, but quickly go back to scanning the ground. Kate whistles once, and both dogs dash to her side. Together they walk the perimeter of the house, scanning the forest in the distance while looking for any signs of the man. The wind is whispering in the tall trees, but she sees nothing out of the ordinary. She swings open the squeaky garden gate and peers inside, then closes the gate again before continuing her search. She circles around to the other side of the garden and, noticing that the padlock on the shed door is still latched, she does not look in.

Coming full circle to the front of the house again, Kate steps up onto the porch, stops, and looks around once more before going back inside. "Nothing's out there," she says.

They all stay inside the house for a couple of hours, trying to keep busy. The children sit with Sarah at the dining room table, working quietly. Kate's ears strain to hear any sign from the dogs as she strings a large bunch of onions together. When finished, she stands on a chair to add them to the dried vegetables that hang from the dining room ceiling, then looks out all the windows again. Returning to the kitchen, she picks up the wooden paddle leaning against the wall and spins the wet clothes in the broken washing machine, then turns the lever to let the water drain outside to the garden.

Hearing the dirty water gurgle through the rigged drain pipe, Kate remembers that she has to go back out to the river's edge. The irrigation weir is still open, and she needs to close it. She pours a large pot of hot clean water into the wash bin, then walks to the doorway of the dining room. "I'm going to take the dogs out to the river. I left the weir open."

Without a word, all three children push their chairs back from the table and rise to join her. "No, you can stay here with Sarah," Kate says, but they are already walking toward the front door.

Sarah stands, too. "Honestly, we weren't getting much accomplished in here. Maybe it would be better if we all came with you." Sarah smiles gently at Kate. "Five sets of eyes are better than one."

Together they cautiously make their way across the yard to the river. The dogs stay close, but Kate can tell they are more relaxed now. Sarah looks across the water to the fields as Kate straddles the weir to screw it closed. The water slowly rises in the pool behind the weir as the small ditch empties. The tall grass in the yard rustles gently in the breeze as they make their way across the bridge. They plod through the stubble and dirt of the north field to the place where Kate saw the man. He is no longer there. No sign of him can be found.

"Should we walk into the forest and look for him there?" asks Sarah.

"No. You're probably right. He's long gone," replies Kate. "Sarah, we'll walk back to the neighborhood with you." The children mill around the field, already distracted. They have started talking among each other, and Kate can hear them laugh from time to time.

"You don't need to do that. I'll be fine."

"It's no trouble, really. Besides, it would be fun for the kids to see their friends." Kate is attempting to act lighthearted, but Sarah is not buying it.

"If you walked with me today, then you have to walk all the way back home. I'm not afraid." Seeing the uncertainty in her friend's eyes, Sarah says, "Really, Kate. I'll be fine. He's long gone."

Kate is not at all as confident as Sarah, but she lets her make the journey alone. Sarah will cross through the swath of rubble and destruction, just as she has done hundreds of times before. As Sarah leaves their house that afternoon, she waves to the family standing on the porch, and Kate prays silently for her safety to a God she's not even sure she still believes in.

~

On Saturday morning Kate rises early to make the journey to the market. She helps Margaret kindle the cookstove fire, laughs with Laura when they discover the two double yolks in this morning's eggs, and hugs Jonah when he finally wakes up and joins them in the kitchen. As the family moves through its morning routine, Kate smiles good-naturedly and hides her worry about leaving them. Once breakfast is over, however, she has no choice but to face the difficult decision. Does she skip the market today to stay with her family, or leave them here to fend for themselves if the man returns?

Margaret seems to sense her mother's conflict. "Mom, we'll keep our eyes and ears open today. You don't have to worry about us."

"I know you will. But I'm still not sure I should go."

"We'll be fine."

Laura nods. "Mom, it's okay. You only saw the man that one time. He's not coming back."

"And if he does, Kiko and Ruby will rip him up and then we'll take care of the rest." Jonah is not smiling as he says this, and Kate suddenly wonders what he really would do if the man attacked them. Would her own son draw a knife on another person? For ten years she has tried to guide him away from violence, but for the first time, he might be faced with the decision to kill another human. She shudders at the thought.

"No, Jonah," says Laura. "Kiko and Ruby will bark, or we'll see the man or something, and we'll all get to the cellar right away." She turns to her mother. "Mom, seriously, we're fine here. We know what to do if he comes back."

"But he's not going to come back anyway," Margaret says firmly. "And you can't stay here for the rest of your life. You might as well just go to the market today and get it over with!"

Well, I can't argue with that logic, thinks Kate with a smile. Yes, she knows her children are well prepared for the slim chance that a man attacks them. The house is safe. The cellar is secure. She will go to the market, but she will be filled with worry the entire time she is gone.

Kate leaves a little later than usual that morning. She makes each of the children go over the emergency plan with her as they harvest fruit and vegetables from the garden. She checks the cellar door to make sure it's easy to slide closed. She walks the perimeter of the house. Then finally, she straps on her backpack and says good-bye. And as she steps off the porch to begin her long walk to the shore, Kate hears the heavy click of the door locking behind her.

Once on the road, the rhythm of her walking begins to soothe her. She'll be happy to arrive a bit late today, because this way she won't have to tell the story of the man over and over as each woman arrives on the beach. Sarah will, no doubt, have already circulated the news, and the women will be eager to hear more.

Fifteen minutes into her journey, Kate leaves the small path from her house and begins the walk along the well-traveled main road from the neighborhood. This time she does not stop to pray for the man recently buried. She simply glances toward the mound and hopes the neighborhood women will not have cause to gather there again anytime soon. Kate has never killed before. She hopes with all her heart that she never has to. Not even a raider.

As she expects, the other women have already gathered on the beach by the time she arrives. Rhia's rowboat is on the shore, and the fish are already laid out for display. The conversation stops when they see her, and they all turn toward her.

Iris is the first to approach, and she wraps her arms around her friend before Kate even has time to take off her backpack. "Are you okay?" she says.

"I'm fine. We weren't hurt at all."

Iris helps Kate set her backpack down onto the sand. Now all the women have gathered around, looking at Kate with deep concern. They all know how vulnerable Kate and her family are out by the river. They'd had no way to know the fate of the family since Sarah left them the day before.

Iris turns to the other women on the beach. "Everyone! I know we are all interested to hear what Kate has to say, so if it's all right, we'll just wait to start the market until after she tells her story." The women all nod in agreement, and Iris turns back to Kate. "Go ahead, Kate."

This is the moment Kate has dreaded. She doesn't want to be the one to tell of a man loose in the neighborhood. She doesn't want to stir up the women or cause fear. And most of all, she doesn't want a replay of what she witnessed four months ago when the last man ventured too close. The way the women had joined together to hunt the man had scared her. Not because of the shared responsibility of the task, but because of the way some women responded to the duty. Even though she knew they had to protect themselves, had to protect their families and their neighborhood, she was frightened by the gleam of anger and anticipation she saw in some of their eyes as they searched for him.

Patrice had been the one to alert them to the danger. She'd come running to the market that morning after he had attacked her. She was shaking and out of breath, with blood covering most of her shirt. Her hand still gripped the knife she had cut him with, and it took Iris a while to calm her to the point where she could describe the location of the attack.

"He jumped out from the tall grass along the road," Patrice had said. "He grabbed at my pack and shouted for me to give him my food. I struggled and yelled, and he hit me until I fell to the ground. I had to stab him before he could kill me!"

They had left their backpacks on the sand, grabbing only the knives and bows they carried as weapons. Trudging up the sandy cliff, they soon found the blood trail the man had left along the road, and they followed it into the tall grass.

"Move quietly now. Keep your eyes open," whispered Iris

as she held her bow.

When they spotted him hiding among the broken bricks and shattered glass of a destroyed building, he was already breathing weakly. He was filthy and gaunt. Fear shone in his eyes, and he tried to back further into the rubble.

"Stay away," he said in a weak, breathy voice. "Leave me alone!"

Kate began to walk toward him, but Iris stopped her by touching her arm. "I can get a good shot from here," she quietly and calmly said.

"Iris, he's—"

Patrice screamed, startling everyone. Her whole body shook as she pulled her knife from its sheath, and Kate watched her run at the man, shrieking with rage. It happened so quickly they hadn't had time to stop her. Patrice was on him in seconds. She drove the blade deep into his chest, withdrew it, and plunged it into him again and again, screaming the whole time. Iris, Sarah, and a few others ran to her and pulled her off the man, pushing her to the ground and holding her there as they wrestled the sticky knife from her hand. Kate could only stand and watch.

Most of the women had been horrified; they trembled and cried at the sight of it, at the sight of their friend weeping in rage and misery on the ground. And later, most of them were somber and silent as they walked back toward the beach to collect their packs. But not all of them. Kate had noticed that two or three of the women seemed proud of what had happened. She had detected the slightest smirk of satisfaction on their faces. She couldn't bring herself to believe they were happy about the horrible thing that had been done, but she'd sensed something in them, something that frightened her.

Kate hadn't talked to anyone about that. The women

were responsible for keeping the neighborhood safe. They all agreed to the laws that forbade men from wandering alone through the country, unprotected and unguided by women. And hadn't she just felt the deep terror of seeing a man near her family's home? There is no question in her mind that a man alone could only mean trouble, but deep in her gut she knows that some of the women reacted too strongly to the last man. Kate doesn't want to think about it. She doesn't want to believe that they might have enjoyed the hunt.

No. That was definitely not the right word. Not enjoyed. That wasn't possible. The women of her neighborhood had suffered so greatly during the Last War. She has been friends with these women for years, and they had helped her build her garden and her fields. Quite simply, these were women. And everyone knew that women, though strong and capable, were not prone to cruel acts of aggression. Women were the peacemakers during the war, the ones who had built a new society free of hatred and free of war. They could not have enjoyed seeing the man killed. They were simply doing their duty and protecting their neighborhood from a criminal. However, there was power in being the protector. And there was always the desire to keep the power once you get it.

And now, Kate knows she must describe her own sighting of a man as delicately as possible. She would try to keep them all calm and simply tell them the facts. The women listen intently, nodding occasionally, asking for extra details several times. When Kate is finished, Sarah speaks up. "That seems to be the whole story. I don't think we'll see him around again."

"We can't be sure of that," says Iris. Some of the women nod. "I think we all need to be on the lookout for a while." Turning to the group, she asks, "Has anyone else seen anything unusual lately? Anything at all?"

No one has. It was likely an isolated event, and Kate feels a little more confident that she will not see the man again.

The market begins, and the women barter their goods, each one going over the facts of the sighting, each one commenting on what might be done to increase security. Kate can feel Iris watching her and knows her friend will try to support and console her while they walk the common road home together today.

When the women say their good-byes and begin the ascent of the cliff, Kate and Iris linger behind to help Rhia load food and the books into the small boat. They push it out into the water as Rhia leaps on board, waving as she confidently rows away.

"Sometimes I think it would be nice to live on a boat, away from everyone," Iris says. "Even though she's all alone out there, she's pretty well protected from everything on land."

Kate understands Iris's implication. "I'm pretty safe at my house, too."

"I know. But it bothers me that I didn't even know you were in danger until Sarah got back to town." Iris lifts her backpack and slides the straps onto her shoulders. "We need to clear the path to your house a bit more so it's easier to get to you."

With a smile, Kate says, "I'm all for it! That way you and I can see each other more often. We can sit on your couch and drink cider." Both women laugh.

"Well, you should at least start carrying your bow," says Iris. "That way you don't have to wait for the man to get to you."

"Iris, you know I'm shit with the bow. I'm more of a catch-food-in-a-trap kind of girl."

"Oh, you're not that bad."

The women stop and look at each other. Kate says, "Haven't you ever noticed that I always serve rabbit when you eat at my house?"

A smirk tugs at the corner of Iris's mouth. "Haven't you ever noticed that I always bring you venison as a gift?"

~ Five ~

KATE AND MARGARET are busy chopping zucchini and carrots in the kitchen when Jonah and Laura come in from the garden with two bowls full of raspberries. "Mom, this is all of them," Laura says. "Should we get peas from the cellar, or do we need to chop?"

"Jonah, please get the peas. That would be great," says Kate. "Laura, grab the two big pots from the cellar, bring them up here, and fill them half-full with water."

The evening sun is streaking through the west-facing windows as they prepare the vegetable soup that will feed the neighborhood children tomorrow. Kate expects about a dozen of the older children to help them till the soil of the south field.

Weeks ago, they had worked together to harvest the peas and beans from this field. Now the fertile ground will be turned once more by children pulling and pushing handheld plows. Other children will follow behind, raking the dirt flat. Some of their mothers will join them, but most are too busy with their own households to spend the whole day at Kate's. However, all the families are willing to send anyone they can spare. The shared responsibility of the task is rewarded by the sharing of the harvest the following year. Only by working together can the neighborhood survive and thrive.

Jonah will spend the planting day running back and forth from the house to the field, bringing food and water to the children as they toil in the sun. Margaret and Laura will help to direct the efforts, ready with tools in the inevitable case that a plow or a rake bends or breaks. Kate loves planting days. The promise of growth and life springing from the earth restores her faith in the goodness of nature. The family is happy today.

When Jonah and Laura climb back up the cellar steps, Kate and Margaret are ready to put the soup on the stove. Most of their regular household duties are done for the day. All that is left is cooking the soup, letting the dogs out for their last patrol, and getting ready for bed.

"Thanks," says Kate, as Laura sets the heavy pots onto the stove. "Okay, Mags, you can start getting ready for bed. Jonah, let Kiko and Ruby out. Laura, you can read for ten minutes tonight."

"Mom, come on. Ten minutes is hardly enough to get started!"

"I know, but it's already late and we have a big day tomorrow. I want everybody in bed soon."

Jonah is on the floor, rubbing Kiko's floppy black ears. Ruby is already waiting at the front door, impatient to get outside. "Jonah, come on, buddy. Let's go," chides Kate.

He slowly stands up and motions to Kiko to follow him. The dogs push past him and out the front door. Their toenails scrape across the wood of the front porch as they head out to the yard. Kate can hear Margaret in the bathroom brushing her teeth. Laura has settled into a chair with her book open in her lap.

"What is this one about?" Jonah asks from across the room.

"It's the story of a girl in New York City a long time ago," Laura responds. She looks up from the book and glances at Jonah. "Her family was poor and didn't have much stuff. She has a little brother that she takes care of while her mom is working around the house and her dad is out at his job." Jonah has always loved listening to his sister tell him about the stories she's reading. Some books she has read so many times she could practically recite the whole story from memory.

"Is this the one where they go to the doctor for vaccines and the doctor thinks that just because they're poor, they won't understand him when he makes fun of them?" Jonah moves to sit on the couch next to Laura.

"Yep. That's the one," Laura says. "I guess a long time ago doctors always had lots of expensive stuff and they didn't like poor kids."

Jonah sits quietly next to his sister; he looks like he's thinking. "Dr. Preston's not like that. She's always really nice to everybody, even though we're all poor," he says.

Laura looks up at the ceiling. "Yeah, who cares about money if nobody has any. Actually, I don't think we're that poor anymore. We used to be when we were little." Laura's voice drops to a whisper. "Mom used to be really skinny." Then, in her normal voice, she adds, "Dr. Preston gets lots of good stuff in trade for helping us, but she's so nice. She'd probably do it even if you had nothing to give. She just tries to help everybody and keep everyone healthy."

Laura begins to read again. Jonah doesn't say anything for a minute. Then, in a whisper, Kate hears him ask, "Laura, do you think Sarah could teach me how to be a doctor?"

Kate stops scooping carrots into the soup pot, not sure of what Laura will say. Will she tell Jonah that he could never become a doctor because he is a boy? Is that even true? Will she tell him they already have a doctor in their neighborhood, so they don't need another one?

Without hesitating, Laura says, "No way. Sarah can't teach you to be a doctor because she's not a doctor. You'd have to ask Dr. Preston to teach you." Jonah seems satisfied with this answer, and smiles.

All the new rules and guidelines, set up for the protection of people and to help the world to thrive under the banner of peace, couldn't answer this simple question for Kate: what if her wonderful son wanted to be a doctor?

Suddenly, barking erupts in the backyard. Kiko and Ruby are together behind the garden, and they sound angry. Kate drops the spoon she is holding and picks up a knife. She steps out onto the small back porch, looking around. She can't see through the thick tangle of branches that climb up the garden fence, so she has to step down onto the ground and walk to the tall garden gate. Her children are right behind her as she unlatches the gate, swings it open, and steps out into the night.

"Kiko! Ruby!" she shouts into the dark. They instantly stop barking and run to her side, but they turn to face the yard and the river beyond. Kate can tell that their hackles are up and they are watching something, seeing more in the dark than she can.

The family is tense, looking for any movement in the yard. But after a few minutes, the dogs settle down. Their tails begin to swing freely again, and they look up at Kate and the children. Apparently, whatever it was is gone now.

"Okay, come on in. It was probably wild dogs, or a deer

trying to get at the garden," Kate says. She holds her arms out to usher her children into the garden, and one by one, they go. Kate takes one final look around the yard, and then latches the gate behind her.

~

The morning sun has already warmed up the yard when Kate sees the neighborhood children running along the path toward her house. She steps onto the front porch, and the dogs run out to greet the children, barking and jumping with their tails wagging. Kiko leaps into the air and twists her body as two of the older boys pat their legs and call to her. Margaret, Laura, and Jonah run outside and call to their friends.

Kate smiles as she makes her way down to the fifteen children gathered in the front yard. Four women have also come along today: Iris, Patrice, Elle, and Denny. Kate greets each of them with a hug. "Peace to you, and good morning!" she says. "I'm so glad you could come out today." Four of Iris's grandchildren have come along, Patrice has brought two of hers, Elle and Denny each have one of their older children, and four other families have sent one child.

"We're glad to be here," Iris says. "I don't get out here often enough."

"I know it's a long walk."

"Have you had any more trouble out here?"

Kate knows she is referring to the man she saw weeks ago. Certainly all the women have been talking about it and wondering if he would show up again. "Nothing. I think he was probably just passing through alone. I doubt he'll come through this way again, now that he knows I've seen him."

"Don't be too sure about that," Patrice says. "You know how sneaky those bastards are. Last time the Carriers came through here, they said they saw a group of raiders that had six little children. They steal the kids from families to add to their numbers."

"Those poor children," says Denny. "The thought of my own kids in the hands of raiders . . ." Her voice trails off.

"And it makes it harder to fight them when they have kids with them," Patrice adds. "Who's going to shoot when they might hit those kids?"

"I wish we could figure out a way to rescue them," says Elle. "We could take them in and raise them right. We took in all the orphans during the war. Half the neighborhood women have children they've taken in. We could do it again. Just think about the horrible things they must have seen!"

Kate doesn't want to talk about the raiders today. These women have been good friends to her, and she respects them for what they have gone through and what they have accomplished, but she doesn't have time to get into a lengthy discussion now. There is too much work to be done. Besides, she just wants to enjoy the company of the women and the happy laughter of the children as they work.

She steps from one foot to the other awkwardly, then says, "Maybe you can try to come up with some ideas about that, and bring it up at the next market so everyone can start thinking about it."

"That's a good idea, Kate," Patrice says. "You of all people should be concerned about this."

"What do you mean?" Kate asks.

"I mean, you're out here all alone. Don't you worry about raiders blowing through here? They'd hit you before the rest of us would even know about it!"

Kate moves toward the side of the house, turning her back to Patrice. "I know. It's something I think about all the time, but—"

"You should move into town. We could set up a system where people take turns tending the field crops. Someone could come out here every day and take care of things, and you wouldn't have to live out here."

Kate is grateful for the genuine concern she hears in Patrice's voice, but she says, "Patrice, this is my home. This is where my children were born. I don't want to leave." She turns to her and smiles. "Besides, I've seen the tomatoes you've been hawking at the market this summer. If living inside the neighborhood means I'd only get nasty fruit like that, I'm staying out here!"

Patrice laughs. "Come on. You know my chickens got into them. Leave my poor tomatoes alone!" The other women laugh good-naturedly, and Patrice adds with a smile, "We've got a bunch of kids ready to work here today, Kate. Should we get started?"

Kate raises her hands to gather the children. "Okay, everyone," she shouts. "Let's head back to the shed and get the tools!" She leads the way, unlocking the padlock and swinging open the shed door so the children can collect the equipment they need.

Jonah pulls three wheel plows out of the dark shed, passing them to hands waiting outside. They are fashioned from bicycles Kate and Iris collected from the rubble seven years ago, sometimes pulling them out of deep craters and banks of dirt.

"Woo-hoo!" Iris had shouted each time she found a bicycle. "Kate, I got one!"

With Jonah napping on her back, tied snug to her body with the long cloth sling she had wrapped him in, Kate had trudged through the bricks and fallen trees to help Iris extract the bike. Laura and Margaret followed close behind, carefully avoiding the exposed chunks of concrete and jagged bits of brick. More often than not, the bicycles were twisted and warped. Only a few frames were found intact.

If a frame was straight, they would break the bike down before reassembling it for its new job. Iris removed the seat and stuck a long metal wedge into the space, tightening up the bolts. Then, flipping the frame upside down, she reinserted the handlebars where the front-tire fork had been, and put the front tire into the space for the back tire. Holding tight to the handlebars, the mothers and older children could push the bike frames through the field, driving the metal wedge deep to furrow and turn the dirt.

Laura and Margaret lift a six-by-six wooden-frame plow from the shed, with metal tines connected to the bottom and long straps of leather and fabric tied to the top. The older children who are gathered around guide the younger ones, explaining what each tool does, how to hold the straps and the rakes, and to be careful for the sharp metal parts.

Inside the shed, two tall metal bins contain the seed they need to plant the winter wheat. Iris, Patrice, and Elle take canvas bags from hooks on the wall and sling the long straps over their shoulders. Denny squeezes in beside them and opens the top of the bins that protect the seed from rodents. Together, they scoop out handfuls of seed and load it into the canvas sacks. When the bags are heavy and full, the women leave the shed.

Finally, the twins gather a group and lead them toward the river, working together to carry the tools. Kate watches as they cross the small bridge and spread out over the south field.

"Okay, Jonah," Kate says. "Let's bring the youngest ones into the house, and show them where all the food is." They lead three children into the house and show them the large pots of soup waiting on the stove, and the bowls stacked on the counter. Jonah will be in charge of helping the little ones distribute food and water to the workers in the field today, a responsibility he relishes.

"Jonah, go show them where the cups and pitchers are, okay?" Kate says.

"Okay. Come on everyone. The stuff is along the side of the house by the spigot," he says as he leads the noisy trio of children out the front door.

~

The children do good work in the field. Within two hours, about a quarter of it is cultivated. The freshly turned earth is dark and cool compared to the brightness and heat of the late September day. Margaret, Laura, and an older boy are using the wheel plows. They each stand behind a bicycle frame, holding tight to the handlebars, aiming the heavy blades deep into the dirt. Other children pull the wooden-frame plow by leaning their weight into the leather-and-fabric harnesses in front. Denny and the other children follow behind with rakes, leveling the soil to prepare it for the seed.

Jonah runs up to his mother with a pitcher of water. "Do you want me to bring out some soup for everyone yet?"

"Not yet, honey. We're just getting started," she says, adjusting the strap of the canvas sack on her shoulder. "When we get about half-done with the plowing, you can call everyone over for a break."

"Got it," he says, and continues into the field to offer water to the children working in the hot sun.

Kate, Iris, Patrice, and Elle start at the four edges of the ready part of the field. Working toward the center, they reach into their canvas bags and pull out small handfuls of seed. They spread the seed by hand, tossing the small grain down to the dirt with half-circle turns of their wrists. A few of the children follow behind them with the rakes, gently covering the seed with just a bit of soil. It would take Kate and her children days to accomplish what they can do in just hours with the help of the neighborhood.

When about half of the field has been plowed, Jonah's voice rings out loud and clear. "Time for a break! Everyone can put down your tools and come over for some food!"

The sweaty children drop their rakes and unharness themselves from the plows before walking to the edge of the field where Jonah has set up the picnic lunch. Bowls are stacked up, with the big pots of soup nearby. Jonah had successfully directed the younger children's effort to haul the heavy pots to the field. They used the wheelbarrows he designed and created from scraps found throughout the area, being careful not to slosh the soup as they crossed the yard and the bridge.

Everyone sits down in the late summer sun as they eat and drink, enjoying the gurgle of the river as it slowly flows past. Sunlight bounces off the surface of the water, playing in the cattails, irises, and other phreatophytes along the bank. Someone decides to take off his shoes and stick his feet into the water, and soon all the other children have done the same.

Kate sits near the top of the bank, watching the children and sipping soup from the edge of her bowl. As the food begins to refuel them, the light of easy laughter begins to surround the children like a soft glow. She smiles when they inevitably begin to splash water onto each other with slaps of their feet. The mothers know it will soon devolve into a soaking wet pile of children.

Patrice stands up and firmly says, "All right, everyone. If you're done with your lunch, let's get back to work."

~

It is late in the afternoon when they are done. The seed has been sown, and the children have watered the field with pitchers, scooping water out of the irrigation ditches Kate filled by opening one of the weirs by the dam. As they pour the water from the pitchers, they separate it with their fingers to sprinkle and splash the earth.

As they finish the last section, Kate pushes her hands into the small of her back, arching her spine in a stretch. She wipes a tangle of hair away from her eyes with the back of her filthy forearm and looks over the field, full of hope for the tiny seeds that will germinate in the dark, rich dirt.

In another hour, the tools are cleaned and dried, and the last of the plows, rakes, and sacks have been put back into the shed. Kate moves to Iris's side and says, "Thank you for all your help today." She sweeps her hand out to the group of women. "All of you."

"You're welcome, Kate," Iris replies. She exhales loudly as her shoulders slump. "I might be getting too old for this."

Kate puts her arm around Iris's shoulder and smiles. "You'll never get old, my friend. You'll be plowing these fields with my grandchildren someday."

Margaret and Laura are off near the edge of the trees, talking to several of their friends, quietly laughing and teasing. Jonah is running around the yard with three of the younger boys.

"How can they still have the energy to run around?" Kate wonders out loud to the women standing near her. "I think if we could figure out how to harness the infinite energy of boys, we would be able to power the world," she jokes. The mothers laugh and shake their heads, but Kate's smile fades a bit as she thinks about what she just said.

In the dappled light, the women gather the children and begin the long walk back to town. Kiko and Ruby run back and forth from the porch to the departing group, wagging and barking and jumping as Margaret, Laura, and Jonah wave to their friends. Kate wraps her arm around Margaret and gives her a little hug. She can hear the children laughing and shouting as they leave her yard and head into the rubble.

~

The last of the evening sun fades as the family prepares for dinner. Jonah is scooping soup into bowls from the dredges of the large pots. Laura and Margaret stand near the table, filling mugs with water and setting out spoons. Kate has saved the last bit of this week's bread for tonight, knowing her children would be extra hungry after the day in the field. She is standing at the kitchen counter, cutting thin slices when she hears Margaret yell at Laura. "I told you not to fill it that full! You get the towel. It's not my fault!"

"Hey, what's going on in here?" asks Kate, moving into the dining room. "What happened?"

Margaret is upset. "Laura filled the cups too full, and then one spilled all over! It's dripping all over the floor, and she doesn't even have the sense to get the towel!"

"Why should I get it? You spilled it!" Laura says to her sister.

"But I told you not to fill them so full!"

"Okay, okay. Girls, it's just water. I'll grab a towel. It's no big deal." Kate steps to the kitchen and returns a moment later with two well-worn towels. "Margaret, you wipe the floor, and Laura, you wipe the table."

Margaret grumbles as she kneels down.

Laura catches her mother's eye and shrugs. "She's probably just mad because she didn't get to see her boyfriend today."

Kate turns to Margaret, who is now glaring at Laura. "Boyfriend? You have a boyfriend?"

"He's not my boyfriend, Mom," Margaret barks. "And Laura should just keep her nose out of my life!"

"Maybe he's not your boyfriend, but you want him to be," Laura teases.

"Shut up!"

Kate's daughters have always had the ability of being the best of friends and the worst of enemies in the same breath. She tries to defuse the growing hostility by saying, "Laura, please don't make fun of Margaret's feelings. If she does like a boy, you should be the one person in the world she can trust with that information." Laura looks sideways at her mother. "And Margaret, you know if you let her get under your skin like that, it just makes you feel worse." Neither of the girls say anything.

When Kate can't stand it any longer, against her better judgment, she asks, "So, do you have a boyfriend?"

Both of her daughters look at her as if she were an idiot. They shake their heads and roll their eyes dramatically. Well, at least they're united again by their disgust with me, she thinks.

"Well, who is it?" Kate says.

Margaret still doesn't answer.

"Is it Rebecca's son? The blond one who doesn't have the sense to tie up their pig?"

"I don't have a boyfriend," Margaret says under her breath.

"Well, I trust you'll let me know when you do." Neither girl says a word. With an exasperated sigh, Kate walks back to the kitchen counter.

The four of them sit down to a simple dinner around the

dining room table. Kiko and Ruby, exhausted from the day of running and playing, curl up on their beds in the kitchen and start to snore softly. It is dark outside, so Jonah turns on the small lamp along the wall.

Apparently done fighting, Margaret asks Laura, "Did you see how Patrick was whining when the plow broke today?"

"Yes," Laura answers, rolling her eyes. "He does that every season. And then I get to help him fix it."

Through half-closed eyes, Kate notices that Jonah is nearly done with his first bowl of soup by the time she starts hers, and she wonders at how much his body is growing and changing lately. "Jonah, slow down. You'll get sick if you eat so quickly." She props one elbow onto the table and leans her head into her palm, slowly scooping up the soft carrots and beans from the broth, already thinking about how good her mattress will feel tonight.

When his bowl is empty, Jonah goes to the kitchen to refill it. He is about to sit down again when he stops. Kate looks up from her soup to see Jonah standing at the other end of the table, one hand holding his bowl, one hand touching the back of his chair. His face is white and his dark eyes wide, looking over Kate's shoulder toward the front room.

"Mom. Mama," he whispers.

She is afraid to turn, but she knows she has to. The sound of the blood rushing into her head fills her ears, and she holds her breath. Margaret and Laura are frozen, their heads turned toward the front room and their eyes full of fear. Kate puts down her spoon and pushes her chair back.

In the faint light of the rising moon, she can see a man standing on her front porch. He is motionless on the other side of the cracked and patched picture window that fills half of the front wall. His dark hair and beard are long and matted. His gray-and-black clothes are torn and filthy. It takes Kate a moment to realize what he is holding. A child hangs limp from his arms.

~ Six ~

KATE SPRINGS INTO MOTION, dashing to the kitchen to grab her long knife before running back to the dining room, where the children are frozen in fear. The dogs, startled awake, scramble to the front room. They erupt in ferocious barking, snarling at the man on the porch. Kate stands in front of the table, putting herself between the man and her children. He has not moved, but he is looking straight at her. Kate doesn't know what to do.

Nearly a minute goes by before Laura whispers, "Mom, I think he has a kid in his arms."

Kate says nothing. She doesn't take her eyes off the man on the other side of the window. It isn't until she sees that Jonah has stepped to her side that she musters the courage to move. "Stay here. All of you. Don't move," she tells them in a quiet voice. "If he does anything, I want you all to get to the cellar. Right away. Don't wait for me."

Move your right foot forward. Just move your foot, Kate thinks to herself.

She manages to lift one foot and take a step. Once her legs begin to move, her mind agrees to move, too. "Kiko! Ruby! Right here," she calls as she walks to the front room. The dogs stop barking and move to her side.

Kate inches to the window and looks at the man. A lump feels lodged in her throat, and she has to force herself to speak. "If you move, I will kill you," she yells, pointing the knife toward the man. "Do you understand?"

He nods slowly, keeping his eyes on her.

"What do you want?" she shouts.

He doesn't speak but looks down at the child in his arms.

Clenching her jaw, Kate stares at him for a minute more. Finally, knowing that she must try to help the child, she moves sideways the few feet to the front door and places her hand on the dead bolt above the knob. "Margaret and Laura, I want you to keep an eye on him."

"Mom! Don't go out there," Margaret pleads.

Her hand still on the lock, Kate turns back to her children. "I have to." She turns the dead bolt with a loud click and then opens the door. Leading with the knife held firmly in her hand, she steps out onto the porch. The man slowly turns his body to face her, cradling the child in front of him. "What do you want?" she repeats, glaring.

The man speaks deliberately and quietly. "This boy needs help. He's sick, and he needs your help."

For the first time, Kate breaks away from the man's gaze and looks down to the boy. He looks about six or seven years old, though in the tangle of his baggy clothes it is difficult to tell.

"Where did you get him?" she asks.

"He's my son."

Kate looks back into the man's eyes. They are blue and,

even in the dim light, they are bright. His face reveals no emotion, but she thinks she hears sincerity in his voice as he simply says, "Please."

"What's wrong with him?"

"I don't know. He was feeling sick the last three days. Today he developed a fever. He's so hot, and I don't know what to do." The man is still speaking calmly, quietly.

Kate knows the man could be a raider. This could be a horrible trick. This could all go bad very quickly. But if he is telling the truth, he has risked his life for the boy. As much as she wants to appear tough and in control, she already knows she will do everything she can to try to help the child.

"You'll put him down on the porch, then step down and walk away," Kate tells the man.

"I'm not leaving him here alone."

"If you want me to help him, you will do what I tell you."

The man hesitates, then bends his knees. He lowers the child gently to the floor of the porch and then slides his arms out from beneath the boy. Before standing, he looks down at the child and brushes the hair from the boy's face. Rising, the man looks back to Kate and says, "I'll step off the porch, but I'm not leaving." He sidesteps to the edge of the porch and backs down the steps to the yard.

Once the man is about twenty feet away, Kate takes a closer look at the boy lying in a heap on her porch. She bends and sets her knife down next to him. She scoops him up in her arms and then picks the knife up again, holding it carefully so the edge is pointed away from the child. Kate backs into the house, her eyes on the man until she closes her front door, locking it.

Her children are still at the table, clumped in a group, watching. The dogs are where she left them, still alert. Kate hurries to the tattered couch lying against the far wall of the front room and eases the boy onto the cushions. His clothes and hair are damp and filthy, but his face and hands have been recently wiped clean. Kneeling beside the couch, Kate can feel the heat of his fever and see the shallowness of his breathing through his wet clothes.

"He must have tried to dip you in the river to cool you off," Kate says to the unconscious boy. "Laura, I need some washcloths and a bucket of fresh water. Jonah, get me some towels."

Margaret moves to her mother's side and kneels next to her. "Is he okay, Mom?"

"I don't know yet. Don't touch him. He has a high fever. If it's from a virus, it might burn itself out and he'll be fine. But if it's an infection, he'll need to see Dr. Preston right away."

Out of the corner of her eye, Kate notices movement on the porch. She looks up to see that the man has returned. He looks around and then slowly walks to the chair set in the corner. The man picks up the chair and puts it directly in front of the picture window. He sits down and looks at the boy on the couch.

"Keep your eyes on that man, Margaret," Kate whispers.

Jonah hands the towels to his mother. She folds one of them up and lifts the boy's body enough to slide it beneath him. When Laura comes in with the water and washcloths, Kate begins to take the boy's clothes off. "I need to look him over to see if he has any obvious injuries."

She peels off his damp shirt, dips a washcloth into the bucket of water, and squeezes it out. Then she begins to wash the boy's thin arms and chest. It looks as if he hasn't bathed in weeks, and dirt quickly cakes the cloth. Though he doesn't open his eyes, the boy whimpers as she moves him, and quietly cries when the cool cloth wipes his skin. A good sign, Kate thinks.

Methodically, Kate works her way down the boy's body, removing his clothes as she goes and covering the cleaned parts with the fresh towels. As she pulls off his thin pants, he urinates into the air. Kate quickly covers his penis with the washcloth, and most of the urine flows onto the folded towel below him. It is concentrated and dark yellow.

When she has examined his whole body, she says, "Jonah, can you get some of your clean pajamas for him to borrow? I'll boil his clothes tonight so they're ready to dry tomorrow."

"Did you figure out what's wrong with him?" asks Margaret.

"I don't see anything obvious. No cuts or bruises. He's definitely febrile, and quite dehydrated." She chews on the corner of her bottom lip as she thinks through the next step. "Laura, could you please get some of the soup from dinner? Just a little bit. Add some water so it's tepid and pretty thin, then bring it in here. We'll see if we can get some fluids into him."

Jonah has returned with some pajamas. "I picked some that were a little small for me. And I brought this blanket and pillow so he can sleep."

"Great. Thanks, honey." Kate slips the fresh shirt over the boy's head, tugging it down onto his body. He cries again. His eyes flutter open briefly, and she notices that his irises are as blue as those of the man on the porch, if not as bright. The boy looks at Kate, unseeing, before he falls back to sleep. She finishes by pulling on the loose-fitting pants, then covers him with the blanket.

Laura comes into the front room with a bowl and a spoon. Kate lifts the top of the boy's body into a sitting position while sliding herself in behind him. He stirs again, and she talks gently to him. "It's okay, honey. You're safe here. I know you don't feel well right now, but I want you to try to drink a little bit of this soup, okay?"

Laura holds the bowl for Kate while she scoops a small amount of broth onto the spoon. She puts the spoon to the boy's mouth and tries to get him to drink a little. The boy's face contorts, and he turns his head away from the spoon. "Come on, love, you can do it. Take just a few sips for me." After several tries, the boy wakes enough to drink a sip of the soup. His eyes open, and he looks around the room at the three children watching him. He seems delirious from the fever and doesn't speak, but Kate manages to get him to take about a half cup of the liquid before he falls back to sleep.

"Thanks, honey. I think that's all we'll do for now," Kate says to Laura. Laura takes the bowl and spoon back into the kitchen, and Kate slides out from beneath the boy, laying him back down onto the couch. "We'll try again in a few hours and just see how he does tonight. Maybe we'll know more in the morning."

"What about the man?" whispers Margaret. "Do you think he'll stay out there all night?"

"I don't know. I'll have to go talk to him."

"Don't, Mom! Don't go back out there. He's been staring at us the whole time."

Kate looks out the window at the man. He hasn't moved; his hands are still resting on the arms of the chair. "It's okay, Mags," she says quietly.

But Kate is not sure that is true. She turns to the children. "I want you three to stay right here by the couch and watch through the window. I'm going to go to the door just to talk to him. If there's trouble, get to the cellar."

"What about the boy?" asks Jonah.

Kate pauses before answering. Will she tell her children to risk their lives for this unknown child? "Leave the boy."

Kate picks up her knife. She looks back at her children and smiles encouragingly, then unbolts the door. Loudly enough to be sure the man outside can hear, she says, "If he tries anything, we'll kill him."

As she steps onto the porch, the man turns his head toward her, but he does not stand. They look at each other for a moment, then he says, "Do you know what's wrong with him?"

"I can't be sure. He definitely has a fever, but I don't see anything obvious that could have caused it. It might be a virus." She needs more information. "Did he get injured lately, or did anything unusual happen?"

"No."

"Did he eat or drink anything that might make him sick?"

"No."

"How long have you been with him?"

"I told you, he's my son." For the first time, the man's voice gets louder. Kate sees anger flash in his eyes, then he quickly regains his composure. "He's been with me his whole life. I don't know what's wrong with him. Three days ago he said he wasn't feeling well and started throwing up. Today he stopped throwing up, but he seemed to feel a lot worse. Then by this afternoon, he was really hot and could barely move." The man has lowered his voice again. "When I couldn't get him to wake up, I came here for help."

The story doesn't sit well with Kate. "But where is your wife?"

He stares at her but doesn't answer.

"What neighborhood are you with?"

Still nothing.

She asks, "Are you with a group of raiders?"

Hostility glows in his blue eyes again, but he simply says, "No."

Kate doesn't want to push the man further, afraid of the anger she saw flash over his face. Trying to hide her fear, she says, "Well, all I can tell is that he's really dehydrated. Maybe if we can get him to drink a bit tonight, he'll feel better in the morning. If not, you'll have to take him into the neighborhood to see the doctor."

"How am I going to do that?" the man asks bitterly.

Before the war, before the new rules, that question would have been easy to answer. But Kate knew the implications of it now. How would the unknown man walk into the center of town without alarming the other women? She knew as well as he did that he could be shot before he ever got to the doctor's house.

"Let's just see how he is tomorrow." She takes a deep breath and glances back into the house. The boy is resting peacefully on the couch. Her children are still standing near him, on guard. "What's his name?"

The man pauses and looks into the house. His demeanor softens at the sight of the small boy. "His name is Evan."

Kate hears the way the man says the name. Gently, with a soft pride and a deep love in his voice. As if he had been saying the name since before the boy was born. As if the name means more to the man than anything in this world. Kate hesitates, then says, "You can't stay here tonight."

"I'm not leaving him."

"You can come back in the morning."

"I'm not leaving him."

He is looking right at Kate, and she knows he will not

back down. So she turns to the front door and steps inside. Before closing the door, she says, "I'm locking the door. Don't try to get in."

~

Kate takes a chair from the dining room and sets it next to the couch. Throughout the night she keeps watch over the boy. Every few hours he stirs, at times calling out nonsensical words or garbled phrases. During those wakeful times, she lifts his body and spoon-feeds him a bit of soup. She sleeps lightly and in short spurts, listening to the boy's breathing and for any hints that the man might be trying to get into the house, even as she dozes.

Each time Kate looks out the window, the man is still there in the chair. Most times, he is awake, watching the boy, watching her, but several times she notices that his head has dropped to his chest and he is asleep.

The long night finally fades as the first glimmer of sun begins to light the yard. Kate opens her eyes, and it takes her a minute to remember why she is on a chair in the front room. The boy is still sleeping on the couch next to her, and she reaches to touch his forehead with the palm of her hand. He's still quite hot, but he looks a little better than last night. Kate smiles at the boy and then remembers the man. She lifts her head to look out the window and sees only an empty chair.

Her stomach tightens, and she strides quickly to the window. Where is he? She is about to turn, ready to run to the bedroom to check on her children, when she spots him across the yard. He is standing still at the edge of the forest, his back to her. Then he adjusts the front of his pants and turns back toward the house. Embarrassed, Kate rushes back to her chair.

The boy's eyes are open, and he is staring at her. She notices again how blue his eyes are, a little brighter today than in his delirium last night. She gently says, "Hey, good morning. Don't be scared. I'm not going to hurt you. You were really sick last night, and we tried to help you."

He doesn't speak, but she can see that he's frightened. "You're in my house. A man brought you here last night. Do you know who that man is?"

Just then, Jonah steps barefoot into the room. Seeing that the boy is awake, he runs to his mother's side. He's usually the last one up, and Kate guesses that anticipation for meeting the boy woke him early.

"Hi," Jonah says, raising his hand in a small wave.

"He just woke up," Kate whispers to Jonah. "I'm not sure he knows where he is or what's going on."

Jonah shrugs and kneels by the couch. "Well, you're in my house and we're taking care of you. You were really sick last night. Are you still sick today?"

"I think he is, honey. He's still pretty hot," Kate says softly.

"Okay, well, you'll get better soon. Don't worry. My mom will take care of you." Jonah is talking to the boy in his regular voice, but his movements are a little exaggerated. Kate can tell he is excited about the boy, curious about him. Jonah stretches his arms over his head and says, "Well, I guess I'll get you some breakfast. I know I'm hungry."

As he leaves the room, Kate sees the man step back onto the porch. He doesn't sit down but looks first at the boy, then to Kate. He wants an update. She takes a long sweater from the hook on the wall and pulls the thick, faded red wool around herself. Reaching out to touch the doorknob, she glances back to the chair where she spent the night and sees the knife lying on the floor. She walks quickly to the spot, bends to pick up the knife, and then goes out into the cool morning air.

Standing on the front porch, Kate crosses her left arm in front of herself, keeping the knife in her right hand pointed at the man. "He's awake now, but he's still pretty hot."

"Is he better than last night?"

"I think so, but it's hard to tell. I'll just have to see as he wakes up a bit more."

"Is he going to be okay?"

Kate takes a deep breath. She is irritated by the man, annoyed that he brought this mess to her, and exhausted from the sleepless night. "Look, I'm not a doctor. I have no idea what's wrong with him. If he's got a virus, his body is heating up to fight it off. Viruses are sensitive to heat, so the body reacts with a fever. The fever will burn off in a couple days and he'll be fine. If it's something else, I have no idea what to do."

"I'm not an idiot. I know what a virus is," he says. "He's been sick before from viruses, and I know how they work."

"Well then, why did you bring him to me?"

His eyes meet Kate's for a moment, then he drops his gaze to the floor. His jaw is clenched and he crosses his arms in front of his chest before answering. "Look. Believe me, I wouldn't have come here if I didn't have to."

This is going nowhere, thinks Kate. "I'll let you know when I know more." She turns to go back inside but adds, "In the meantime, you can stay on the porch, but stay away from my family." She dead-bolts the door and slides her knife into its sheath.

Jonah is sitting on the couch with the boy, holding a bowl of soup and a spoon. Margaret and Laura are sitting on the floor in front of them, talking to the boy. He is sitting up a bit, propped up against the pillow in the corner of the couch.

Kate takes the bowl and spoon from Jonah. "Honey,

move off the couch," she tells him. "I want you to give him some space." Jonah slides down to the floor, and Kate squats in front of the boy, balancing her arms on her thighs.

"Hey, are you feeling any better?" she asks.

He looks at Jonah and the girls before answering in a quiet voice. "A little."

"He ate a couple sips of the soup," Jonah says.

"That's good." Kate glances down at the bowl in her hand, then points out the window at the man sitting on the porch. Quietly, she asks, "The man who brought you here—do you know him?"

He nods and looks out the front window. He gives the man a little smile and says, "That's my dad."

Kate is glad to hear that. She wants it to be true. "He said your name is Evan, right?" The boy nods again. "Well, Evan, I think if we can get some fluids into you, you might start feeling even better. Is there anything I can bring you to make you more comfortable?"

He looks at the girls again and then leans over toward Jonah. The boys put their heads close together, and Evan whispers something into her son's ear. Jonah nods and holds his hand to the side of his face to keep his sisters from seeing the words he mouths. "Mom, he has to pee."

~

Throughout the morning, Jonah helps Kate tend to the boy in between doing his regular chores. He takes charge of the boy's freshly boiled clothes, hanging them to dry on the line in the kitchen, and peeks into the front room often to see if he's awake. Evan, still feverish, fades in and out of sleep but is willing to sip soup or tepid tea when awake.

Margaret and Laura walk warily through the house, still fearful of the man outside. When the dogs begin to whine,

Kate ties rope leashes around their necks and takes them out through the rear entrance, asking her daughters to keep an eye on the man to make sure he stays put.

The man doesn't budge all morning. Each time Evan wakes, he turns to look out the window, as if making sure his father is still there. He smiles weakly, and the man smiles back and lifts his hand in a small wave.

At lunchtime, the family sits down together at the table while Evan sleeps on the couch. They eat leftover chicken-salad sandwiches, and preserved plums from the cellar. Kate talks about housework, trying to ignore the obvious questions they all have about the strangers. "Margaret, the lever on the drain of the washing machine is dripping again. I'd like you to try to tighten it up. Jonah can wring out the load that's in there and hang it to dry. And Laura, we haven't checked the traps yet today. We have to do that right away in the morning, or—"

"Mom, I'm not going out there while he's on the porch," Laura says.

Kate sits back in her chair, wiping the corner of her mouth with a worn gray napkin. "I know. I guess we could go out together if Margaret makes sure he just stays there—"

"No. I'm not doing it. What if there are more of them out there? What if they come running out of the forest?"

"We can take Kiko and Ruby," Kate answers calmly. "We have to check the traps. If there's something in there, it will just attract rodents and wild dogs if we let it sit."

"You can't take the dogs," Margaret blurts, her voice trembling. "What if he tries to get in here while you're outside? Or what if that boy tries to hurt us?"

Jonah says, "How can he hurt you? Evan is really sick, and he needs our help."

"Jonah, you don't know everything! They both probably

want to kill us all," Laura says, and Kate notices tears welling up in her eyes.

"Okay, honey," Kate says as she stands up and moves behind Laura's chair. She puts her hands on her daughter's shoulders. "We're all a little worried about this, but we need to try to stay calm and figure out what to do. I'm not going to let him hurt us. We know what to do if somebody tries to get in here. The cellar is very safe."

"But he's sitting on our porch right now! Why did you let him stay here? Why did you take that kid in the first place?"

Kate kneels down next to Laura and looks into her eyes. "Laura, Evan is really sick. We have to help children who are sick. If we didn't take him in last night, we would be no better than the raiders."

"But what about the man?"

"I don't know." Kate takes a deep breath and looks around the table at each of her children. "I'll go talk to him. I'll try to figure something out." She walks to the front door. Before she opens it, Jonah runs to her with a plate. Half of his sandwich is still on it.

"Here, take this out to him. I'm not that hungry."

Kate begins to protest but stops herself. She takes the plate and goes out onto the porch.

The man stands but stays by the chair. Kate can see holes in his thin overcoat, the ends of the sleeves are frayed and too short for his long arms. The shadow of dark circles below his eyes blend with the dirt matted in his scraggly beard. And even from across the porch, she can smell him. Kate takes only one step toward him and sets the plate onto the porch rail. "Here's a sandwich. You must be hungry."

His eyes follow the plate as she put it down, but he doesn't move toward it. "How is he?"

"I think he's feeling a bit better. He's eating and drinking a little bit, but he's still warm. Sometimes, they feel better in the morning but then get worse as the day goes on." She shrugs and waits for the man to speak again.

"I can take him now."

Surprised, Kate just looks at the man. This could be an easy solution to the problem. The man could take the boy and be gone from their lives.

From where she is standing, she can see the couch through the window. Evan is awake again, and Jonah is sitting near him, holding the wooden deer he carved two winters ago and showing the boy the details of his work. They are talking and smiling.

"I don't know. He's still feverish."

The man does not speak for a moment. Then, glancing off into the yard, he shrugs and says, "I know you don't want us here. If he's getting better, I can take him and you won't have to deal with us anymore."

"You're right. I don't want you here. But he's just a little boy, and it's my responsibility to make sure he's okay."

"No. He's my son. He's my responsibility." His blue eyes flash.

She wants to know more about them. She wants to ask him a hundred questions about the boy's life and figure out how to help him. She has already begun to wonder how she can get the child away from this man to save him from the filth in which he lives.

"I know he's your son. I just want to make sure he's okay. I think he should stay here at least until his fever is gone."

The man looks unconvinced.

"If he has a bacterial infection," she says, "he might still need a doctor. And you're right—you can't take him into town.

But we could."

Looking defeated, he sits back down in the chair and folds his hands on his lap. Kate goes back inside, feeling like a prisoner inside her own house.

That afternoon, Evan's temperature rises again and he sleeps. Kate and her children try to accomplish their normal tasks, but everything is made more difficult by their fear of the man on the porch. Margaret and Laura are sitting at the table, working on their lessons, and Jonah and Kate are in the kitchen kneading flour into bread dough when there is a knock at the front door. The dogs explode into barking and rush to the front room. Kate runs after them, shushing them. She glances at Evan, but he does not wake up. She opens the door slowly, only wide enough to see the man.

"I have to leave for a while," he says. "But I'll be back soon. If Evan wakes up looking for me, will you tell him that?"

"I'll tell him."

He backs up two steps and places the empty plate on the porch floor before turning to go. She opens the door a bit more and watches him step into the yard and around to the back of the house. She hurries to the kitchen window and watches him go through the backyard, across the small wooden bridge, and through the fallow field. When he disappears into the trees, she knows he is the same man she saw weeks ago. They must live out there, she thinks.

Ten minutes later, the family goes outside full of trepidation, but there is no trace of the man. The children work together to clean the chicken coop and check the traps, and the dogs sniff around the perimeter of the yard. Kate is relieved to be out in the fresh air and open space. She moves between her children, helping them with their chores, grateful to be free of the walls they have been bouncing off of inside the house.

It's Margaret who alerts them when she sees the man coming back across the bridge nearly an hour later. Kiko and Ruby run toward him, barking wildly, and Kate calls to the dogs to come back. They stay close to the man as he crosses the yard, sniffing his legs and jumping away from him every few steps. Margaret and Laura quickly head indoors, but Jonah moves to his mother's side. They stand close together near the shed.

"Kiko! Ruby! That's enough. Quiet down now. It's okay," Kate says as she pulls out her knife again, angling her body so she is between the man and Jonah. Kiko stands near her, keeping watch, but Ruby soon lies down a few feet away. In the man's right hand are two skinned rabbits. When he gets to Kate, he lifts his arm, holding the rabbits out to her.

"These are for you."

She slowly takes the rabbits from him and hands them to Jonah. "Thank you."

"You're welcome."

Kate notices that the man's hair and beard are wet. He is wearing the same dark clothes, but his face and hands are clean. He looks at her uncomfortably, then drops his gaze to the ground.

"Look, I understand how difficult this is for you. I'm sorry if I scared you and your family last night, but I didn't know what else to do. I couldn't wake up Evan, and I had to do something, so I brought him to you." He is still speaking slowly, deliberately, as if he'd been practicing this speech during the last hour. "I know you've been taught to fear strange men, but I have no intention of hurting you or your children. I'm not a bad man."

"Okay," is all Kate says.

His shoulders slump and he exhales loudly. He puts his hands on his hips and looks first at Jonah, then back to her. "What's your name?" he asks.

"My name is Kate Decker. And this is my son, Jonah." The man looks at her expectantly, and she knows she should reciprocate. "What's your name?"

"I'm Michael MacGregor." He holds out his hand and says, "It's nice to meet you."

It was the old formal way, from a time when men and women might meet each other unexpectedly, but Kate remembers it. It was the way she'd met her husband. She lifts her hand to take his and says, "It's nice to meet you, too."

Releasing her hand, he asks, "How is Evan? Has he been sleeping this whole time?"

"I think so. I'm sure Margaret and Laura are checking on him now. He's been sleeping a lot this afternoon."

"Can I see him?"

It's the moment Kate has dreaded. It goes against everything she's been taught to invite a strange man into her home, but how can she refuse to let him see his son? "Let me go in and check on him. If he's still sleeping, I think we should try to not disturb him."

There is hesitation in her voice, and the man looks disappointed. "I understand."

"Mom, let's get these rabbits in, and I can start cooking them up for dinner," Jonah says. He turns and walks toward the garden gate. Kate follows him and, when she reaches the garden, turns to the man. "You can go up to the front. I'll check on Evan and let you know." Without waiting for an answer, Kate pulls the heavy gate closed behind her and latches it.

Evan sleeps for much of the rest of the day. Each time Kate goes into the front room to check on him, she sees Michael sitting in the chair outside. She is thankful the boy stays asleep but knows he's bound to wake up soon. When he does, she will be put in the difficult position of choosing to let the man in or asking him to stay out. Either choice could lead to catastrophe.

The family eats a dinner of roasted rabbit, along with a late-season salad of kale and apples. Jonah prepares a separate plate for the man and sets it next to his mother at the table. When they have eaten, she takes the food out to him.

"Here's a bit of dinner for you," she says, crossing the porch to where he sits.

"Thank you."

"You're welcome." She leans against the porch rail and looks into the house to where Evan lies. "How old is he?"

"Eight." Michael eats quickly, using his fingers to stuff the juicy meat into his mouth.

"Do you live out in the hills?"

Michael takes few seconds to chew his food before answering. "Yes."

"Do you have a house out there?"

"No."

"Where is his mother?"

Michael stops eating and turns to face Kate. "You don't really want to know all this. You want to get him healthy so you have a clear conscience, and then you want us to disappear. You don't have to stand here asking me all this to make yourself feel better."

"Please don't presume to know what I want," Kate says, irritated. "I am genuinely concerned about Evan, and I'm trying to learn more about him so I can help him."

"I don't need you to help him."

"What?"

"It's not your job to help my son."

"It's my job to help anyone in need. And, no offense, but he sure looks like he is in need."

"We're fine."

"Do you even hear yourself? You came to me. You came to me with that little boy lying senseless in your arms, filthy and feverish. Maybe you need to think about what's best for him."

He looks at her for a long time before speaking. "Evan is my son. I take care of him. The last thing I need is a woman I don't even know trying to take him from me, claiming it's for his own good. Just because you're female doesn't mean you can take my child."

"I'm not trying to take your child." When she speaks the words, she hears the lie in her own voice and is disgusted with herself. That's exactly what she had been thinking when she saw the boy last night. But Michael's thoughts flew so quickly to the idea, she suddenly wonders if someone tried to take Evan away from him before. Curious, she waits in silence while he eats the rest of his food.

He stands up and turns to her, the plate extended in his hand. "Thank you for the food."

She takes the plate, and he sits back down. She wants to say more, but he has turned his back. Kate walks back into the house and locks the front door.

~ Seven ~

KATE WAKES EARLY the next morning, sore from another night in her chair. Even in the soft dawn light, she can see that Michael is gone from the porch. Evan, starting to stir on the couch, opens his eyes and looks at her.

"Good morning," she says, smiling.

"Good morning."

"How are you feeling today?" She walks to the corner and turns on the small lamp on the side table before moving to the edge of the couch. Kate touches Evan's forehead, pushing aside his reddish-brown mop of hair. His fever is down, but he is still warm. His cheeks are less flushed, and his eyes are bright.

"I feel okay." Evan sits up and looks around. "Where's Jonah?"

"He's still sleeping, but he'll probably be up soon. Is there anything I can get you? Are you hungry, or thirsty?"

The boy clears his throat. "I'm pretty thirsty."

Kate goes into the kitchen to get him a cup of water.

Jonah meets her there, still in his pajamas. "Is Evan awake yet?"

"He is. And he asked for you. Why don't you take this water in to him."

The two boys begin to talk as she kindles the fire in the cookstove and fills the heavy black pot with water. She overhears Evan telling Jonah about his favorite place to swim in the river. Jonah reciprocates with his ideas about the best places to fish. Kate notes that Evan referred to a location nearby, just a twenty-minute walk from their house.

Soon Margaret and Laura come into the kitchen, both dressed and ready to start the day. As the sun slowly drifts in through the kitchen window, they help Kate prepare breakfast.

Margaret asks, "Mom, is that man still here?"

"I think so. I talked to him last night and told him Evan should stay until he's well again."

The girls shoot sideways looks at each other. "How long will that be?"

"I don't know. I think he's feeling better today. We'll have to wait and see." The girls are quiet, and Kate knows they want the man to leave, but she feels a strange obligation to defend him. "His name is Michael. I think they live out in the forest. That's why he's so dirty."

"Aren't you scared of him?" Laura asks.

"I don't know," Kate says, honestly. "I think we have to be cautious, but I also think he really loves Evan, and is trying to do what he thinks is best for him. I think we need to just see what happens, and at the same time, be careful."

The girls sit down to breakfast, and Kate calls to Jonah to join them. He comes into the dining room with Evan at his side.

"Hey, you're up! Come have breakfast with us," Kate

says.

As they eat, Kate notices the way the boys talk to each other, the way they smile and laugh. Margaret and Laura are unusually quiet at the beginning of the meal, but eventually they start to laugh and joke with the boys.

"Mom, can I take Evan out to the river to show him the weir?" Jonah asks.

"Not yet, honey. He's been pretty sick. I want him to stay inside today. Maybe tomorrow."

"How long is he going to stay?" Laura asks.

Kate catches the bitter tone in Laura's voice and responds firmly. "Laura, Evan can stay here as long as he needs to. We don't throw out children."

Laura drops her eyes to her plate.

Jonah scoops scrambled eggs and a slice of toast onto a plate and heads toward the front door.

"Jonah, stop," Kate shouts, jumping to her feet. "Don't go out there. I'll do it."

"I was just going to give him some food."

"I know. But I'll do it. I don't want —"

Evan's small voice interrupts Kate. "My dad's not going to hurt Jonah."

Kate looks at the skinny boy sitting at her table in Jonah's baggy pajamas. Trying to apologize, she says, "I know he won't hurt Jonah. I just want to . . . I just want to talk to your father. He's not even out there now anyway."

She smiles at Evan and takes the plate from her son. "I'll just put this out for him. You sit down and finish your breakfast."

She steps onto the porch and sees Michael walking across the yard. His arms are full of thick logs and sticks. He veers to the side of the house and she hears several loud clunks as he adds them to the wood pile. Returning to the front of the house, he gives Kate a strained smile.

"I brought you some breakfast," she says as he steps onto the porch.

"Thank you again." He takes the plate from her but does not sit down. "Where's Evan?" he asks as he looks in through the window. There is a hint of panic in his voice.

"He's okay. He was feeling well enough to eat, so he's at the table with my kids."

Relief washes over Michael's face. "He's better? Can I see him?"

Kate hesitates, then says, "I suppose. I just . . . I'm not sure how."

"Kate, I'm not one of the raiders. I'm not going to hurt you." He is speaking slowly and quietly again.

Looking into his bright eyes, she wants to believe him.

"I just want to see my son. I've been with Evan every day of his life except these last two. I just want to talk to him."

"Of course. Yes, of course you can see him," she says, but she does not move toward the door.

Michael shakes his head and sets the still-untouched breakfast on the porch rail. "I know it's hard for you to believe me. I know what raiders can do, and I don't blame you for being careful. Why don't you go in and ask him to come back to the couch. I'll just wait here, and then you can let me in when you're ready." When she doesn't answer, he says, "I know it's a leap of faith."

Kate nods and then steps back inside. The four children are sitting at the table, finishing their breakfast. Jonah is teaching Evan a song he sings with his friends from the neighborhood. It's about dogs passing gas, complete with various noises to illustrate the concept. Kate thinks it's a stupid song. Evan is cracking up. Margaret and Laura are rolling their eyes and laughing. Jonah reaches the end of the verse, and all four join in the chorus—"So, don't give your dog a bean, 'cause you don't know where it's been. Dogs are really smart, but they really love to fart!" Then they all make the required loud noise with their mouths.

When Evan sees Kate, he stops and stands up. "Is my dad out there now?"

"He is. He's going to come in to see you, but I think you'd better head back to the couch for a bit. I don't want you to push it too hard today. You're still a little warm."

Evan hurries back to the couch, and Jonah rushes after him.

"Hold on, Jonah," Kate says. "I want you to get dressed and help clean up the breakfast dishes. There's also laundry to do, and the garden needs weeding. We've been slacking on our chores the last couple days, and we need to catch up."

With a sigh, Jonah turns around and walks down the small hallway to pick out some clothes from the shelf.

"You girls can bring the dishes to the kitchen. Then I want you to feed the chickens and check the traps. And I haven't seen you working on your lessons much this week. You have school tomorrow, so make sure you're ready."

Evan is waving at his father through the window, clearly happy that he's finally being allowed in. Before Kate turns the doorknob, her fingers touch the handle of the knife in her belt. When she opens the door, Michael is waiting there.

"Okay, come in," she says.

Without a word, Michael strides across the room to his son. "Hey, buddy, how are you feeling?" He squats in front of the couch, putting one hand on Evan's leg and the other hand on his forehead.

"I'm okay."

"You're still a little warm. Did you eat something?"

"Yes. I think I'm better, Dad. I think we can go." Evan looks up at Kate, standing on the other side of the room. Evan seems to sense the tension between Kate and Michael. He must know how risky it is for them to be in her house, and he has heard the wariness in her voice when she speaks to his father.

"Not just yet," Michael tells him. "I think Kate is right. We need to make sure you're all better before we go." Evan looks confused, but Michael pats his leg and nods.

"Hey, I brought you something," Michael says. He reaches into his pocket and pulls out a shiny black rock.

"My obsidian! I thought I lost it." The boy turns the stone over in his small hands.

"I found it at home, next to your bed. It must have fallen out of your pocket."

"Thanks, Dad. I can't wait to show Jonah."

Michael turns around and looks at Kate. "I also brought some of his clothes. I wasn't sure what you did with the ones he was wearing."

"We washed them. They're fine. But leave the other ones, too."

"Do you mind if I just sit with him for a while?"

"No. That's fine. Call if you need anything." She walks to the kitchen to give them some privacy.

~

Michael sits with Evan on the couch for nearly an hour. Kate can overhear most of their conversation—Evan talks a lot about Jonah and the things he has shown him—but at times, their voices drop to a whisper. Once, Michael says something inaudible to his son, and Kate hears the boy reply, "No, Dad, don't worry. She's been really nice."

When the girls are done with their morning chores and are ready to work on their lessons, Kate goes back into the front room. Michael is sitting on the couch next to Evan, his arm around the boy. They are smiling and talking. Michael looks up as she enters, and gives Evan one last squeeze before standing up.

"Dad, when can you come back in?"

Michael looks at Kate, the same question in his eyes.

"Why don't you try to rest now, and then your dad can come back in a little while," Kate says. She is already moving toward the door to let him out. Michael starts to cross the room, but he abruptly stops in front of the battered old upright piano standing against the wall. The wood on the top left corner is broken, it's scratched in many other places, and the bench is missing.

He looks at the piano for a moment before asking, "Do you play?" He lets his hand softly fall onto the closed lid over the keys.

"No. I can sound out a few simple melodies— 'Jingle Bells,' 'Happy Birthday,' things like that. But I don't play."

"Your children?"

"No, none of us. This belonged to an elderly couple who used to live nearby. When they died, I brought it here."

"Why?"

"It just seemed like something that should be saved. Do you play?"

Michael glides his hand across the surface of the piano. A sad smile flickers across his face and then disappears. He pulls his hand away. "No."

They walk together out to the front porch. He sweeps his arm in the direction of the yard, silently asking her to follow him. When they are down in the grass, out of sight of his son, Michael folds his arms across his chest and steps close to her.

"I want to thank you," he says quietly, looking into her eyes.

His clothes reek, a foul combination of mold and body odor, and Kate takes a step back, trying not to crinkle her nose. He notices and drops his gaze to the ground.

Embarrassed, she tries to make up for it. "You're welcome. I do think he should try to sleep a bit, though. If there's something you need to do for a while, go ahead, and then maybe you can come back later and see him again."

He nods once, still looking at the ground, and walks away. She watches him cross the bridge and the field, and enter the hilly forest. When he has passed beyond her sight, she notices that the first golden leaves are beginning to drift to the ground.

Inside, Kate sits next to Evan on the couch. He is playing a domino game Jonah set out for him. "How are you feeling?" she asks.

"Okay," he says without looking up from the game.

"Your dad says he'll try to come back and see you later." The boy doesn't answer, so Kate continues. "It looked like he was going back to your place in the woods. Do you have a house out there?"

"No."

"Do you have a tent or something?"

"No."

"Well, where do you live?"

Evan stops playing dominoes and looks up at her. "I'm not supposed to tell you about it. My dad says not to tell you anything about us."

Kate is offended by this, but part of her understands Michael's need for secrecy. Undeterred, she presses Evan for more information, trying to be less obvious. "Oh, that's okay, if your dad told you not to. I was just trying to figure out if you needed anything. If you're feeling better, maybe tomorrow you can go back home. Do you want to bring some blankets, or food or anything?"

"Um, maybe."

"I know this couch isn't that great, but it's better than sleeping on the ground, right?" she says with a laugh.

"We're not on the ground. It's okay. As long as it's not too rainy, it's okay."

"And I bet if you asked Jonah, he'd let you borrow some of his toys if you wanted."

"Really?"

"Sure. You can ask him. Do you have sleeping bags out there? Maybe I could see if any of Jonah's old clothes would fit you. Do you need some more clothes, or a hat maybe?"

"Dad said we'd have to find some more stuff before it gets colder. We usually have enough food, though." At this, Evan stops and looks quickly at Kate, a glimmer of fear in his eyes. "I mean, we find food sometimes. And my dad is good at hunting." He looks back down at the dominoes intently, avoiding Kate's gaze.

"Do you have any other friends out there?"

"No."

"Does your mother live out there?"

Evan shakes his head a little, still looking at the game.

"Well, I think Jonah and the girls like you. They could be your friends. And they know what it's like to have just one parent. They only have a mom, and you only have a dad." She watches as one of his bony knees bounces up and down a few times, but he says nothing.

Kate bends to look into Evan's eyes. "Even when you're

back home with your dad, you are always welcome here. Do you understand? You can always come here if you need anything."

He gives her a small smile, and she tries to smile back.

The entire family joins Michael and Evan that night in the living room. Michael has left his heavy coat hanging on the porch rail outside, and Kate is pleased to notice that the coat must be the source of much of his stink. Michael and Evan are on the couch, and Kate has brought in chairs from the dining room so everyone can sit. Laura is reading from one of Jonah's favorite books in *The Chronicles of Narnia* series, acting out the different voices and moving around the room like the waves that bob the ship in the story. Holding the book in one hand, her free arm reaches out and her head lolls from side to side as she animates the idea of a seasick boy.

"'What he saw was blue waves flecked with foam, and paler blue sky, both spreading without a break to the horizon. Perhaps we can hardly blame him if his heart sank. He was promptly sick.'"

With this, Laura leans over and makes a retching sound, sending Jonah and Evan into a giggling fit. Kate's heart is warmed by the sound of their happiness. She looks over to see that Michael is smiling as well. He must feel her eyes on him, because he looks in her direction, but Kate's glance darts back to her daughter.

After an hour of the children taking turns reading out loud from their chosen books, Kate stretches her arms up over her head. "I think we should probably start getting ready for bed now." All four children groan, but she ushers three of them toward the bedroom.

Jonah turns to Evan as he leaves the room. "Good night,

Ev. See you in the morning."

Kate instructs the kids to hurry up with their teeth and pajamas. "I'll be back in a few minutes. I'm just going to make sure everything is okay for the night."

When she returns to the living room, Michael is already on the front porch, sitting in his usual chair. Kate sits down next to Evan on the couch and says, "Give the girls a few minutes to get changed, and then you can go brush your teeth and get ready for bed, too. Is there anything else you need tonight?"

"No, I'm fine." He is already moving the pillow and blanket into sleeping position, but he glances up at Kate and smiles.

"Have you been comfortable here?" she asks.

"Yes."

"Well, it's been nice to have you around. I know you've been sick, but I bet if you were healthy, you and Jonah would have had even more fun. It would be great to have more help around here, too."

Evan pulls back the blanket and sits down on the couch. "Yeah, Jonah is fun. I think tomorrow I'll feel even better, and maybe we can play outside."

"That would be great. Okay. I'll let you know when it's your turn in the bathroom, then." She leans forward, intending to give his back a quick rub, but he leans close and hugs her. Kate smiles again and gives him a good squeeze. "Good night, Evan. Sleep well." As she pulls away, she notices Michael sitting in his chair, watching her.

~ Eight ~

THE NEXT MORNING, Kate sleeps longer than she expected. It was the first time she'd slept in her own bed in three nights, and her shoulders and back ache. She lumbers to the kitchen to find Margaret and Laura already working on breakfast. They have warm buttered toast and chamomile tea waiting for her.

"Ah, thank you, thank you," she says, kissing both girls on the cheek as she holds the steaming mug between her hands. She pads into the front room in thick socks, rubbing the sleep out of her eyes. Evan is still sleeping, wrapped in the warm blankets she tucked around him the night before. Michael is asleep in the hard chair on the front porch, wrapped in his dark coat. Kate heads back into the kitchen and helps her daughters prepare the meal.

When all the children are awake, they sit down at the table. Evan eats a hearty breakfast. His fever is gone. Kate watches the boy's small hands as he eats, wondering what will happen to him now that she can't justify keeping him here any longer.

"Mom, can Evan come with us to school today?" asks Jonah.

"What?" she says, breaking out of her reverie. "Um, no, I don't think so. I don't know. We'd have to ask his father."

"Well, he says he hasn't been to school in a long time," Laura says. "But I'm sure the teachers wouldn't mind if he came along. Sarah is always saying that every person has the right to an education."

"She's right, Mom," says Margaret. "Maybe his dad would be scared to bring him to school, but he could come with us, and we could bring him back here after."

Evan looks hopefully at Kate, nodding.

"It sounds like you four have been thinking this all through," Kate says, raising one eyebrow. "I don't know. I'm not sure how that would work." The idea of getting Evan into school had crossed Kate's mind. But, unlike her children, she thought of it as a future plan. Something that could happen after she figured out how to tell the neighborhood women about the strange single man living in the woods around them. "Look, I'll talk to his dad about it, but I don't think Evan can come with us today. I'd want to let the teachers know beforehand, so they can be ready for another student, too."

Among the children's disappointed groans, she hears a knock. The dogs leap up and run to the front door, but they only bark a few times. When Kate opens the door, Michael smiles at her and says, "Good morning."

"Good morning."

"I saw that Evan is up, so I was hoping to see him."

"Come on in. They're all at the table."

Michael crosses the room and squats next to Evan. "Hey, buddy! How are you feeling today?"

"I feel fine, Dad," Evan answers with a smile. "What do you want for breakfast?"

Michael looks embarrassed at his son's assumption, but Kate quickly says, "Have a seat. There's enough for all." She motions to a chair, and Jonah hands him a plate.

As he scoops scrambled eggs, Jonah says, "We were just talking about when Evan can come to school."

Michael looks first at Jonah, then at Evan. "School?"

"Yeah, Dad. Jonah and Margaret and Laura all go into town once a week and go to a school. Plus, one of the teachers comes out here on another day."

Before Michael can say anything, Kate interrupts. "That's true. We were going to ask you if you wanted Evan to go to school with us sometime, but I wanted to ask the teachers about it first."

"Um, I don't know, buddy." Michael says to Evan. "I'll have to think about it awhile, okay?"

"But Dad, I could go with Jonah, and—"

"I said I'd have to think about it." Michael takes a few more bites of his food. "And since you're feeling so much better today, we're going to head back home."

Evan and Jonah exchange disappointed looks. Michael finishes his eggs and pushes his chair back. He turns to Kate and says, "Can I talk to you outside for a minute?"

"Sure," she says. Kate smiles at the children and then follows him out to the front porch.

"So, he's all better? No fever?" Michael asks once Kate has closed the door behind her.

"That's right. He seems fine."

"Then I'll take him home now." He is facing her with his hands on his hips. She can see he's angry.

"Look, I didn't ask Evan to come to school. The kids

thought that up on their own."

"That's fine. I just want to get him home."

"You're not acting like it's fine. In fact, you're acting like you're mad at me for something I didn't do. I told them that he couldn't come to school with us today and that we'd have to talk to you first. And considering how much I've gone out of my way to help you and feed you the last three days, I have to say, I don't really appreciate your attitude right now."

"I'm sorry," Michael says. "I just don't want him to get excited about school since it can't happen."

Kate's shoulders drop, and she looks away from him. They both stand still before she breaks the silence. "I have to go back inside. We have to get ready to go."

"Okay."

"Evan's clothes are all clean and folded next to the couch. I'll ask him to get dressed after he's done eating."

"That's fine."

She pauses on her way in, her hand on the doorknob. "I think Evan and Jonah have become friends. They seem to really like each other. We all like Evan. He's a great kid." Kate turns to look at Michael. "He's welcome here anytime."

Michael's expression softens. "Thank you," he says.

~

As they leave the yard to begin the walk to school, Jonah turns back to wave at Evan. Michael is standing behind him, still on the porch, a small bundle of clean clothes tucked into his arm. Some are his own, and some are borrowed from Jonah.

"Mom, when do you think Evan will come back?"

"I don't know."

"Did you ask his dad?"

"I told him that Evan is welcome to come back anytime."

They cross the old road, broken up long ago by bombs,

103

and more recently by the tall weeds and grasses that incessantly push through the old blacktop. Kate doesn't often think about the families who used to live in the destroyed houses around them. In the beginning, she couldn't stop thinking about them. She would imagine the mothers and fathers reaching for their children as the bombs fell, pulling them close in a futile attempt to save them. Countless times in the first few years after the war, she woke up crying in the middle of the night from the nightmare of those days.

In those old dreams, she is standing in her own kitchen, wearing a light-blue dress and an apron. Margaret and Laura, only two years old, sit in their high chairs eating cooked peas and carrots. David sits between them with Jonah on his knee. She opens the oven door and the smell of roasted turkey wafts up to her face with the heat. She pulls out the turkey, already on a serving tray, and turns to take it in to her waiting family. David smiles as she enters the dining room and is about to speak, but baby Jonah turns and puts his tiny hands over David's mouth. The baby looks back at Kate and, in a clear adult voice, he says, "It's all over." Kate feels the turkey slide off the edge of the tray as she hears the faraway scream of the first bombs beginning to fall.

~

Within five minutes, they enter the area that used to be the college campus. They can see shattered remnants of stone buildings, demolished by the missile strike a dozen years ago. The tall oaks and evergreens that once shaded students and faculty as they crossed the quad lie toppled and decomposing all around them. The path the neighborhood helped to clear is littered with twigs and sticks that continue to fall from these trees, along with many larger pieces of stone and wooden beams that are too heavy to move. Kate and her children carefully make their way through the debris, keeping quiet.

Ten minutes later, they reach the top of the small hill that use to hold the campus church. The only thing left of the structure is a part of the crumbling foundation. They always pause here during their walk to the center of the neighborhood. Margaret likes to sit quietly on the large stones. Laura and Jonah like to rummage through the tall grass and burned-black beams, looking for small pieces of the tile that used to make up the beautiful mosaic at the front of the church. They collect the pieces and use them to make a sort of puzzle back at the house, trying to re-create the angels and saints that were shattered.

Kate stands, getting a good view of the surrounding area from this elevation. She can see her house from here, the sparkle of the light on the river as it meanders across the land, and the forest beyond. She looks a long time at the hilly forest today, wondering where Michael and Evan live, wondering for the first time if they can see her house from those hilltops. After a few minutes, the family regroups and starts down the hill into the town below.

As they enter the neighborhood, the children shout to friends they see who are also walking to school. Mothers standing in front yards say good-bye to their children, and wave to Kate as she passes.

"We're a little early," Kate says to her children. "I'd like to stop at Sarah's house first."

"I thought you needed to use Elle's sewing machine today," says Margaret.

"I do, but I want to talk to Sarah first."

"About Evan?" asks Jonah.

"Shh. Yes, but, hey Jonah, don't mention Evan to anyone just yet, okay? We need to keep him a secret for a little bit."

Laura nods. "Think about it, Jonah. It would scare everybody to know a strange man was living out there."

"Okay. I won't say anything. But will you ask Sarah about him coming to school?"

"I will, honey. Don't worry. I plan to."

They round a corner and walk down the road toward Sarah's house. They pass several yards, most with clothes drying on the lines, and chickens pecking at the dirt behind makeshift fences. Kate carries some of the children's torn clothes in her backpack today, which she will mend with fabric scraps she has saved over the years. Most of the kid's clothes are hand-me-downs from older children in the neighborhood, and have been through several mendings already. The resulting patchwork doesn't stand out, however, since the colors have faded to gray.

Sarah lives in a small house near the center of the neighborhood. The light-green paint on the wooden siding is peeling, but the house was left mostly intact after the war. Sarah and Eric moved in here when they married, and welcomed Sarah's mother into the house a few years later when her father died. A dozen cloth diapers hang on a clothesline in the front yard, drying in the sun, and as Kate enters the yard, she can hear a baby crying inside.

Kate's knock on the front door is answered by Sarah's mother. "Ah, Kate! Peace to you, and good morning. Good morning children! Are you ready for school today?" she asks with a warm smile.

"Peace to you, Helen," Kate says. "We were just headed to school, but I wondered if Sarah was still here."

"She is. Hold on a minute and I'll get her." The woman holds the door open. "Come on in."

Sarah's three young daughters run out from other rooms

when they hear their grandmother shout, "Girls, come on out. Some friends are here!" The children all spill out into the yard, talking and laughing. Margaret lifts the youngest of the three into her arms, and carries her to a waiting swing that hangs from the tall oak along the side yard.

Inside, little Thomas toddles over to Kate and holds up his arms to her. She scoops him up and says, "Hi, sweet baby! I heard you crying. Are you okay?"

The boy smiles at Kate but says, "No."

"Don't worry about him. He just doesn't know how to say yes yet," Sarah says as she comes into the room. She takes Thomas from Kate and snuggles him close. "I didn't expect to see you here. Is everything okay?"

"Sorry. Yes, everything is fine. I just wanted to talk to you about something, but if you're too busy getting ready for school, I can come back later."

Part of her is hoping Sarah is too busy, and she's unsure how to continue when her friend says, "No, it's okay. I'm pretty much ready. I just have to top off Thomas before I go." Sarah moves to the couch and sits down with the baby. She lifts the front corner of her shirt and pulls up her bra as he lies down in her lap to nurse. "Come sit down. What's going on?"

Kate takes off her backpack and sets in on the floor. "I brought you some honey from our hives." She pulls the plastic container from a pocket in her pack.

"Thank you! That's so nice. You always bring something for me."

"You're welcome. I just like to make sure you know how much I appreciate what you do for my children." Kate sets the honey on a nearby table and sits down on the couch next to Sarah before she begins.

"How are the kids doing?"

Sarah smiles. "Everyone is fine. How about yours?"

"They're good." Kate pauses and looks around the room.

"Kate, there was something you wanted to talk to me about?"

Kate takes a deep breath and says, "First of all, I don't want you to be worried about us. We're fine." Sarah doesn't say anything, but Kate sees worry creep into her eyes. "Three days ago a bunch of kids from the neighborhood came out to my house to help plant the winter wheat. After they all left, a little boy came to our house." Kate looks down at the arm of the couch and begins to pick at a loose thread at the edge of a tear in the fabric. "He was sick, so we took him in and helped him. I think it was just a virus, but he had a high fever for a couple days. He's fine now, though."

"Which boy was it? Nobody said anything about their son staying with you. I didn't even know."

"No. It wasn't one of the boys from the neighborhood."

"What?" Sarah looks confused. They can hear even more kids playing in the front yard. Other children on their way past Sarah's house have stopped to join them.

Kate continues her censored description. "The boy lives in the wild. I'm not sure where."

"Oh my God," Sarah says. "He just came to your house? Where is he now?"

Kate notices Thomas looking up at her with his large brown eyes. The corner of his mouth curls into a smile, though his lips and tongue maintain their hold on his mother's breast. She smiles back at the sweet baby, then says, "He wasn't alone. His father was with him."

Sarah waits a long time before saying anything. Kate can see that she is trying to process what she has just heard, and trying to formulate a rational response. Kate is grateful for this.

Finally, Sarah takes a deep breath and says, "Did you know this man?"

"No."

"Is he one of the raiders?"

"I don't know. I don't think so. He seemed to just want help for his son. He didn't hurt us or steal anything. The boy was better this morning, so they left."

"Wow," Sarah says. "Well, I'm glad you're okay. Have you told anyone else about this?"

"No, you're the only one. I don't want to scare everyone and get them all worked up. Maybe he was just passing through, or something."

"Do you want me to come home with you today? Are you sure you feel safe there? You can stay here, you know."

"No, no. It's not like that. I don't think we're in any danger. I wanted to talk to you about it because Jonah wants Evan to start coming to school. I'm not sure if that's okay with his dad, or anything, but I wanted to ask you about it."

"Evan is the little boy?" Sarah asks. When Kate nods, Sarah continues. "He's welcome to come to school if he wants to. I think everyone should be allowed to come to school, and I'd be happy to have him. But, Kate, if you're talking about having him start school, it doesn't sound like you think the man is just passing through."

"Hmm," Kate says.

They both look up as a tall man walks into the room from the kitchen. It is Eric, Sarah's husband. His friendly eyes sparkle from under a thick mop of dark-blond hair as he says, "Peace to you, Kate! Sorry to interrupt, but I can take Thomas, honey. You should probably start heading to school."

Kate can't help but watch him as he crosses the room and bends to scoop Thomas out of Sarah's lap. His strong arms lift the baby high, and he blows noisily on his belly, to the delight of the boy.

"Is everything okay?" Eric asks, noticing the worried looks on the women's faces.

"Yes, we're fine," Sarah says. "I should get going, though. Kate, do you want to come with me to school?"

"No, I need to go to Elle's to use her sewing machine. But I'll walk out with you."

They walk together to the front door, and Kate watches as Eric puts one arm around Sarah while holding Thomas in the other. "Have a good day at school," he says, and then kisses her on the lips. Sarah gently touches Eric on the cheek as she says good-bye. Uncomfortable, Kate looks at her hands.

Once outside, Sarah turns to Kate and says quietly, "Are you sure you don't want me to come home with you later?"

"I'm sure. And Sarah, I know it's a lot to ask, but could you not say anything to anyone until I find out more?"

"I don't know. I mean, if this man turns out to be a threat, it's wrong of us not to warn everybody about him."

"I understand that, and believe me, I've been thinking the same thing for three days. But what if he's not a threat?"

"Kate, do you know anything about this guy? Where he came from? Where the boy's mother is?"

Kate sighs and looks out into the yard where the children are playing. "You're right. I don't know anything about him." Margaret is standing close to one of the neighborhood boys. He leans toward her and whispers something in her ear, which makes Margaret laugh. Kate says, "Just give me until Saturday. I'll tell everyone at the market."

She watches Sarah lead the children in the direction of the old grocery store. It is now used as a school, church, and general meeting area. It was the only large building left fully intact after the war, though even by then, there was no food inside it. The neighborhood had since cleared out the shelving, using much of the material to repair broken houses and fences, and now, the children gather there twice each week to be taught by several women who volunteer for the task.

Kate plans to work at Elle's house for five hours before making her way to the school to pick up her children. Some days, she crosses the neighborhood to Iris's house during school hours. Today she thinks about her friend as she ambles along the road in the warm morning sun. She thinks about the day she met Iris, nearly twenty years ago.

They were assigned to be partners in an advanced chemistry lab, and disliked each other instantly. Kate thought Iris was old, arrogant, and bossy. Iris thought Kate was just another aimless rich kid. Their first month as partners was awkward, but once they began to see each other as strong, intelligent women, a mutual respect was formed. The tenuous bond that was forged between them during this time became solid the day their professor told all the women in the class they were no longer welcome there.

During the next years, they would see each other in passing, less and less frequently as the sanctions against women deepened. Once the war began, David would pass along rumors about Iris and her stealthy subversion of the rules. After he was taken away, Kate sought out Iris, asking for her help. The shared horrors of the Last War and the struggles of the years that followed drove many women together, and Iris was a heroic leader through it all. She was instrumental in helping them regroup and restructure the neighborhood. And, like most of the women, her personal tragedies did not stop her from surviving. If anything, they made her stronger, smarter, and tougher than she ever thought she could be.

Kate respects Iris and understands her desire to keep peace at all costs, but she also knows Iris to be uncompromising in her beliefs. It is a quality that has undoubtedly helped their neighborhood to thrive over the past ten years. It is a quality that Kate admires. And yet, it is the quality that is preventing Kate from seeking Iris's advice about Michael and Evan. Although Iris is one of her best friends, a part of Kate is glad to have something else to do today.

~

It is late afternoon when they arrive back home. The dogs bound up to them as they approach the house, wagging and barking a welcome. The first thing Kate notices is that the broken railing on the side of the front porch has been fixed. Three years ago, a six-foot piece had begun to crumble. It was on the side of the porch that got the most direct rain exposure, and, because there was no new paint or stain to protect it, the wood had quickly rotted through. Kate had removed the rotten section, thinking it was better for them to deal with a missing part instead of relying on a rail that could buckle at any time. She hadn't found the time to replace it, though.

Now, where there used to be an open space, two thick, straight branches span the distance, meeting in the middle above a perpendicular support. The bark has been shaved off the branches, and the wood is attached to the support and the house with straight gray nails. The porch chair sits in that corner, now empty. Michael must have noticed the missing railing the whole time he sat there.

Margaret says, "Hey! The railing's fixed. Mom, check it out."

"Yes, I see it." Kate scowls.

"What's wrong?" Margaret asks.

"Does he think we need his help? This is my house."

Then, under her breath, Kate mumbles, "Unbelievable."

"Mom, why are you so mad about this?" Margaret asks. "He did something nice for us."

"I know. But he should have asked first. Maybe I didn't want that fixed."

"Really? You've been complaining about that rail for years. I bet he just wanted to repay you for helping Evan. It seems like a nice thing, to me."

Kate sighs, her anger beginning to fade. "You're probably right, Mags. Besides, it's no big deal. It's just a porch rail."

Kate walks to the rail and silently admires the smoothness of the new wood, her hand sliding slowly over the length of it. He must have worked on the pieces over the past three days, during the brief times he left the porch. She imagines him sitting on a stump in the forest, one end of a branch resting on the ground in front of him while bracing the other end between his legs. As she glides her hand over the few knots and curves of the rail, she imagines him sliding a small plane down the length of the wood, rhythmically smoothing it, working it into the right shape.

She pushes the thoughts of him from her mind. "It's just a porch rail," she says. Suddenly anxious about what else he might have done, she goes into the house. Kate walks through each room, scanning them for any changes, but finds nothing out of the ordinary.

Margaret and Laura easily fall back into their daily routine, building up the fire and filling the pot with water. As Jonah hangs up their coats on the hooks near the front door, Kate notices him take a quick look at the couch where Evan had recovered.

"Hey, Jonah. Are you okay?" she asks.

"Yes, I'm fine."

"I know you liked having Evan here. Maybe he'll come back again sometime."

"I hope so. It was just fun to have another guy around, you know?"

"Yeah, I know." Her son gives her a weak smile and heads into the kitchen. Kate wonders if Jonah was referring to Evan or Michael. Then she wonders the same thing about herself.

The children are busy working on the evening meal, their talk light and happy. "I'm going to pull beets and kale. I'll be back in a minute," she says as she goes out the kitchen door. She steps down off the small back porch onto the path, and winds her way through the garden.

Kate knows she'll need to spend some time over the next few weeks putting the garden to sleep for the winter. The few crops that can survive the coming rain and cold don't take up much space, so she will be able to turn the ground, fertilize, and mulch nearly all of the fenced in area. Fall is her favorite time of year. It's the earth's final display of life and warmth before the darkness sets in, like the magnificent last gasp of air a body musters before death steals away a soul.

Reaching the small section of beets, Kate squats and begins to dig the dark-red roots from the ground. As the fifth of the large round bulbs pops out of the dirt, a thought crosses Kate's mind and she stops, the stem still in her hand and the juice staining her fingers like blood. She quickly walks to the garden gate. She circles around to the long shed behind the garden, then inspects the heavy lock on the shed door. The padlock is secure, but she opens the shed anyway and checks the inside. Nothing is out of place. Nothing is missing. Maybe Margaret is right, Kate thinks. Maybe he was just trying to be nice.

Feeling a little guilty, Kate leaves the shed and locks it behind her. Then, she turns to look out over the yard to the fields beyond, pulling her sweater a little tighter around her body to keep out the cool air. The wind has strengthened during the last hour, and she looks up to the sky, checking the movement of the dark clouds. There can be some strong storms this time of year, and Kate hopes the winter wheat can get a little more established before a heavy rain hits.

She walks along the edge of the fence. There are beets to wash, clothes to fold and put away, dinner to make, and countless other small tasks to be done before she can finally rest tonight. Kate pushes the tall garden gate open and walks back toward the waiting vegetables. The gate swings closed behind her. Halfway through the garden, she pauses midstep. She pivots on her heel and quickly walks back to the gate. She opens and closes it, looks closely at the hinges, and then smiles. He has smeared some sort of grease on the hinges, maybe rabbit fat, from the feel of it. She is finally free of the annoying squeak. Kate smiles at the thought of Michael sliding the thick goo around the hinges, and returns to her work.

~ Nine ~

KATE DESCENDS THE STEEP, SANDY CLIFF down to the beach, where she can see that several women have already gathered for the market. She unbuckles her pack and takes out several jars of pickled beets and eight small sugar pumpkins she has brought to trade, laying the bright-orange orbs out on the sand in a neat row. They were heavy to carry, and she's looking forward to a lighter walk home. The women talk about the week as others emerge from the path through the tall grass.

Kate smiles as she sees Sarah. "Peace to you, and good morning, Sarah," she says to her friend.

"Peace to you, and good morning, Kate. How are you today?"

Kate hears the concern in Sarah's voice, and touches her arm as she answers. "We're all fine, thanks. Though we did miss you yesterday."

"I'm sorry," Sarah says. "I planned to come out, but something came up. I'll be there next Friday."

Kate hears the lie in Sarah's excuse but doesn't push it.

116

"Okay. I'll tell the kids. No problem," she says, smiling at Sarah.

Iris takes a step to the middle of the group and says in a loud voice, "Good morning, everyone! It's so nice to see you all again today. We can tell it's fall, because our packs are getting quite a bit lighter, but thanks to the work of our community, we've done a good job putting away food for the winter. As always, if anyone has any concerns, or is in need of anything, please don't hesitate to ask. You can talk to me privately, or you can always ask the group. The great compassion and generosity of our women is the thing that helps our neighborhood to be truly great."

Everyone nods and smiles. Some of the women reach out, touching a friend's arm or shoulder.

Iris continues. "Now, does anyone have anything they want to say today before the market begins?"

It is the moment Kate has been dreading. She musters her courage and raises her chin. As she is about to speak, Patrice steps forward and says, "I have something I want to talk about."

"Okay, Patrice," says Iris with a smile. "The floor is yours."

"Well, we've all been hearing these stories about the raiders, and I think we should have a discussion about it. I'd suggest that we do something to increase our security a bit. The last time the Carriers passed through here, they said it's been getting worse. They've also told us about some groups they've seen that have a bunch of children held hostage. I think we really need to do something about this."

There are some nods from the women, and others shake their heads sadly with the thought of kidnapped children. Kate, initially relieved to have a reprieve from her confession, now wishes she had spoken up before Patrice's fearmongering.

One of the women asks, "What do you think we can do, Patrice?"

"I don't know, but I think we should figure something out. Maybe we can start some armed patrols around the outskirts. We could set up a schedule for women to serve two or three days each month. Or we could at least have some plans in place for how we will get the word out to the whole neighborhood if the raiders do attack."

Denny steps forward. "Patrice and I have been thinking about this all week, and we're not sure what would work for everyone, but we'd like to get some ideas out there. I'm sure everyone agrees that we could use more security. Maybe we could build a tower in the center of the neighborhood and have somebody in there all the time as a lookout."

"Would there be an alarm?" asks Iris. "Maybe we should contact the neighborhoods around us and see if they have set anything up."

"Or we could talk to the Carriers the next time they're here to ask what other places are doing," suggests Patrice.

Kate has felt Sarah watching her during most of this discussion, and she tries to subtly shrink farther back into the crowd with each security suggestion. When Patrice says, "It might be a good idea to set up a central armory that we can all get to in an emergency," Sarah raises her hand and steps forward.

"Hold on a minute," Sarah says. "I think we might be rushing into this before we know all the facts. So far, we have had no evidence of aggressive raiders in this area. I know the Carriers tell a lot of stories about them, but sometimes I feel like they might be exaggerating a little. They trade in neighborhoods all over the region, so maybe they've seen raiders elsewhere, but not around here."

"No evidence? I still have the blood stains on my shirt from the man who attacked me in the spring," Patrice says, her voice rising. "What more evidence do you need? Do you want to wait until there's another attack before we do something to stop them?"

"No, I'm not saying that. I want my family to be safe just as much as the next woman. But the man who attacked you was just one man, not a big group of raiders. I'm just saying I don't think we should rush into armed patrols." Sarah sighs, looking around the circle of women. "We need to try to avoid a violent conflict, not build up an army."

"I never said anything about an army," insists Patrice. "Nobody said anything about an army."

"I agree with Sarah," says Iris. "I think the best course is to first find out more details from the Carriers. They should have the best overall information about what dangers are out there." She turns to Sarah. "I know you usually talk to them when they come into town. Would you be comfortable asking them for more information?"

"If Sarah already thinks they are exaggerating, I'm not sure she's the best one for the job," says Patrice. "No offense Sarah. I'm just saying maybe we could have a couple people talk to them about this."

Sarah shrugs and says, "I understand. It's fine if we have a few people together. I agree that we can't just listen to one person's opinion on this matter."

Trying to defuse the tension, Iris says, "What if the next time they pass through, three or four women who have the time to spare can meet with them?"

"Okay," says Sarah.

"I can talk to the neighborhoods on my fishing route,"

Rhia says.

"That would be great. Thanks," Iris says.

Patrice nods in agreement before adding, "I also think it would be a really good idea to take a couple trips to the surrounding inland neighborhoods."

"It's been about five months since we did that," Iris notes. "It was right after that man attacked you."

"Yes, I remember," Patrice says. "I'd be willing to volunteer to lead a group."

"I can go, too," says Iris. "I think we should go to New Hope first, since they're the closest to us." Looking around at the crowd, she asks, "Who else would be able to go? I know you'd lose a whole day of work, but I'm sure other women would try to help your family that day."

Several women raise their hands to volunteer, and the crowd begins to break up into small groups. After a few minutes, five women have been chosen to make the two-hour walk to the neighborhood to the east. They will go the following Wednesday morning, when most of the children are in school. Other mothers have offered to take care of the children after school until the women return.

Iris raises her hands above her head to quiet the group and says, "I want to thank Patrice and Denny for bringing this up today. I think it's always a good idea to talk about our safety, and I'm looking forward to finding out more from the Carriers and from New Hope."

Kate has remained silent throughout the entire discussion. No one had expected her to volunteer for the journey because of her location on the outskirts of town, so her hesitation to contribute to the discussion didn't seem unusual. Only Sarah caught Kate's eye. Kate couldn't read what Sarah was thinking, but she hoped her friend would understand.

Iris asks, "Are there any other things we need to talk about today?" When no one speaks up, she smiles and says, "Well, then let's start the market."

~

Kate crosses her front yard under darkening skies. When she left home this morning, the sky was a crisp blue with white clouds streaking across it like mare's tails blowing in the wind. By the time she had split from the group of women leaving the market to walk along the smaller path to her home, the clouds had begun to gather into thick gray bunches. She can feel the chill in the air and is looking forward to the warmth of her house.

Kiko and Ruby wag their bodies as she reaches down to pet them on the front porch. "Good girl, Kiko," she says as she presses her palm into the dog's right ear, rubbing in firm circles.

The savory scent of cooking onions and mushrooms meets her as she opens the front door. She can hear the children talking in the kitchen, and the sizzle of the food sautéing on the stove. As she rounds the corner, she sees Evan standing at the counter next to Laura. He is smiling as he slices raw rabbit meat into small cubes and passes them to Laura, who drops them into a small bowl of flour seasoned with rosemary and thyme.

"Evan," Kate says, surprised. "I didn't know you were here." She looks around the room and out the window against the far wall, scanning the yard.

"Hi, Mrs. Decker," the boy says, turning to her.

"Mom," Laura says, "His dad brought him a little bit ago. I told him you weren't here, so he left. He said he'd come back after lunch."

"Is that okay, Mom?" Jonah asks as he steps to her, and

quickly hugs her around the waist before returning to the stove.

"I suppose so," she answers, not exactly sure that's true. "How are you feeling, Evan?"

"I'm fine." He puts the knife down on the counter and wipes his hands with the wet cloth hanging over the spigot in the sink. "My dad said I had to bring back the clothes I borrowed from Jonah last week, so we did."

"Oh, Evan, you can keep those clothes," Kate says, walking through the room to kiss each of her children on the top of their heads. "Jonah doesn't fit into them anymore."

"I told my dad that, but he said we can get our own clothes."

Kate smirks and shakes her head at the man's stubbornness and pride. "Well, when your dad comes to pick you up, I'll talk to him about it."

Jonah has dumped the meat into the pan on the stove, and is stirring it into the sautéed vegetables. "OK, everybody. This is almost done" he says.

Kate moves to the dining room. The table is already set with plates, cups, and forks, and Kate now notices a fifth place setting. They are about to sit down at the table when they hear the sound of heavy boots stomping up the front porch steps. Kate sees Michael pass by the front window, a look of fear and anger on his face. A moment later she hears a loud knock.

"Where's Evan?" he says as she opens the front door.

"He's right there," Kate replies, motioning toward the dining room table. She sees him look at Evan, then scan the room before turning to look out over the yard. "What's wrong?" she asks.

He doesn't answer right away, and she sees he is out of breath from running. Then, with his back to Kate, he says gruffly, "Did you go to the market today?"

"Yes."

"And?" Michael turns to her, and she sees an accusation in his eyes.

"And what? What are you getting at?" Kate is angry now, too. Still standing in the doorway, she puts her hands on her hips and stretches herself to her full height.

He backs down a bit, and turns to look out at the yard again. "Did you tell them all about us?"

If he were looking at her, he would have seen guilt flash over her face, and she is glad he cannot see her reaction. Struggling to regain her composure, she simply says, "No."

She sees his shoulders slump a bit as he sighs. He remains facing the yard, but his voice is softer now as he says, "I left Evan here because he wanted to hang out with Jonah again. He's been asking to come and play ever since we left the other day. After I dropped him off, it suddenly dawned on me that you were at the market this morning."

Michael turns, and Kate sees that the anger has left him. Fear and sadness now burn in his blue eyes, and she struggles to hold onto her own anger, to hold onto her position of control. His arms hang by his sides as he quietly says, "I came running back here, expecting to find him gone."

Now she understands. He'd been scared that Kate had told the women at the market about them, and he knew as well as she did what their reaction would have been. They would have surged from the beach like a tidal wave, sweeping up the cliff and over the roads to Kate's house. The women would have broken down the door, if necessary, to get to the boy. They would have taken Evan, locking up Michael or forcing him to flee, all in the name of saving the boy from the horrors of living with a man they would assume was a raider. Kate would not have been able to stop them.

Looking into Michael's eyes, Kate loses the moral superiority that she has claimed since the moment she saw the man. She knows the deep fear he must have felt when he realized he had left his son in danger. She finally understands the terrible jeopardy he put himself in the night he decided to ask for her help. And she knows how close she came this morning to destroying their lives forever. Michael and Evan would never be safe now that Kate and her family know about them.

"He's not gone," she says quietly. "He's right here. I didn't tell them about you. He's right here." Kate steps aside, out of the doorway, and lifts her arm toward the table.

Evan is standing close behind her, looking down at the floorboards. All the children have overheard the conversation, and their faces are locked in expressions of fear and anxiety. Slowly, Evan raises his head. Kate can see that he is full of sadness, but he steps forward and smiles—first at Kate, and then at his father. It is a smile of courage and trust, and Kate feels the sting of tears prick her eyes as he says, "Dad, are you going to eat with us? You can have some of mine."

~

After the meal, the boys work together to clear the dishes and clean up the kitchen. Margaret and Laura take the dogs and go outside with the short-handled ax to chop wood into kindling for the fire. Michael pushes his chair back from the table as Kate comes in from the kitchen with a broom and dustpan. "Here," he says, standing. "Let me do that for you."

"You don't have to," she says.

"I want to." He reaches out to take the broom from her hand.

Kate pulls the broom closer to her body. "I said you don't

have to."

"I know I don't have to, but I want to," he says, smiling. He steps closer to her and puts his hand on her wrist. The muscles in her arm tense, and she turns her head to the side to avoid his gaze.

Michael is standing so close, Kate can see the rise and fall of his chest as he breathes. Her eyes are drawn to a missing button near the top of his faded blue shirt, the collar lying open at an angle across his clavicle. The rugged scent of his body mixed with cedar and autumn leaves catches her by surprise, and she suddenly jerks her wrist away from him, stepping back.

Michael looks hurt, his eyebrows knitting together. "I'm sorry. I was just trying to help," he says.

"It's okay. You've done enough . . . the porch rail . . . and the gate hinges. I can do this," Kate stammers as she bolts to the corner of the room and begins to sweep.

"Kate, I'm really not trying to usurp your authority or anything. I just feel like I owe you for everything you've done for Evan."

"You don't owe me anything. Anyone would have done the same."

"That's not true." He has moved to the farthest corner of the room, away from her. "You have been much kinder than most women would be. At least to me. Most women would have tried to help Evan, but they would have run to town the next morning to tell everyone about me. Some would have even killed me that first night and just taken my son."

Kate stops sweeping and glances into the kitchen where the boys are working. She leans on the broom, looks back at Michael, and whispers, "Wait a minute. You're talking about women who are my friends. We're here to keep the peace.

Nobody would just kill a man without reason. That's the sort of violence we've worked hard to eliminate."

"Have you? Eliminated it, I mean. It feels like the violence is still out there, just redirected. I know you've tried to set up all these new rules to keep yourselves safe, but most women are still just as scared of men as they ever were."

Kate narrows her eyes and takes a step closer. "No. For the first time in the history of the world, we don't have to be afraid. Not of the good men in our neighborhoods, at least."

"If you're not afraid, then why keep the men locked away in your houses? Why take away all our rights and freedom?" His eyes flash, and there is the hint of venom in his voice.

A tight knot forms in Kate's stomach at the truth in his challenge, and she has to steel herself. She takes a small step backward, and sees his eyes dart quickly to her feet. Then, trying to sound in control, she calmly replies, "Nobody has taken away your rights or freedoms. You agreed to the new rules."

"You changed the rules after you took over."

"Some rules have evolved. But everyone is just trying to do what's best."

"Best for you."

"Best for the neighborhood," Kate responds firmly. "Finally, we are able to live and work in peace, because we don't have to worry about strange men wandering around town trying to hurt us. And best for the men. The men here are taught to respect women and work alongside them. To honor and protect them."

"To serve them."

"No! Not at all." Kate shakes her head. "And our children are being taught how to be good and kind, too. Our teachers help the boys learn how to resolve conflicts without violence.

How to respect a woman's body. How to be a decent and supportive husband."

Michael walks into the front room shaking his head. Over his shoulder he says, "Good men were always taught that. That's nothing new."

"That is something new," she says, following him. He leans against the far wall and watches her as she steps closer. "Women all over the world have lived in fear of men for millennia. We've feared things like social repression, date rapes getting brushed away by the police, and in some countries, genital mutilation and acid attacks on young girls who refused arranged marriages.

"Men have always been physically bigger and stronger than women, and they kept us down by both their pure physical strength and their position of power. Now, finally, there aren't enough men around to keep us down. Now women have taken hold of the power they were always too afraid to use.

"Think about how different our world is going to be when this generation of boys grows up, having been allowed to grow into whole, good, decent men. Nobody is going to tell them that they have to go through life being some stupid caricature of masculinity anymore. They can talk about feelings and beauty and love, and still be respected. We haven't taken away your freedom, we've given it to you. You should be thanking us."

"Thanking you? Because you've taken all the power?"

"We didn't take all the power. We've just finally balanced the power. The men in our neighborhood are respected, and loved, and cared for. The difference is, the women are also respected, and loved, and cared for."

She shakes her head and adds, "No, I'm not scared of

you. Because I know that if you hurt one hair on my head, or one hair on my children's heads, the women of my neighborhood would hold you fully responsible. You're the one living out in the woods. You seem to be the one who's afraid."

Michael's brow furrows, and he takes a step toward Kate. "Of course I'm afraid. All your talk about freedom and balance . . . Do you really think it feels balanced to me? What would happen if I tried to walk into town today? What would those balanced women think of me?"

"We have to protect ourselves from the raiders," Kate says.

"And who are the raiders? Do you think they *like* roaming around hoping to come across women to hurt? Do you think they're all just bloodthirsty killers? Or could it be that some of them are men whose homes and lives and families were destroyed by the war? Who, thanks to your new rules, have no way to break into this glorious new society."

"That's bullshit," Kate says. "There are men out there who hate the new ways, but not because they can't find homes. It's because they can't stand the idea of not being in control. They can't stand the idea of women having any power. Any. And those men *are* out there roaming around, and they'd love to come into my house and take everything I have. There are men who would come in here and kill me and my children without a second thought."

"I'm not one of those men."

"Maybe you're not, but how would we know that? You're out there in the forest, living like a wild dog. You just show up on my porch . . ." She hesitates and looks around the room. "If you know what people are going to think of you, why are you out there? Why aren't you part of a neighborhood?"

He throws up his hands and says, "It's complicated."

"Complicated?" She moves the broom from one hand to the other. "I'll tell you what's complicated. Keeping an eight-year-old boy alive in the woods is complicated. How long do you think you'll be able to keep him out there? Were you just thinking he'd live out there with you forever? Don't you want him to have a normal life?"

"Normal?" he says in barely a whisper. "You don't know anything about us."

"Okay, so tell me."

"I don't have to tell you anything."

"No, you don't. But you should. You should be doing whatever you can to help your son live a normal life."

They stare at each other for a long time. Finally, Michael says, "It was a terrible idea for me to bring Evan here today. I'm sorry."

He heads toward the kitchen, but Kate steps in front of him, blocking his way. "Where are you going?" she asks.

"I'm going to get Evan, and we'll leave. You won't have to see us again."

"Wait," Kate says firmly, sidestepping to remain in his path. She tries to think quickly. "You don't have to do that. There are other options."

"I don't think so. If he keeps coming here, eventually everybody is going to know about us. We have to leave."

"I told you, I didn't tell everyone at the market today."

"Eventually you'll tell someone." Michael stops and takes a step backward. He tilts his chin up to the ceiling and sets his hands on his hips. She watches as he slowly breathes in, holds his breath for a moment, and then exhales. When he looks back at her, a gentle light has returned to his eyes and he softly says, "Look, I don't blame you, Kate. You've gone out of your way to help us. You've taken my son into your home, you've given us food. Do you know what he told me after we left here the other day? He told me it was nice being part of a family again." Kate hears the slightest sadness in his voice.

"Kate, I can never repay you for what you've done. Or, more importantly, for what you didn't do. Trust me, there aren't many women left who would have had that courage. But I can't expect you to keep us a secret. Besides, even if you don't tell, one of your kids will. Not on purpose, but it will slip out. You know it's true."

Kate's shoulders slump, and she looks away from him, feeling guilty. Only hours ago, she was ready to turn him over to the group, so confident in her assessment of the situation. Now she just wants to buy time so she can figure out how to help Evan. And with Michael standing before her, somehow believing she is a better person than she feels, she wants to help him, too.

Thinking quickly, she says, "Well, Evan and Jonah have become friends. How can you take that little bit of normal away from him now? You can't keep Evan out there in the woods. You're going to have to figure out a plan sooner or later. Let us help you." Her eyes soften, and she says, "Michael."

She sees him draw in his breath and watches as his posture changes. He blinks slowly and exhales. The hard creases that line his forehead smooth out, his shoulders relax, and his face opens up. He looks like it is the first time anyone has spoken his name in a long time. With that one word, she has transformed him from being a strange creature living in the woods into a man again.

She studies his eyes, and what she sees in them makes her want to hold his gaze, but Michael looks away and shakes his head. "I just don't see how it could work." He steps around her, and she lets him pass.

Before he enters the kitchen, he pauses, listening to the boys. They are talking and laughing. Michael leans on the doorframe, and a subtle, sad smile tugs at the corners of his mouth. Jonah and Evan have finished the lunch dishes, and are busy kneading flour into two small balls of soft dough on the surface of the counter.

Evan is standing next to Jonah, who explains, "It works best if you push it with the heel of your hand, like this. Then you can just flip it with your one hand, while you spray this little bit of flour on the counter to keep it from sticking so much."

"Like this?" Evan asks, trying to mimic Jonah's movements.

"Sort of, but you really have to try to stretch it instead of whack it."

Evan laughs and looks up. "Dad! Jonah was asking if we could go fishing after the bread is done. He says there's a place he goes just upstream of here that's really good."

"I don't think so, buddy."

"Please, Dad? You can work on the roof, like you said."

Michael quickly says, "I didn't say I was going to work on the roof. I just mentioned that there are some old-looking shingles that will need replacing soon. Evan, I don't think today's a good day for fishing."

"It's okay," Jonah says. "I'm almost done with my housework, and I was planning to go this afternoon anyway. He can come along."

Just then, the kitchen door bangs open and Margaret and Laura enter, their arms loaded with kindling. As they stack it in the bin next to the cookstove, Laura says, "Cripes! It is really getting windy out there. I think it might rain tonight, Mom."

"Yeah," Margaret adds. "I think we should scramble to get the rest of the ripe veggies in today. Otherwise, it's all going to get knocked off. And we need to get the boards up on the chicken coops so they stay dry. Jonah, are you almost done with the bread?"

"Yes, but Evan and I are going fishing after."

"Jonah," Kate says, sliding sideways past Michael into the kitchen. "You might not get to go fishing today. It sounds like there is a lot to get done."

"Aw, Mom. Please? Me and Evan can catch something for dinner. We need to eat, don't we?"

"How come Jonah gets to go fishing and we have to do all the work?" Laura asks, irritated.

Kate holds up her hands. "I didn't say he could go fishing. Everybody slow down."

"She's right, JoJo," Margaret adds. "We have to get stuff done. And it's going to rain anyway."

"We can fish in the rain," Jonah protests. "Fish love rain."

Michael is still in the doorway, watching the family argue. His smile grows as they bicker about chores and fish and weather, and he soaks in the sights and sounds of normalcy. His son leans against the counter, his flour-covered hands pounding the sticky ball of dough. Evan nods each time Jonah makes an assertion in favor of the fishing trip.

"Fish might love rain, but it makes no sense for you to get soaked," Kate tells Jonah. "Besides, Evan's just getting over an illness. He certainly doesn't need to sit in a cold river in the rain."

"We also need to draw down the dam before the rain starts, too," Margaret adds. "There's too much to get done today for fishing."

"I can help," Evan says as he turns from the counter. "You've helped me a lot, so now I can help you. And my dad can help, too. I bet if we all work together, we can get it done fast."

"Thank you, Evan," Kate says, smiling. "It's really nice of you to offer, but I don't think—"

"You're right, buddy," Michael sighs. "It will get done a lot faster if we all help."

Kate turns to him, a puzzled look on her face. She recognizes the confusion she sees in his eyes, having felt it ebb and flow within herself over the past week.

Michael shrugs and asks, "What do you think?"

"I don't know. I mean, I thought . . ." She lets her words trail off, putting the question back to him.

"Maybe a little bit of normal won't hurt."

As she looks into his eyes, she thinks she sees a spark of hope where, before, there was none. Has he begun to trust her? She wants to be the person who saves Evan from a life in the wild. Her own spark of hope ignites, and the resulting warmth that floods her body makes her so happy, she is able to ignore the thing in the back of her mind that is screaming out a warning.

~

Michael and Evan work alongside the family during the afternoon. As expected, the chores get done quickly, and Kate knows the boys will soon renew their campaign for the fishing trip. As the children put the tools and equipment away in the shed, she stops to survey the sky, looking for signs of the coming weather. Michael crosses the yard and stands beside her.

"Do you think it's going to rain?" he asks, his arms folded over his chest.

"Yes. The clouds have been accumulating all day. I feel like I can smell the rain coming in on the breeze," she replies. "I don't think they should go fishing today."

"They're going to be mad." Michael turns toward the house. Out of the corner of his eye, he looks at her with a smirk. "You tell them."

Kate smiles and watches him walk away.

~

It's after dark when the first drops finally begin to fall. Kate is lying in her bed, listening to the dull ticks of rain as it hits the corrugated plastic window next to her head. Though exhausted as usual, she is unable to fall asleep, plagued by a thought just out of the reach of her conscious mind. She pores over the day, trying to wedge the mystery free from its hiding place, but she just can't do it.

Thoughts of Michael distract her. The light she saw in his face, if only briefly. His smile, so easy and warm every time he heard Evan laugh. When she closes her eyes, she can see him lifting a heavy sheet of plywood and placing it along the side of the chicken coop. He braced it with his body while she tightened the bolts to secure it. She had stood close behind him as she turned the screwdriver, close enough for her raised elbow to brush against the back of his shoulder. Close enough to hear his quiet grunt when he adjusted his hold on the board.

"Mom," Jonah whispers.

It startles her, and she is afraid to speak, as if her voice will reveal her thoughts.

"Mom, are you awake?"

"Yes. What's wrong?"

"Nothing. I was just thinking about stuff."

"What stuff?"

Jonah hesitates, then says, "Well, it's starting to rain out."

Kate hears Margaret and Laura softly breathing in their bed across the room. "Yes, I know it's raining. And?"

"Well, I was just thinking about how it's raining, and how it's going to start getting colder at night, and how it would be awful to be outside right now."

Kate doesn't say anything for a minute, waiting to see what else Jonah will say. She can see his next question coming, and suddenly wishes she had pretended to be asleep.

"Mom?"

"Yes, honey?"

"Maybe Evan and his dad could live here with us."

"I don't think that would work," she says.

"Why not?"

"We don't have enough space. We couldn't fit any more mattresses in here. And, besides, I don't think Evan's dad would want to do that."

"Why not?"

"Um, I don't know. I just don't think he would."

"But why not? I mean, Evan says they live in, like, a tree house, and that they get wet when it rains, and that it's cold in the winter. Don't you think his dad would rather live in a real house?"

"Jonah, I don't know. I think his dad is doing his best, and he might be offended if we told him he had to live here. It's a big deal to live in someone else's house."

Jonah is quiet, and Kate hopes she has convinced him to drop the idea. After a while, she relaxes and starts to feel tired again. Her heavy eyelids close, and she takes a slow, deep breath. She notices the feel of the mattress below her back and shoulders, and allows it to support the weight of her body, letting go of the day, letting go of control. As sleep finally drifts over her, she hears Jonah softly whisper, "Okay, Mom."

~ Ten ~

MICHAEL AND EVAN came by twice more during the week, and Jonah ran to the front door to welcome them both times. On the first day, Kate made it clear to the boys that Jonah wouldn't be allowed to neglect his usual household duties just because a friend was there. Jonah grumbled but quickly agreed to her terms. Evan could work with him, and when the chores were completed, they'd be allowed the freedom to explore the river and the edge of the forest until dinnertime.

"I want you to keep your eyes open when you boys are outside," Kate tells Jonah, pulling him aside.

"For what?"

"We rarely get visitors, but you never know."

"Okay." Jonah tugs at the unraveling bottom hem of his sweatshirt. "But we were going to build a fort in the forest. There are all those big rocks at the edge of the field, and we can use some of the long bamboo poles stacked out there."

"That's fine. Just try to stay alert."

Kate is glad to see Jonah so happy. He has a few friends in the neighborhood, but there are no boys so close to his age. Jonah had been born at a time when there were few men left alive in the neighborhood, and the husbands who were around were starving alongside their wives. It wasn't a good time to make new mouths to feed.

During the first years following the war, some men did trickle back to the neighborhoods as they made their way home from the front lines. As they were acclimated into the roles that husbands would take in the new society, babies began to be born again.

During the afternoons Jonah and Evan spend together, Michael stays at the house. Kate tells herself it is because he feels obliged to offer his help, but she senses that he is still wary of leaving Evan alone with her. Whereas Jonah and Evan work together as a team, Michael and Kate find ways to work around each other, getting as much done as they can while coming into as little contact as possible.

However uncomfortable his presence in her home makes her feel, it is empowering to be able to direct Michael, giving him the jobs she wants to get done. She feels like she is regaining control of her house and family, after feeling so frightened and powerless when he suddenly showed up on her doorstep just two weeks before. And Kate has to admit it's nice having the extra help.

"Since I'm here, are there some jobs around the house I could help you with?" Michael asks while standing in the backyard one day.

She notices him look around the yard and at the shed, and waits for his eyes to dart to the roof of the house. As soon as they do, Kate says, "That would be great. There's a whole load of laundry to wash. Jonah can show you where it is."

Michael stiffens but smiles politely and follows Jonah through the garden gate and into the house.

When he volunteers the next day, Kate allows Michael to butcher a chicken, but then asks him to spend the next hours in the kitchen, preparing the evening meal. He proves to be quite adept at cooking and watches Kate closely to see her reaction to the dinner he made. She tries to conceal how delicious it is, and only smiles politely.

After dinner, the children gather in the front yard to say good-bye to Evan. Kate moves to Michael's side on the front porch, and together they watch the boys tell Laura and Margaret about their fort, and their plans for the next visit.

"Tomorrow another woman from the neighborhood is coming here," Kate tells Michael. "She comes out on Fridays to teach."

Michael looks out into the yard, then he drops his eyes to the wooden floorboards of the porch and asks, "What are you saying?"

"I'm saying, maybe tomorrow isn't a good day for Evan to visit."

"Right. Okay."

"What did you think I meant?" Kate asks.

"Nothing."

Bullshit, she thinks. There was some accusation in his tone, and it angered her. "No, not nothing," she tells him, turning to face him with her arms crossed in front of her chest. "What did you think I meant?"

"I don't know. You're the one who said Evan should go to school. I thought maybe this was your way of trying to make that happen." He looks up at her and meets her gaze. Kate had almost forgotten that she had told Sarah about them, and to hide her guilt she becomes even more defensive.

"If I was trying to make something happen, I'd just come out and say so. I was just . . ." Her voice trails off. She lowers her voice as she turns to look out at the children. "I was simply telling you that Sarah will be here tomorrow. I assumed you wouldn't want to come while someone else was here."

He shifts uncomfortably. "Fine. We won't come tomorrow." Whatever small comfort they have gained with each other over the last few days disappears, leaving only the distance and mistrust that was there before.

~

On Friday, Kate hurries to get the children fed and ready for their lessons with Sarah. She usually shows up around nine o'clock, and they are all anxious to see if she will make it this week. Kate made up an excuse for Sarah's absence last week, and the children didn't question it, though Kate could clearly see that they knew the real reason as well as she did.

Kiko and Ruby begin to bark as the family finishes up the breakfast dishes. Margaret runs to the front room and looks out the window.

"It's Sarah!" she shouts toward the kitchen. "And Eric's with her!"

Everyone moves to the front room and crowds around the window to see. "I didn't know he was coming," Kate says, crossing to the front door. She steps outside and waves as they approach the house.

"Peace to you both, and good morning!" she says.

"Peace to you, Kate," Sarah says. "I'm sorry I'm running a little late today." She gives Kate a hug.

"No problem. You're not late at all. We're just glad you could make it this week." Kate turns to Eric and smiles.

Sarah slips her hand into her husband's. "I hope you don't mind that Eric joined me today."

"No, of course not. We're glad to see you, too, Eric." Turning back to Sarah, she asks, "Is your mom watching the kids today?"

"Yes. My older girls are big enough to help out a lot, too, so they'll be fine for a few hours. But there are some things I wanted to talk with you about, so I thought Eric could entertain your kids for a little while."

"Sure, that's great," Kate says. "Come on in."

"Hi, Eric!" Laura says warmly as they enter the house. "What are you doing here?"

"Well, Sarah and your mom need to talk about some things, so I thought you could take me on a short hike. Maybe we could work on some plant identification. Sarah has been teaching me about it, too, so we can quiz each other."

The children happily put on their sweatshirts and follow Eric outside. Once they have left, Kate looks at Sarah and asks, "Is everything okay?"

"Yes, everything's fine. I'm sorry to bring Eric uninvited."

"No, don't worry about it. The kids have known Eric their whole lives. They know he's a good man."

"Thank you," Sarah says. "To be honest, he didn't want me to come out here at all. I told him about the man."

Kate had expected this. Everyone knew that Sarah and Eric shared everything, and thought of each other as equals. Without openly questioning her about it, many of the women in the neighborhood thought Sarah gave her husband too much leeway, allowing him to participate in the decision-making of their household, allowing him to help with many of the outdoor chores. If Kate were being honest with herself, she would have to admit that the reason she chose to tell Sarah about Michael was because she hoped that she, of all people, would be sympathetic.

"I see," Kate says. There is an awkward silence as Kate and Sarah search for what to say next. Finally, Kate adds, "It's okay, Sarah. I thought maybe you would tell him. I know Eric is a good man. And I understand that you'd need to talk to someone about this."

"Thanks, Kate," Sarah says, visibly relieved. "It's a difficult situation, and I didn't want to lie to him about why I was nervous to come here. Has the man been back?"

"He's been back a few times. Actually, the boy and Jonah have become friends." There is no benefit in lying. Kate is desperate for a confidant, and longs to tell Sarah everything. "Oh, Sarah, I'm not sure what to do."

Sarah sighs. "I don't know."

They move to the dining room, and Sarah sits down. Kate says, "I have water boiling. Can I get you some tea?"

"That would be great, thanks."

She goes to the kitchen and pulls two mugs down from the cupboard. They clink together as she sets them on the counter, then scoops tiny, dry chamomile flowers into each. A moment later, she returns passing Sarah a steaming cup. They sit in silence for a minute, both looking into their mugs, as if the detritus at the bottom could really tell them the future.

"Well," Sarah says, breaking the tension. "Last time we talked about it, you had mentioned you might want to get the boy into school. Have you thought about that any more?"

"Yes, but I don't think it's going to happen just yet. I don't think the father is ready for that. He's really protective of Evan. To be honest, I don't even know much about them yet." Kate looks around the table as she thinks about the times Michael and Evan have sat here. "But, Sarah, Evan is a really great kid. I guess I've been trying to just let them get used to us a bit, you know? I don't want to push it too quickly."

"That's understandable," Sarah says. "And I can see how you might need to go slowly with them to earn their trust. Do you know where they come from? Or where they're living?"

"I don't know exactly. It sounds like they live in the woods, but I'm not sure." Though she trusts that Sarah wouldn't intentionally cause harm to Michael or Evan, she is hesitant to tell her much more. "But the man has been helping out a little bit around here, and Evan fits right in. Jonah loves having him around."

"Aren't you scared?"

Kate looks into her friend's eyes. She sees only concern, without a hint of hatred or prejudice. "No." It is as much of a revelation to her as it is to Sarah. "No, I'm not scared of them. His name is Michael. The man's name is Michael."

Sarah watches Kate for a moment, then gives her a small smile. "Well, I hope your instincts are right. Who knows, maybe I won't even have to drag Eric out here next week. Though he didn't mind a bit. He loves getting out of the house. And, it was nice to go for a long walk with him, just to be with him. Without any of the other women watching."

Kate nods, understanding the jealousy some of the younger women feel toward Sarah for having such a strong and handsome husband, and the rebuke some of the older women give her for letting him speak freely at the monthly meetings. "Well, I don't blame you for bringing Eric along. If it's too difficult for you to come out here on Fridays, maybe I can figure out a way to get the kids to you. Though Eric is welcome here anytime."

"Thanks. Why don't we just see how it goes. You can come to school a few minutes early next Wednesday and let me know what you think. Okay?"

"Okay. Thanks, Sarah."

"You're welcome. But, Kate, there is still the issue of telling the rest of the neighborhood."

"I know. I've thought about that, too. I was going to tell them last week at the market, but everybody seemed too riled up. I didn't want to throw this into the mix."

"Yeah, that got a little weird, didn't it?" The women smile at each other, trying not to say anything overtly negative about Patrice, or the tension at the market. "Seriously, though, it makes me a little nervous when everyone starts talking about putting up defenses and forming an army to fight the raiders. Kate, I know I'm younger than most of the other women, but that seems like the beginning of something pretty scary. Isn't that the kind of thinking that got us into the war in the first place?"

Kate hesitates a long time before answering. It is a delicate question. She has vivid memories of the years before the Last War, the fearmongering, the buildup of the military, the demonization of the enemies. And, like every person who survived the war, she can still feel the thud of the bombs in her chest, and can smell the burning wood and flesh in her nostrils. There is no doubt in her mind that the men of the world induced and perpetuated the violence that nearly destroyed the human race. There is no doubt in her mind that there are men out there still, roaming the country with anger and hatred in their hearts, willing to kill any women in their path in the hopes of regaining control.

"I agree that we need to be careful," Kate finally says. "We have to be able to protect ourselves from raiders, but we also have to make sure we don't turn into the thing we fear so deeply. I don't know the answer, but I'm willing to trust in the wisdom and goodness of the women in our neighborhood to figure out a good solution."

Sarah nods and looks back down at her tea again. "They went to New Hope on Wednesday."

"Oh, that's right. What did they find out?"

"Well, I didn't go along because I was teaching, but there was a meeting when they got back that evening. Iris did most of the talking. It sounds like the women there are nervous about raiders, too, and some of them would be willing to help develop some sort of alert system. It seems like the lack of communication between the neighborhoods it one of the biggest issues. There were a bunch of ideas put out there—smoke signals, carrier pigeons, trying to get a horse so someone can be a messenger—things like that."

"Hmm," Kate says. "Carrier pigeons?"

Sarah smiles. "I know, but I think they were just trying to brainstorm some ideas. And I'd rather train birds to carry notes instead of training people to shoot weapons."

"I suppose. Was anything decided at the meeting?"

"Not really. Both neighborhoods are going to try to come up with ideas and then meet again in two weeks. In addition, we are going to head south to Bellwether, and they're going to go north to Prenshaw. If we get a bunch of neighborhoods involved, maybe we can make a whole network."

"I like that idea," Kate says. "I think the more neighborhoods we can contact, the better. Rhia should be able to help. We should talk to her about her fishing route."

"Well, I've actually saved the biggest news for last," Sarah says, a sneaky smile on her face.

"What?"

"The Carriers passed through two days ago!"

"Oh, that's great! Did they have any baking soda?"

"Not this time. Lots of soap, though. And big barrels of oranges and avocados. Bolts of fabric. Some tools and nails.

Jugs of olive oil. Next time you come into town, have the kids bring their backpacks."

"Wonderful! My mouth just started watering," Kate says, laughing.

"A few other things, too. We had to give them a goat, lots of preserved food, and two packages of paper in trade."

"One of Iris's young goats?"

"No. One of Colleen's. A few of us went out when we heard their carts coming, and we talked to them a long time about the rumors of the raiders, what other places are doing, and if the government has any new plans to help us out."

"And?"

"And they had to admit that they haven't heard of any big groups close to us. There were some bad attacks a year or two ago in California, and there have been some smaller groups moving north from there, but they haven't seen anything up this far. Raiders do seem to be a serious problem in parts of the country, but it doesn't sound like they're around here yet."

"That's great!" The news makes Kate feel more comfortable about Michael, and more hopeful about keeping peace in her neighborhood.

"Still, they did emphasize the idea that it is a problem elsewhere, and thought it was a very good idea to try to come up with a warning system."

"So, maybe we have some time to really work this out. Maybe everybody can calm down a little bit and come up with a peaceful solution." They both nod, confident in the good intentions of women.

"Can I get you some more tea?" Kate asks.

"Sure."

When her cup is refilled, Sarah sips the hot liquid, warming her hands on the mug. She sets the cup back down onto the table and says, "They had a new pamphlet, too."

"What's it about?"

"It says the government is still working on getting things up and running. The iron mines in Upper Michigan are sending boatloads of ore down Lake Huron to Detroit, and there's another foundry working near there. Plus, they recently sent out another large crew of workers with stoves, paper, cloth, goats, and pigs."

"Wow," Kate says. "That's wonderful. We haven't seen a big crew in two years."

"Right. The pamphlet says they plan to get to Utah before winter, then start out again in the spring." Sarah is smiling brightly, happy to be able to share this news with Kate. "There are a lot of mountains to cross, but they should get here by next summer."

"I want a big fat mama pig. I want her to have lots of little piglets, and listen to them squealing all over my yard."

Sarah smiles. "Just invite me over for dinner when you slaughter one."

Kate suddenly wants to tell Michael the news. She wishes he were here, sitting at the table with them, participating in the conversation. Or outside with Eric and the kids, walking and laughing with them. She can't wait to see him again.

While Sarah goes over the children's lessons at the dining room table, Eric puts together a pot of soup from vegetables and beans. Kate works near him in the kitchen, folding a pile of laundry. Although clean, the clothes are dingy and gray. She notices how Eric moves through the kitchen, comfortable in his job, only occasionally asking where an ingredient is. As the onions and carrots begin to simmer in the pan, he turns to Kate and says, "We found something special for the soup today."

Kate looks up from the laundry. Eric is smiling at her, his hand open. She moves closer and looks at the small seeds he is holding. "What are those?" she asks.

"They're mustard seeds," Eric answers. "We found them this morning out in the woods, on the other side of the fields. Laura was the one who identified the plant. She's really bright, you know."

"I know she is. But I didn't know we had mustard out there."

"You never know what wonderful things are out in the woods. A couple years ago, we found that rosemary plant, and now half the people in the neighborhood have some growing in their gardens." He has turned back to the counter, and is working with the mortar and pestle to grind the seeds into powder. "I'll save a few of these for you. You can plant them in the spring and have mustard whenever you want. It's great for soups and as a marinade for chicken or rabbit. I've even read a recipe for potted rabbit that uses mustard. It sounds really good. But don't put it in your main garden. I've read that it spreads really quickly and can end up taking over."

"Thanks, Eric. That would be great. I'll get a little container for the seeds."

As Kate listens to him go on about gardens and seeds, she is taken by the ease with which he speaks to her. With all the housework men do, they have little time to socialize, and rarely speak to women outside their family. Kate knows the system is designed that way. To keep them busy and keep them separate, to keep them out of trouble. She smiles, noticing his ease of movement, his open expressions, and most of all, the feeling she gets from him. He isn't frightened of her, and he manages to be both confident and compassionate. She can also hear

Jonah in the other room, talking with Sarah about his lessons, and Kate cannot help but compare the two. She is comforted by the thought that Jonah might grow up to be like Eric. She is comforted by the hope she feels in her heart.

Later, the family says good-bye to their guests, and Kate waves from the porch as they leave. The children disperse into the yard, already beginning to tend to their chores. It is a beautiful fall day, just a bit crisp. Kate pulls her wool sweater tightly around her shoulders, looks to the trees in the distance, and is happy to see that the rain last week didn't knock all the leaves to the ground. She closes her eyes and takes a deep breath, pulling the scent of the earth into her lungs. Standing here, still and quiet, she can almost feel the season changing, with light and life ebbing slowly into winter. Opening her eyes, Kate smiles as she sees Sarah slip her hand into Eric's. She watches a moment longer than necessary as the young couple walks down the path that will lead them home.

~ Eleven ~

IT IS MORE THAN TWO WEEKS before Kate decides to tell Iris. Michael and Evan have been coming to her house regularly, and Evan grows closer to her family with each visit. Kate knows it is only a matter of time before Jonah, Margaret, or Laura slip up and mention him during school. She has considered simply waiting for it to happen and dealing with it then, but she knows it makes more sense to manage the situation proactively. Perhaps, she thinks, if she can talk to Iris alone, she can help her to see that Michael is not a threat. Perhaps she can create another ally for when she will have to broach the subject during the market.

She has a script prepared. She has thought through every possible reaction Iris could have, and is ready with a rebuttal for each one. She believes she will be able to convince Iris that what she has been doing is not crazy, is not dangerous, but rather, is the generous and kind thing to do.

After leaving her children with Sarah at the school building, Kate walks the twenty minutes to the opposite edge of the neighborhood to get to Iris's house. She passes several friends along the way and stops to speak briefly to each of the women, trying hard to act casual while inside her body the tension continues to build.

At last, she sees Iris's single-story house at the end of the road. It is a pale mélange of faded wooden boards, most salvaged from other houses that were destroyed during the war. The resulting patchwork is shaded by several tall apple trees that stand just a little too close to the house, their branches scraping the sides and roof with each pass of the breeze. Kate swings open the gate at the front of a five-foot fence, which encompasses not only Iris's yard, but also a portion of the forest behind it. Inside the fence, six goats wander. Their heads pop up and down as they pull tough grass from the ground, methodically mowing the area.

Kate steps up onto the front stoop and lifts her fist to knock on the silver metal storm door. After a few seconds, Iris appears behind the screen, a smile spreading over her face at the unexpected sight of her friend.

"Kate! What a surprise! Oh, come in. Come in!" Iris holds the door open. "Peace to you. I didn't expect you today," Iris says. "Is everything okay?"

"Everything is fine," Kate answers. "I just dropped the kids off at school and wanted to stop by and see you. How are you today?"

"I'm great, thanks. I'm just working in the cider room. Come on back and we can talk there." She leads the way through the kitchen to a small dimly lit room. A hole in the wall shared with the kitchen serves as a heating vent to warm the room. Several large oak casks are lined up on tables set against the wall, with an array of funnels and tubes positioned among them. Large windows are set into three of the exterior walls, but two of them, long broken, have been covered with wooden boards. The third is slightly open, allowing air circulation.

Iris picks up a small cup as she walks to one of the casks. A corncob is wedged into a round hole in the top of the barrel, with a stub piece of grapevine inserted lengthwise into the center of the cob. A long plastic tube stuck into the center of the grapevine dangles from the cask into a bucket of water on the table next to it. She turns a wooden spigot stuck into the bottom of the barrel, and golden brown cider drains into the cup. As she works, she says, "It's so nice to see you! How are the kids? Are they doing okay in school?"

"They're all doing great," answers Kate. "How are your grandchildren?"

"They're such good kids. Even the youngest one knows how to milk the goats now, and can help her mother process the cheese they're working on. Between you and me, I think the stuff still tastes like old socks, but what can you do. There are a lot of details to work out, I guess."

Kate laughs and nods. "They'll figure it out. Maybe someday a nice Swiss family will move into our neighborhood and teach us all the secret to making good cheese. Until then, I guess the old socks will have to do." Iris is examining the cup of liquid she drained from the casks when Kate asks, "How's the cider this year?"

"This is my first batch. We got a bumper crop of apples in September, so the presses were busy. This barrel looks like it's almost done, so I'm giving it a taste test. You can tell it's done because the bubbles have stopped. See, I have this tube that comes out of the top of the cider barrel, and as the cider ferments, carbon dioxide is released. It goes through this tube into the water jug next to it and makes bubbles. When the bubbles stop, you've got hard cider!"

"Well, I'm glad those college chemistry lectures paid off.

Imagine what you would be doing now if they hadn't kicked us out."

"Who needs lectures," Iris says. "I've got books." She smiles at Kate and then lifts the cup to her nose, sniffs the cider, and finally takes a small sip. "Mmm. Yeah. That's just about perfect. Do you want a taste?"

"Sure, thanks."

Iris gets another cup from the shelf and pours some for Kate, refilling her own cup as well. Iris says, "Right on schedule. This batch will go into the other barrel by the window. I can just pour the cider through the funnel on top, and in a couple months, it'll turn into vinegar. Speaking of which, can I give you some today? How's your supply?"

The hard cider produced in Iris's barrels is passed among the women of the neighborhood during special occasions: weddings, funerals, and holidays. But the vinegar made during the second step of the process is used almost daily for pickling, marinading, and even cleaning. A natural disinfectant, the vinegar has been an invaluable part of keeping families healthy since the war.

"I'd love some, if you have a little extra. But I didn't bring anything to trade. Can I bring something to the market this week for you?"

"Don't worry about it. Well, actually, are your bees still awake?" Iris asks as she rummages around the shelves, eventually finding a dented plastic bottle and a lid.

Kate smiles. "I'll bring you some honey. Thanks, Iris."

"No problem. I'm hoping to get few kids from my goats in the spring, too, so . . ." She looks slyly at Kate. "You know I have a sweet tooth."

Kate laughs and says, "I'll start stockpiling honey for you! Oh, Iris, it would be so great to have a couple of goats at home."

"I know. I feel bad that it's taken us this long to get you some. If it weren't for the wild dogs, you would have had them last year. You'll have to do a lot of work on your property before they come live with you, though. You've got to build a strong fence, and an outbuilding. Plus, I'll have to teach you how to raise them. You've got to know how to trim their hooves, and dehorn the new ones, and when to milk them and when to let them be dry."

"Maybe Margaret and Laura could start coming here once a week to help you out. They could do a sort of goat internship with you," Kate says as she sips her cider.

"I'd be happy to have them here. That's a good idea!"

The women nod, and Iris fills the bottle with vinegar. Then she sets it down on the table and picks up a large plastic pitcher. Turning back to the cider barrel, she begins to fill the pitcher from the spigot. With her back to Kate she says, "You know, you could make this stuff at your house, too. I could give you some mother of vinegar, and you'd have your own supply."

"I'd love to, but I don't think I have a barrel like yours."

"You could just use a big crock or something. I'll keep an eye out for a container, if you want."

"Thanks, Iris. If you don't mind, that is. I mean, the vinegar is sort of your thing. You get a lot of good trades for it. Are you sure you're OK with me setting up my own supply?"

"Oh my goodness," Iris says. "Kate, I know a lot of people think they need to keep control over some of the specific things they grow or make, but I don't think that way. I think the more people in the neighborhood who are self-sufficient, the better for us all. Especially with you living so far out of town. You should have one of everything, as far as I'm concerned."

"Well, thanks again. I'll keep my eyes open for a crock, too." Kate leans back against the table and watches Iris as she pours the hard cider into the vinegar cask and stuffs a wad of old white cloth into the hole of the funnel.

"This used to be a piece of my wedding dress," Iris says, holding up a scrap. "Can you believe that? After all these years, it's about as fancy as cheesecloth. But, oh well. I get more use out of cheesecloth than a wedding dress anyway." She laughs and walks back to where Kate stands, refilling her cup along the way. Iris asks, "Did you really come here just to visit? I get the feeling there's something on your mind."

Kate is happy to have the cider in her hand. She has always felt more comfortable talking to people with something to hold, something to keep her hands busy. She runs her fingers over the side of the cup. "Well, yes, I guess there is something. It's a rather . . . difficult thing to talk about, though."

Iris stops drinking and looks at her friend with concern in her eyes. "What is it? Are you okay?"

"Yes, I'm fine. We're all fine. I just . . ." Her words trail off as she looks down into the cup, trying to sound relaxed.

Iris holds her cup in one hand and puts the other hand on Kate's arm. She moves a step closer and leans her hip onto the table next to her. "Kate? What is it?"

Kate musters her courage and looks at Iris. Knowing that the longer she waits, the more difficult it will be, she blurts out, "Something happened at my house a while ago. We're all fine." She pauses and tries to smile, hoping to calm Iris's fear and steady her own pulse. "But we met someone."

Iris takes her hand off Kate's arm and knits her eyebrows, a puzzled look on her face. "You met someone? What do you mean?"

"Well, there was a little boy. He's only eight, and his name is Evan. He was really sick, and we took him in for a few days to help him get better."

"What? What boy? Whose boy?"

"He's been living in the wild, and he needed our help, so, of course, we helped him. He's really a wonderful child, and it seems like he's been well cared for, well taught."

"But who cared for him?"

Kate can see the hardness in Iris's eyes, a cold look of confusion and fear.

"Cared for by his father."

Iris sets down her cup, sits back on the table she has been leaning against, and crosses her arms in front of her chest. She looks at Kate a long time before saying, "Kate, did you see the man?"

"Yes. And I've talked to him, too. His name is Michael. He's not a raider. He's just a regular father, trying to take care of his child." She is speaking very calmly and quietly, trying to use her voice and her eyes to show Iris that there's no need to be afraid.

"Where are they now?"

"I don't know." It's not a complete lie.

"When was this?"

"A few weeks ago."

Iris shakes her head slowly, and Kate can see that she is about to speak. Before she can, Kate says, "I didn't say anything because the boy needed our help. I didn't want to get everyone alarmed and then have Michael run away with him while he was still sick. I thought it was best to help the child first, and figure out what to do about the man later."

"Figure it out? What's to figure out? Jesus, Kate, he could

have killed you all and we wouldn't have even known about it."

"But he didn't kill us, Iris. He didn't even try to hurt us."

"Well, consider yourself lucky. Christ. I can't believe you waited all this time to say something." Iris has moved farther away from Kate and is looking out the open window into her yard.

"I told you, I didn't want to scare them off. Isn't it our job to help children in need? Iris, you would have done the same thing. You would have tried to help that boy, right?"

"I would have helped the boy by rescuing him!" Iris says, her voice rising. "So, what, you got him healthy and then sent him back out there with that man? That man who probably isn't even his real father. Kate, when that boy grows up, he'll join the raiders. What did you think? Maybe when they sweep through here, that sweet little boy will remember you and not murder you in your sleep? Jesus, Kate."

"Iris, will you please listen. First of all, the man *is* his real father, and they *aren't* raiders. He's just a regular man. They're living out in the wild, just trying to survive."

"Oh, come on. What kind of father would keep his child out there? A decent father would get his son into a neighborhood so he could be cared for."

"And how exactly would he do that, Iris?" Kate asks. She had expected Iris's anger, but she hadn't expected to feel so defensive about Michael. "Do you think he could just stroll into town? He probably thinks we would try to take his son. And he's probably right! Could you just give up one of your children?"

"I did give up one of my children! I gave up my daughter to a man who beat her and raped her and took away every bit of dignity she had. I gave up Rose to a man who pretended to be kind and wonderful, but the moment they were married and he 'owned' her, he started to show his true nature." Iris's eyes glisten, but her voice is firm. "Kate, that bastard made my beautiful daughter have eight babies in ten years before she finally died trying to have the ninth. And there was nothing I could do to help her. So don't tell me about a 'regular man.' I know exactly what regular men are like. And I thought you did, too."

Kate sighs, her shoulders slumping. "Iris, I know what Rose went through. And I agree with you that there have been a lot of terrible men out there. Awful things were done to all of us. And we're doing our best to fix it all. But there must still be a few men out there who are okay."

"Kate, you know what men were like before. The way they spoke about women, and the way they thought about women . . . Do you think this man roaming around the forest is somehow magically exempt from that?"

Kate moves to Iris and gently touches her elbow. "Iris, not every man is bad. The men in this neighborhood are kind and decent. My husband was wonderful. Isn't it possible that there are more good men out there?"

"Not every man in this neighborhood is decent."

"What do you mean?"

"You don't see everything I see." Iris looks deep into Kate's eyes, and her posture and voice soften. She sighs. "It wasn't up to you to decide what to do with them. You should have told us right away so we could decide how to deal with him. If he was a good man, we would have done our best to help him integrate into our neighborhood."

Kate shakes her head and looks away. "I'm still not sure how that would have worked. After what happened with Patrice . . . I mean, what would the women in this neighborhood have done if they saw him?"

Iris hesitates before replying. "What are you saying? Do you think we would have swooped in and slaughtered him without even talking to him? We're not just an angry, irrational mob, ready to attack anyone we see."

"No, of course not. But lately I've been sensing a lot of hatred out there. A lot of hatred of men. After what we've gone through, it's understandable. But sometimes it just feels like some people go too far. All this talk about building up our defenses and making an army? Honestly, Iris, if I were a man, I'd be pretty scared to go anywhere near our neighborhood."

Iris blinks once, as if Kate had just slapped her face. She looks aghast, then whispers, "Kate, we are not building up an army. And that man attacked Patrice. We had to find him before he hurt anyone else."

Kate looks down at the ground. "I know."

"Maybe you don't know."

They stand in silence for a minute. Kate had no idea what else to say. Finally, Iris takes a deep breath and looks around the room. In a conciliatory tone, she says, "Look. I know it was really difficult to see what Patrice did. None of us enjoyed that. I guess I can understand why you kept the man a secret.

It's true that there's been a lot of talk lately about raiders and we're all trying to figure out how to best protect ourselves, but I think you've got the wrong idea. Maybe because you aren't in town with us, you don't get to hear all the information." She looks at Kate. "We aren't trying to build up an army. I don't want to hurt anyone. Patrice sounds tough, but you have to understand where she's coming from."

"I do," Kate says.

"I know you know her story, but try to really see it from her perspective. Besides, she isn't the only person making decisions in our neighborhood. That's the beauty of it, Kate.

No one person can make decisions for us. We're all in it together. We're all going to work together to make our neighborhood a safe and wonderful place to live. It's what we've been doing this whole time, isn't it?"

"Iris, I know we have a great neighborhood. And you know that I love all the women here."

"And it's not just our neighborhood. We're going to work with all the neighborhoods in the region. You know that, don't you? You trust us, right? I mean, you have to admit that we have a pretty great group of women here."

"Of course," Kate says. "I do trust the group. But I just didn't know how to protect that man and his son." She shrugs. "If this man lives out in the wild, maybe there are others like him. Other men who aren't trying to hurt people or destroy things. Shouldn't we be helping them, too?" Kate sets the cup of cider down on the table next to her and looks at her empty hands. "And what about that boy? Do you think he'd be able to integrate into our neighborhood? At what age should a little boy be considered too dangerous to help? And what about our own boys?"

"What do you mean?" Iris asks. "Our boys are doing great. They're taught to be kind and good, generous and loving. We're helping them to be fully aware of all their feelings and emotions, to be wonderful parts of our society. Our boys are going to grow up without all the anger and hate and cruelty that men used to have."

"I just want to make sure my children grow up in a better world than we did. I just want Jonah to grow up in a better world."

Iris steps to Kate and reaches out her hand. Kate takes it into her own, and they each smile, a little sadly. Iris says, "He will. That's the whole point. I'm sorry I yelled at you before. I know you, and I know you're doing a great job out there. I guess I just got scared. For you, and for all of us. I'm just glad you're okay."

"Thanks. I'm sorry, too. I'm sorry I didn't tell you sooner."

"It's okay."

"Iris?"

"Yes?"

"I don't want everyone to get scared. Is it okay if we don't tell anyone else about this?"

Iris lets go of Kate's hand and takes a step back. She looks at Kate for a long time before finally dropping her eyes to the floor. Quietly, she says, "Okay, Kate. If that's what you want."

"Thank you, Iris. And thanks for everything. I'm so glad I could talk to you about this."

"Me too."

Iris picks up the bottle of vinegar and hands it to Kate before putting one arm around her. They walk together toward the front door and then hug. Iris holds the door open.

On the front steps, Kate turns and says, "Good-bye, Iris. Thanks for listening." She smiles and holds up the bottle. "Thanks for this, too. I'll bring the honey this weekend."

"Sounds good," Iris says, a weak smile curving her mouth. Kate starts walking down the steps. As her foot lands on the ground, Iris calls through the screen door, "Hey, Kate—one more thing. Promise me that next time you'll come to me right away if you see a strange man roaming around the neighborhood."

Kate turns around to look up at her friend. "Sure."

~

A cold wind meets the family as they crest the hill between the neighborhood and their home. Jonah, Laura, and Margaret are chattering happily, relaying the stories and lessons they learned during school today. They seem to barely notice the wind. But to Kate, who has been silent for most of the trip, it feels as if the wind is passing right through her clothes, chilling her to the bone. She tightens the belt around her coat, and turns her collar up to protect her neck.

When they arrive home, the children bustle to get dinner prepared while Kate goes outside to haul in wood from the covered pile. As she stacks dry pieces onto her arm, she goes over the conversation with Iris in her mind. With each clunk of wood, a new thought rings through her head. It wasn't ideal, she thinks. But at least she did it. She feels relieved that she finally told Iris the truth. At least, most of it. Iris won't tell. Will she? She has to protect Evan and Michael. She has to protect her neighborhood. And her family.

Her arms full to the limit, Kate walks back into the warm house. The smell of roasting pumpkin drizzled with honey fills the kitchen. She drops all the pieces of wood at once into the box next to the stove, and with them, she drops away any notion of talking about Michael at the market. She has made up her mind to keep him a secret, and manages to squelch the guilt that has plagued her over the past month.

~

It is late October, and the leaves have all been battered down by the cold rains that patter the roof and windows some nights. Kate has heard these rains while lying in her bed. Sometimes, she hears Jonah sigh from his bed on the other side of the room. Tonight, she falls asleep wondering if Michael is warm.

~ Twelve ~

MICHAEL SQUATS DOWN on the kitchen floor and opens the cupboard door. He begins to pull out pots and pans, setting them on the floor beside him. "There you are," he says, lifting the heavy frying pan, and standing to set it onto the stove top. He puts most of the pans back into the cupboard, reserving an eight-by-eight square baking dish. "Hey, Kate," he calls to the next room. "Do you have dried corn?"

"Of course," she calls back. "In the large silver tin, second drawer from the bottom. If there isn't enough, I'll send Jonah down to the cellar for more."

"Any milk?"

"Only evaporated. Glass jar in the fridge."

"Thanks," he says, and begins to gather the ingredients.

Jonah and Evan sit together in the front room, busy darning the inevitable holes that form in the family's socks and sweaters. At Kate's insistence, Evan brought all his clothes with him today to be cleaned and mended. It wasn't even enough for a whole laundry load, but there were plenty of her children's clothes to add to the tub.

The boys had gotten the wet clothes onto the drying line

early in the morning while the sky was clear, and were frustrated when they had to run out into the first drops of rain this afternoon to bring them back into the house. Now, the cold rain is falling harder, and dark clouds block most of the late autumn light.

Michael has to maneuver around the damp pants and shirts strung over a cord that runs the length of the kitchen, slowly drying with the heat from the stove. He finds the corn and carries it to the counter, then opens the refrigerator. He grabs the milk and some butter, closing the door quickly to conserve energy.

Kate softly smiles as she sits on a chair in the dining room, four freshly sharpened kitchen knives lying on the table in front of her. She holds an old, long knife in one hand and a smooth rectangular stone in the other. She lifts the stone to her mouth and spits on it. Then, with a rhythmic circular motion, she slowly grinds the edge of the knife at an angle onto the surface of the stone. After a minute, she flips the knife and polishes the other side, her body slightly rocking in time with the soft scratching sound from the stone.

It is a motion that stays with her for the rest of the day when she sharpens a lot of knives in one sitting. She has found herself rocking gently while brushing her teeth, hours after finishing the knives. When that happens, Kate smiles. It reminds her of the perpetual sway her body used to have when her children were young. Hours and hours of holding her babies, rocking them in her arms as they fussed, gave her strong muscle memory. Even now, if she hears a baby crying, she finds herself swaying.

Michael is humming as he chops carrots, and Kate listens to the rhythm of his work. Clunk, clunk, clunk goes his knife as it hits the counter. She can see him out of the corner of her eye, and notices the up and down thrust of his arm. Scritch, scritch, scritch goes her knife over the small stone. Clunk, clunk, clunk. Kate feels a tingle go through her. Their bodies are working in the same rhythm.

She stops grinding the knife and begins to pass it over the length of the stone. Turning her wrist, she pulls the blade, swiping one side after the other, honing it into a fine edge. Kate sets down the stone and turns the sharp side of the blade away from her. She wipes it dry with an old cloth and then picks up a long piece of dark leather. One end of the strop she ties to the knob on the back of her chair, then holds it taut with her left hand. She counts in her head as she passes the blade over the length of the leather, flipping it at the bottom and the top of each pass. When she gets to twenty, she releases her hold on the strop and looks closely at the knife blade. Even in the dim light of the room, it shines.

Kate folds the knife into an old cloth, wrapping it loosely like a burrito, and carries it with the other knives into the kitchen. Michael stops chopping and looks up at her as she enters, a small smile flitting across his face before he looks back down to his work at the counter.

"How's dinner going?" Kate asks, opening a drawer and placing the wrapped knife inside. She slides the other four knives into a wooden rack above the kitchen sink.

"Good," he answers as he scoops the carrots into a pot waiting on the stove.

"I've been wondering what your thoughts are about getting Evan into school." When she says it, Kate notices that his body stops moving, if only for a split second, before he continues his work.

"I don't have any thoughts about it," he replies.

"Well," she says, "we talked about it when you first got

here."

"I remember."

"Maybe Evan can come into town with us this week and meet Sarah. She teaches on Wednesdays, and she's really great."

Michael pulls a small container of chicken broth from the refrigerator. He pours a bit into the pot with the carrots before saying, "I'm sure she's great, but that's not going to happen."

"We would be with him the whole time. Nobody's going to hurt him. And it would be so good for him to—"

"Sure," Michael says as he puts the container of broth back into the fridge. "I'll just let you take my son into town with you. That would be great." He stirs the pot on the stove and looks at Kate. "And you can leave your daughters here with me that day."

The smile on Kate's lips disappears, and her body stiffens. She quietly and firmly says, "That's not going to happen, either."

"Okay, good. So we understand each other." Michael begins slicing an onion, a little more forcefully than is necessary.

Kate thinks fast, trying to keep the conversation alive. "Okay, look. I know you're hesitant to have him come into town with us. That's understandable. But maybe he could be *here* this week when Sarah comes. Maybe he could start with lessons at our house once a week. That way no one in town would have to know, but he could start learning something."

Michael's eyes look so directly into hers that she can almost feel his thoughts. It doesn't take long for him to find the answer he's looking for.

"You told Sarah."

She knows there is no point in lying, with the truth so

plainly written across her face. "I did." She watches him take a very deep breath, the kitchen knife clenched tightly in his fist, before he slowly lowers it to the countertop and releases it. He turns to face her, and his face is full of anger and betrayal. If she were not already pressed against the edge of the sink, she surely would have taken a step back.

"How could you do that?" he asks quietly.

"Look, before you get so angry, you need to know that Sarah hasn't told anyone else."

Michael's eyes roll as he turns his palms to the ceiling. "Jesus, Kate. Don't you know what this means?"

"It doesn't mean anything. Yes, I talked to Sarah about Evan. But if you knew her, you would understand. Michael, she's not going to hurt him. She's not scared of Evan. Sarah has a wonderful husband, and children of her own. She has a son, too."

"That's not the point, Kate. I don't think she's going to hurt Evan. I don't think any of the women in your neighborhood want to hurt Evan. But you know they'll want to take him away from me. And who knows what they'll do to me. They'll probably come out here with torches and pitchforks. Christ, Kate."

"I already told you, she hasn't told anyone."

"How do you know? How do you know they aren't on their way out here right now?"

"God, Michael, calm down. Not every woman is evil, you know."

They look at each other, and she knows what Michael will say before he says it.

"And not every man is evil, either."

Her shoulders slump, and she nods. "I know."

"But all your friends don't know that, do they? What do

you think they're going to do? Come out here and say hello? You tell them there's a man living out in the woods by your house, and they're going to be scared. They're going to be scared, and mad, and they're going to—"

"Just exactly what do you think they're going to do?" Kate asks, trying to keep her voice quiet so Jonah and Evan can't hear the conversation from the front room. "You think I would suddenly run into town one day and start shouting, 'Hey everybody, there's a strange man by my house. Let's all go get him!' Is that what you think of me?"

"No," he says, his body animated. "It's not about what you would do. It's about what you can't do. What do you think you could say to stop them."

"We're not just a senseless mob! These are the women of my neighborhood. They're good people. Mothers and sisters and friends."

"Give me a break," Michael says under his breath.

"You're wrong about this, Michael. I'm one of those women. I'm just like the people that you're claiming would want to hurt you, and you know that's not . . ." Her voice trails off with her unwillingness to reveal any more of herself.

He watches her for a moment, and seems to be searching for the meaning of her silence. "Kate, I know you're not like that. But I think you're giving them more credit than they deserve."

"Could you just try to trust me on this?" she asks, looking into his eyes. "I know it's difficult. I know how dangerous this is for you."

"Do you?"

"I do."

He shakes his head slowly and looks back down to the floor with a sigh. "I don't know."

After a few seconds, Michael steps closer to Kate and leans against the counter next to her. He folds his arms and stands quietly before he asks, "When did you tell Sarah?"

"Weeks and weeks ago. Right away, really." Kate sighs and folds her arms, her gaze lying lightly on the worn wooden floor in front of her. "I'm sorry." She says the words to pacify him, knowing that she should be sorry for her deception. "But I needed to talk to someone."

Kate turns to Michael and says, "I do understand what this means for you. That's why I didn't tell you about it. I didn't want you to be worried. I know you don't know Sarah, but she's kind and good."

Michael sighs and says, "I'm sure she's very nice. I just don't know what to do." He looks at Kate and smirks. "And that's as tough for me to say as it was for you to apologize."

She blinks, slightly taken aback by this, but then reaches out to touch him. His blue eyes soften as she rests her warm hand on the back of his arm, and his smirk fades into a gentle smile. His voice is kinder as he says, "Kate, I'm not ready for Evan to meet anyone else yet. I hope you can understand that."

"I do. Just . . . keep thinking about it, okay?"

"Okay."

The front door bangs open as Margaret and Laura come inside. Kate quickly lets go of Michael's arm and pushes away, straightening the sides of her shirt with her palms before walking to the front room to greet her daughters. Their coats, shoes, and hats are wet from the rain, and they peel off their gear by the door.

"Here, girls, let me take your things to the kitchen to dry," Kate says, holding out her arms to collect the wet clothes. "Sorry you got stuck out there. Were you able to get some wood chopped before the rain started?"

"Yes, Mom. Here," Laura says, handing Kate her heavy coat.

"We stacked a bunch," Margaret adds. "We didn't get to chop much kindling, though. We'll have to do more tomorrow."

"Well, come on in, and get yourselves some dry clothes," Kate tells them. "I'll find room for the wet stuff in the kitchen. Michael's in there making dinner."

"Oh, thank goodness!" Laura says, relief washing over her face. "I'm starving!"

Kate's lips smile, but her eyes do not. Her children seem to love Michael's cooking. If absolutely forced, she would have to agree that it is delicious, but she hates to admit it. In the beginning, she reveled in the fact that he was doing some of the cooking. But when it turned out he was better at it than she was, it wasn't nearly as much fun anymore.

"Well," Kate says, "I'll let him know you're hungry."

As she enters the kitchen, her arms full, Michael looks up from the stove and grins. "I heard them. You can tell the girls it will be ready in about five minutes," he says, stirring the vegetables in the frying pan with quick, short strokes. "I'm making some corn pudding, too. That won't be ready until later, but we can have it as a dessert."

"Mmm. That sounds nice. Thank you," Kate says as she begins laying the wet coats over the line. She feels Evan and Jonah's clothes, and, deciding that they are dry, takes them off the line and piles them up on the floor. When she gets to the last piece of clothing, an old sweater of Jonah's, she is surprised to find it still quite wet. She is puzzled for a moment and then sees a drop of water fall from above onto the sweater. Looking up, Kate sees a dark circle of plaster surrounding a soaked section of ceiling.

"Shit," she says under her breath.

"What's wrong?" Michael asks, glancing over his shoulder at her.

Her shoulders slump as she sighs. Kate looks around the room and sees the empty bowl Michael used to mix the corn pudding. She crosses the room and picks the bowl up off the counter, quickly returning to the leak. Michael turns and watches her as she bends to set it on the floor below the drip. A second later, they hear the first plunk of water as it falls into the bowl.

"The roof's leaking?" Michael says.

"Uh-huh."

"Makes sense. This is the first really heavy rain we've had this fall. Don't worry, I can scavenge some shingles from abandoned houses around here. Next dry day, I'll get up there. It'll be good as new." He waits for her to reply, but she only looks at him, her hands on her hips. "Don't worry, Kate. We'll get it fixed."

"I can do it myself," she says, defensively, instinctively. Michael subtly shakes his head and turns back to the stove. Each time they manage to break a brick from the wall between them, she somehow finds a way to build it back up again.

He lifts the pan off the burner and dumps the stir-fry into a large melamine bowl. "Kids, dinner's ready," he shouts as he carries the bowl to the dining room.

Jonah and Evan are the first to arrive. Jonah removes the few books and papers from the table and asks Evan, "Can you get the dishes from the kitchen?"

"Sure," Evan responds, already turning to complete the task.

Within moments, Margaret and Laura are also there, and

170

they help the boys pass around plates, forks, and spoons. Kate fills a pitcher with water, and as she brings it to the table, she passes Michael in the doorway. Their bodies turn sideways to avoid bumping, and she looks down to avoid his eyes.

They all sit together, the food waiting before them. Kate picks up a long wooden spoon and begins to dish out the stir-fry.

"Margaret, here you go, honey. Laura, here you go. This should help you warm up. Jonah, here's your plate, sweetie. Evan, here you are. And thanks for your help again today." Kate reaches out to take the plate Michael is holding up for her. She scoops some seasoned chicken and vegetables onto his plate and hands it back to him without a word.

"Thank you," Michael says without smiling.

She glances at him, and then quickly drops her eyes. "You're welcome."

As they eat, Margaret and Laura discuss the books they have been assigned to report on during school next week. They speak freely, and Kate sees how comfortable they have become with Michael and Evan. As the girls talk about the characters in their stories, Kate steals glances at Michael. He is smiling, listening to the children, and asking questions from time to time. He seems genuinely interested in what they are saying. His questions are insightful and challenging.

"So," Laura says, "the man freezes to death. The dog stays by him for a bit, and then just leaves. Isn't that great?"

"Great?" Margaret asks.

"Well, not great that he froze to death, but I think that's a great ending," Laura replies.

"I don't think it's great. I think it's terribly sad," Margaret says.

"Mags, there can't always be a happy ending. That would

be so boring," Laura teases. "I like the ones where reality comes and kicks you in the butt." She smiles and nudges her sister with her elbow.

"You're right. But I do like happy endings. I like to think that if we do our best, and be our best, and live our best, we might just get to have a happy ending," Margaret says.

Kate watches her daughters, so beautiful and bright. Their youth, their vigor, so brilliant she can almost see it shine out of them. Margaret is so much like her father, Kate thinks. David always thought we'd live happily ever after, too. She feels the familiar melancholy begin to creep through her, and struggles to fight it off before it takes hold.

"Evan and I have been talking about something," Jonah blurts.

All eyes turn to him, and Kate asks, "What's that, buddy?"

"Well, remember how you said Michael and Evan can't live with us because we don't have room?

"What?" Kate feels her heart skip a beat as a mixture of panic and embarrassment surges through her body.

"You said they probably wouldn't want to move in to our house, because it's too small." Jonah is trying to avoid his mom's eyes, aware of the manipulation he is undertaking.

"Um . . . yes . . . I said I didn't know where they could sleep. I mean . . ." She looks to Michael, who seems just as taken aback as she is. "I said we don't have any more mattresses." Though Jonah's question had embarrassed her, the flimsiness of her excuse leaves her mortified.

Kate and Michael stare at each other for what feels like minutes. The dull splash of water echoes from the kitchen as it drips from the leaky ceiling into the bowl, like a metronome marking the measures of their discomfort.

Finally, Jonah says, "Well, Evan and I have been talking

about it, and we've figured it out!"

"Figured what out?" she says, turning back to Jonah.

"They can stay in the shed!" Jonah looks triumphant, as if he'd solved a mystery that had been troubling him for weeks. He turns to Evan, who is sitting beside him, and the two boys beam at each other. "There's plenty of room for them, and we can make a mattress out of the empty canvas sacks out there. We've already started sewing them together."

Jonah and Evan look proudly at Kate. Her mouth is slightly open, and she stares at them with a blank look on her face.

"Guys, you need to talk to us first before you make plans," Michael says. "You can't just assume it's okay."

"But, Dad, why wouldn't it be okay?" Evan asks.

Michael looks at the walls, the ceiling, and the table, and finally settles his eyes on Kate. "Well," he replies, "maybe Kate was going to use the shed for something else."

"No, she wasn't," Jonah says. "It's mostly empty all winter. It's full during the harvest, or when we're collecting materials, but there's not a lot in there now. We can easily rearrange it and make plenty of space."

"But Jonah," Kate says, finally able to speak, "I'm not sure Michael and Evan want to live in our shed. They have a home in the woods. It's asking a lot of someone to move out of their home."

"It will be simple," Evan says. He smiles brightly, looking back and forth between his father and Kate. "We don't have much stuff. We could get it here in just a couple loads. Maybe less if we use Jonah's wheelbarrow."

"But sweetie," Kate starts, "Your father—"

"He won't mind, will you Dad? There's a good roof on the shed, so we won't get so wet and cold. You said it was just going to get colder out there. This way we'll be warmer."

Michael looks at his son, a mixture of sadness and pride in his eyes. Kate imagines them together in the woods, the cold rain beating down around their ramshackle fort, and the words he must use to console the boy during the long nights. Her empathy for him runs deep, having lived through many cold, lonely nights with her own children in the first years after the war.

"It's a really good idea," Margaret says. "I can help you move stuff around in there."

"I can help with the sewing," Laura says. "If we all work together, we can set it up in no time." She turns to Kate and asks, "What do you think, Mom?"

She thinks her children are better people than she is. She sits before them now as if in judgment. Will she become the person they believe she is, or will this be the moment her children realize she is only human, flawed and fearful? She is at a crossroads, faced with a choice that could either solidify all the goodness and generosity she has tried to instill in them, or one that will forever lower their expectations of the capacity of the human heart.

"I think that's a wonderful idea," Kate says, to her own astonishment. She smiles at her daughters, then turns to the boys. "You boys came up with this idea all on your own?" They nod and beam. "I'm proud of you both."

"Yes!" they both shout, pumping their fists into the air.

Kate looks across the table at Michael and holds his gaze. His brow is crinkled, as if he's trying to decipher what new form of trickery or subversion this might be. She senses his mistrust, so familiar with that feeling that she can almost smell it on someone else. Her shoulders rise and fall as she takes a deep breath, and with her exhale, a soft smile shines in her eyes. She silently asks for his trust.

His cheeks flush red, and Kate notices the subtle change in his posture as he sits up a little straighter. Across the length of the table, she can his body relax, and she sees the light appear in his eyes.

"Well, I guess it's all settled then," Michael says, turning to the boys. "We'll start working on it tomorrow."

"After dinner we can show you what we're going to do," Jonah says with excitement. "We can even start moving stuff around."

"Honey," Kate says, "I think Michael's right. Maybe we should wait until tomorrow to start. It's raining pretty hard out there."

"But that's the point, Mom. It's raining like crazy. We can't let them go back out into the woods in this," he says, motioning his hand toward the dining room window.

"I already have all my clothes here," Evan adds. "And my dad doesn't have much out there except tools and cooking stuff."

"But," Kate begins, "we'd have to find you some blankets, and work on the mattress, and—"

"I'm done!" Margaret shovels the last of her dinner into her mouth and says, "I'll go get some blankets."

Laura scoops up her food and says, "Me, too. I'll help!"

"Wait! Wait just a minute, you two," Kate says, holding up her arms to stop Margaret's exit. "I don't want you scarfing down your dinner like that. Slow down."

"Mom," Margaret says, putting her hands on her mom's shoulders as she stands behind her chair. She bends down and presses her cheek against Kate's before continuing. "Don't worry. It's going to be okay."

Yeah, maybe it is, Kate thinks.

~

Three hours later they all crowd into the small space of the shed. Round bins are piled high in the far corner, and tools hang congested from relocated hooks on one wall. A single small lantern hangs from the ceiling, its golden glow casting shadows around the room. A large thin burlap and cloth rectangle lies on the floor in the opposite corner, stuffed with a hundred lumpy sacks, and covered with extra bedding from inside the house.

"Sorry I don't have any extra pillows," Kate says, putting her arm around Evan.

"We can make some," Margaret says confidently.

"And some shelves for their clothes and stuff," Laura adds.

Jonah moves to the side of the new bed and sits down on the low edge. "This is great!"

"It will do for tonight, I guess," Kate says. "You boys can finish sewing the mattress tomorrow and, if it's not raining, Michael and Evan can go get their stuff."

The shed is warm from body heat and the work that has been done here tonight, but Kate knows it will get much colder soon. She looks at Michael and says, "Maybe we can come up with a little woodstove or something in here. It's going to get pretty cold by three a.m."

"I don't know," he replies. "It's so small. It would take a while to figure something out, and we'd have to vent it." His eyes dart around the room, already working on a solution.

"Hot water bottles?" Margaret asks. "At least they could get the bed warmed up before they get in. Once they're snuggled in there, they'd be okay."

"Maybe," Kate says, squeezing Evan closer to her side. "At least that's less of a fire hazard. But I know I don't have

176

anything like that right now. I'm afraid it might still be pretty rough tonight."

He smiles up at her and says, "Don't worry. We'll be okay. This is perfect."

"It is great," Michael says. "We have a couple sleeping bags we can bring tomorrow, too. They keep us pretty warm."

"Bring them to the house first," Kate says as crinkle pulls at her nose. "You can wash them." The words are out before she can filter them, and she immediately regrets them. She looks up at Michael. "I mean, if you want to. If they're dirty."

He smiles at her, easy and honest. "They're definitely dirty. Thank you, Kate. In fact, if you don't mind, maybe I could wash my clothes, too."

"Okay. If you want," she says with all the false nonchalance she can muster.

"You all did so much work tonight. I really want to thank you for this," Michael says, sweeping his chin in a subtle arc around the shed. He smiles at each of the children before looking at Kate. "Thank you."

"You're welcome," she says, smiling. It feels right. "Well, we should get back to the house. It's time for bed, and we should let you settle into your new space." Kate lets go of Evan and takes a step toward the door. The children all bustle around, saying good night, maneuvering in the small space to line up behind Kate.

She opens the shed door and ushers them out into the rain. They run one at a time into the darkness, making a break for the warmth and security of their house. As she turns to close the door behind her, she sees Michael staring at her. She cannot read the look in his eyes, and it makes her pause. "Good night," she says, the rain dripping down onto her head and shoulders. She pushes the door closed.

~ Thirteen ~

"WHAT IF WE USED one of the old microbatteries?" Elle asks. "I bet we could scavenge a car horn, too. If the lookouts see something, they hook it up and sound the alarm. We'd all hear a car horn."

"That's a great idea, Elle," Iris says. "It will take some engineering to get a microbattery charged up, but there must be a way. We could hook up solar in the watchtower, and—"

"Wait a second, Iris. There might be a simpler way," Rhia says, holding up one hand. "I used to have a horn attached to the top of my boat. It broke a few years ago, and I pulled it apart and tried to fix it. I don't know for sure, but I bet we could make a sort of siren for the tower."

"Wouldn't we still need a battery, though?" Iris asks.

"Look," Rhia says, a sly grin on her young face. "I know it's hard for you to believe that not everything requires chemistry or electricity, but I think it could just be mechanical."

Iris laughs, along with many of the women gathered together in the old grocery store. They all sit in a circle in two rows of chairs and benches. Three women from New Hope and three from Bellwether have made the long journey to meet here today, and they sit in the front row near Iris and Patrice.

"It's a pretty simple device, really," Rhia says. "Just a metal tube with a fan inside that we could spin with a hand crank. There are rectangular holes inside the tube, right above where the fan spins, and as it goes around, air is forced through the holes in bursts."

"Why would that make sound?" asks a woman in the back row.

"Think about a flute or a whistle. Those make sound by forcing air through holes. When the fan is spinning, sometimes air goes through the holes. Other times it's blocked by these fins that are attached to the fan blades. When it's blocked, it builds up air pressure. When it's allowed through the holes, you get sound."

Rhia holds both her hands up in front of her face, cupping them together with her thumbs pressed parallel to each other. She places her lips gently against the small hole between her thumbs and blows. A low, mournful sound echoes through the room, and Rhia's dark eyes twinkle above her cupped hands. "See?" she says. "Force air through a hollow space, and you get sound."

Joy, a woman from New Hope, raises her hand, and everyone looks at her. "I remember we used to have an air raid siren in my hometown. It was on top of a tower, and would go off every Friday at noon. The sound went pretty far, but I don't know if it you could hear it all the way in the next neighborhood."

Rhia shakes her head and says, "I don't know either. Maybe it depends how big the siren is, or how big the cone in front of it is."

"Like a megaphone?" Iris asks.

"Something like that," Rhia answers.

"If it works, that would be a great solution," Joy says. "But we would still have to come up with a way to get information from town to town."

They all sit for a minute, quietly talking to each other, trying to come up with viable options. Kate watches the women from the other neighborhoods, curious about them. They will be staying here tonight, with women who have volunteered to host them, and Kate is a little jealous. What a wonderful honor and privilege to have visitors! To hear about their neighborhood, their challenges and triumphs. Just to talk to someone new would be so unusual and exciting. There is great comfort in knowing the same group of people for most of your life, but meeting someone new can force you to see the world in a new way.

Thoughts of Michael cross her mind, as she considers how her life has changed since he first stepped onto her porch. Trying to understand his point of view has forced her to reevaluate her own. Suddenly, things in her home, her life, look different to her, as if she sees them now through his eyes. She was so sure of everything before he came to challenge her. So sure of everything before he turned her world upside down.

Then again, she thinks, sometimes it's good to turn it all upside down. She remembers a junk drawer at home, full of things she has collected over the years. Most of it is worthless, but she can't bring herself to sift through it. Anything valuable in there is covered by so much detritus that she's forgotten all about it. But if she would just take out the whole drawer and turn it over onto the floor, she could sort through the mess. Turning it upside down would force her to finally throw away the useless, half-broken bits. Turning it all upside down would help her find the things that really matter.

"Well," Iris says with a sigh, pulling Kate back to reality. "Why don't I recap some of the ideas that we've brainstormed already. I'm not sure any of them are a perfect solution, but it's a good start." She walks to the large chalkboard that leans against the front wall. Reaching high, she writes one word for each idea, verbally filling out the details at the same time.

"Horses: We petition the government to give us a few horses. That way if something happens, we ride to the next towns to warn them, or to get help. Boats: Use the water to get to the next towns faster than by foot. That is, if the wind is in our favor. Runners: Train people to run the distance between neighborhoods. Bells: This is similar to the siren idea, but maybe sirens are better." She erases the word "Bells" with the sleeve of her shirt and writes "Sirens" in its place.

Sarah raises her hand, but Iris's back is to her and she doesn't notice. Iris continues. "If we set up sirens along the way and take shifts at them, we could sound them as soon as we hear another one, like a chain. Smoke: Again, this would work be like a chain—I'm not sure exactly how this would work. But obviously, if we saw a lot of smoke in the distance, we would know something has gone wrong."

"Iris," Sarah says.

Iris turns and looks at Sarah before saying, "Yes?"

"If we were going to petition the government, don't you think it would be best to ask them where the raiders are a problem? I mean, maybe they have some objective information that we don't know about." When no one speaks, Sarah looks around the room uncomfortably, then adds, "Or maybe *they* have some ideas on how to best protect our town."

"We can't rely on anyone but ourselves," Patrice says, shaking her head. "Someday, maybe the government will be able to eradicate this problem, but we need to come up with a solution on our own. Right now."

"I think Patrice is right," Iris says. "If we petition the regional government now, it's possible they could get us horses sometime soon. I've heard they have a lot of horses, but so few people know how to care for them, they don't like to give them out, because it takes so much training. It's really the training time that we would have to ask them for."

Joy speaks up again. "I think horses would be great. And not just for security. They'd be useful for plowing the fields, and fertilizer. Personally, I'm not sure I could learn to ride one, but I know some of the young people in New Hope could do it."

"That's a wonderful point," Rhia says. "This could be a great way for the young women to really step up to the task. A way for us to pass some of the responsibility on to them as they come of age."

"In that case, we would need a couple horses in each town," Patrice says firmly. "I'm not sending just one person out there alone. No offense to you," she says, jutting her chin toward the visiting women, "but I don't care enough about your town to throw one of my own grandchildren out there on a patrol, just to be slaughtered."

Several women shift uncomfortably in their seats. The visitors raise their eyebrows or look down at the floor. Iris steps toward them and tries to repair the damage. "I think what Patrice means is that we would want teams of three or four people to ride together between the towns. I agree with her that it would be safer that way. Even if it's just to deliver news, we wouldn't send just one person alone."

Many of the women nod. They begin to talk and mutter among themselves, working through the ideas before them, trying to come up with more. After a few minutes, Iris raises her hands to quiet the group and asks, "Does anyone have any other ideas to share? Anything?"

When no one answers, she says, "Well, let's take a vote. Everyone in favor of trying to develop an air raid siren for their neighborhood, raise your hand." Almost all the hands go up, and Iris smiles. "Rhia, we think that's a great idea. Since you seem to know the most about it, would you agree to lead the project?"

Rhia nods. "Sure. I can't guarantee I can make a siren, but I'll try."

"Great. Stay at the chalkboard after the meeting. Anyone who wants to help Rhia with this project, see her after." Iris looks out over the crowd again and says, "We'll get to work right away on a watchtower in the center of town. And the women from New Hope and Bellwether will work on their towers.

"Now, everyone in favor of petitioning the regional government for horses and training, raise your hand." Every last woman raises her hand, and Iris smiles again. "Well, that was easy. Now I don't even have to count," she says with a laugh. "Can I have three volunteers to work on writing a petition? We'll send it the next time the Carriers come through town."

"I'd like to help with that," Joy says, raising her hand. "And I think it would make sense for one of the women from Bellwether to help, too. After all, we want to make sure we're all in it together."

"I'll do it," says Jennifer, one of the women visiting from Bellwether. "I'm not going to let New Hope have all the fun," she says with a smirk.

"I'd be happy to work on it, too," Sarah says.

"Great," Iris says, clapping her hands. "Four weeks from

today we'll have a group meeting in New Hope. Patrice and I have agreed to make the trip there. Joy, is there is any way you could get in touch with the neighborhood north of you? Maybe they could join us then?"

"We'll work on it."

"Thank you. Well, if there is nothing else anyone wants to add . . ." Iris pauses and glances sideways at Kate. "Nothing? Well, then I guess this meeting is adjourned."

The women stand and stretch as they begin to move around the room. Kate walks toward Iris, but upon seeing her approach, Iris turns and moves away. Kate stops and pivots to the right, wandering instead to the chalkboard, where Rhia is already surrounded by a small group.

Rhia turns to Kate with a bright smile. "Hi, Kate! Will you help with the siren?"

"I'd be happy to. What do you need?"

"Well," Rhia says to the group, "I'm not entirely sure how to do this, but I think I understand the basic idea." She begins to draw a diagram on the chalkboard, making circles and fan blades, with long sweeping arrows to indicate the inflow of air and outflow of sound. As she talks, others slowly join the group, until Rhia has assembled a full task force for the enterprise. Kate takes mental notes about the materials needed, where they might look for parts, and how big the siren might need to be.

"Maybe a section of culvert?" Kate asks.

"I don't know. They're usually corrugated, aren't they?" someone asks.

"How would we attach the fins?" another adds.

"We have welding equipment in New Hope," Joy says. "We can share it if you can come up. It would be complicated to bring the equipment here."

They work together for nearly an hour, each woman offering up insights and ideas until a fully formed plan has developed. Tasks are assigned, and they agree to meet up again next month. Rhia and Kate will make the long journey to New Hope with the materials they have gathered, and together with the women there, they will attempt to assemble a siren. If it works, others will be made for the surrounding neighborhoods.

As they wrap up their meeting, Rhia thanks each of them and shakes their hands. "Well, I'd better get back to my boat. The fish don't just jump in on their own, you know," she says with a smile. She turns and starts to walk quickly toward the door, but Kate catches up with her.

"Rhia," Kate says, walking out into the cool November drizzle with her. "An air raid siren is a great idea. How'd you learn so much about them?"

"I told you, I took my boat horn apart when it was broken."

"But"—Kate presses—"boat horns are different from sirens, aren't they?"

Rhia shrugs. "Sure, they're different."

"Do you have a book about them, or something?"

"No. But I think we can figure it out."

"Don't get me wrong," Kate says. "You obviously know what you're talking about. I was just wondering where you learned about it." They take a few more steps down the road together. "I know your father taught you about boats. I was just curious what other useful things he taught you."

Rhia stops walking and turns to look into Kate's eyes. Kate smiles and gently touches Rhia's arm.

"My father taught me about sirens," Rhia says quietly. "He helped me take my horn apart, and told me all about it."

"Sounds like he passed on some valuable knowledge."

"He did." She begins walking through the neighborhood again, and Kate keeps step with her. Kate stays silent, letting Rhia stew in her own thoughts, waiting until the younger woman feels the need to speak, to fill the space between them.

After several minutes of silence, Rhia says, "I guess sometimes the old men have redeeming qualities."

"What do you mean?" Kate asks.

"I just mean, maybe they know some things we don't know. Maybe they could still have something to contribute."

"I think you're right, Rhia. Every person has something to contribute. No one doubts that."

"I know that's what everyone says, but . . . I just think . . . maybe . . . some of the men don't think we all feel that way." Rhia is walking faster now, her pace getting longer as the muscles in her legs warm and the conversation heats.

Kate takes a deep breath, loud enough for Rhia to hear. Then she nods and says, "I think I know what you mean. And I've been wondering about the same thing lately."

"You have?"

"Yes. I believe in the changes we've made to heal all the pain and sadness from the Last War. I do. They were necessary. Without them, we would have been lost. But sometimes I wonder where we go from here." Taking a big risk, she says, "I wonder if we've taken too much away from the men."

Rhia stops walking and turns to Kate again. They look at each other for a long time before Rhia says, "Well, you and I are different from everyone else in this neighborhood, then."

"Maybe. Or maybe there are others who feel the same way. We won't know if we're too scared to talk to each other about it." Kate can see hope flicker in Rhia's eyes, and tries to reinforce the tenuous connection she has established. "Can I tell you something?"

"Of course."

"My son, Jonah, is ten years old now." Kate lowers her voice. "I don't want him to grow up thinking he's bad. Rhia, he's such a good person. I want him to be able to be whatever he wants to be. I want him to grow up knowing he's just as wonderful as my daughters."

Rhia smiles gently and nods, letting a small stream of cold rain drip off the edge of her hat. "He *is* a good person, Kate. Jonah is a wonderful boy."

"But what about you? What about your father?"

Rhia's eyes drop, and though she is looking at the ground in front of her, Kate knows she is thinking of a place far away. "It's too late for my father. He died about six months ago."

"Oh, Rhia, I'm so sorry." Kate reaches her hand to touch Rhia's arm and takes a small step closer to her.

"He was a wonderful man, Kate. He was good and decent, gentle and kind. And he was so smart. He knew everything. And for the last ten years of his life, he wasn't allowed to show any of it."

"Was he with you on the boat?" Kate asks.

"Yes. After the war, when everything changed, he got scared, I think. He knew he wasn't going to be able to keep his mouth shut, and he'd go off trying to teach people and help people, and he'd get himself in trouble," Rhia says with a small sad laugh. "And, he was scared people would find out that he'd been in the military."

"Oh," Kate says.

"See, it even scares you to hear it."

"I'm not scared, just surprised."

"My father was a mechanical engineer for the Army

before the war. During the war, he worked on communications. That's how he knew so much about sirens. When everything started falling off the grid, they had to revert back to the basics." Pride shines in Rhia's eyes, and Kate is taken aback.

"I . . . I'm sorry," Kate mutters. "I didn't know."

"I don't talk about it much." Rhia takes a deep breath. "It's not a popular topic these days."

"That's for sure," Kate says. "But I don't think you should be scared to talk about your father. Many of us had wonderful fathers. Many of us would understand. And—try to understand—anyone who is too scared to even talk about these sort of things might still just be too hurt and sad to be able to talk about them. But, Rhia, we can't stop talking about the past. What's the old phrase? If you forget the past, you are doomed to repeat it?"

"I suppose. But we still have to be very careful these days. I mean, you can't just walk through the neighborhood spouting the glories of military knowledge. Most people assume all the men in the military were evil. I understand that, but . . ." She hesitates and seems to gather her courage. "My father said there was a time, long ago, when people were proud of the military. That soldiers used to try to help people, and build things. That was before things got so bad, I guess. He said men and women who served their country were welcomed back as heroes. Men *and* women! Believe it or not, one of my grandmothers was in the Navy. Maybe that's where I get my love for boats." Rhia lightly laughs as she looks down the path.

Kate tries to smile, and says, "Maybe."

The smile fades from Rhia's lips, and she lowers her eyes again. "Look, I know things have changed a lot since then, and I'm just as opposed to war and fighting as every woman." A sad shadow passes over her face. "But sometimes I wonder if more of the men who fought in the Last War had returned home, then maybe we would have a different idea about them. Seems like, since almost all of them died out there, we never had to try to understand them at all. We buried all of them. Even the ones who survived."

It is an idea that has occurred to Kate from time to time—how different the world would be if more men had returned. Would the women have been able to take over the governments so easily? Would they have felt the need to? If we all had fathers and brothers and sons who returned to us, broken but breathing, would we have been willing to build a greater mutual society—of both women and men—instead of so quickly agreeing to force men out of it?

Men trickled back into the neighborhoods in the first years after the war. Several times each month, a small group, maybe just two or three, would pass through town, trying to make their way back to demolished homes and devastated families. For years, Kate waited, hoping one day to see David, walking back from the dead. How different her life would be if he had survived.

"Some men did return," Kate says. "But most of them were the ones who had been *forced* to fight. They were happy to be home, and ready to be a part of peace."

"Peace, yes. But at what price?" Rhia asks as she begins to walk again.

"Rhia, wait." Kate touches her arm, and Rhia turns to face her.

"Look, Kate, I'm sorry if I upset you. I shouldn't have said anything, and—"

"No, don't be sorry. I'm glad you told me. And I'm glad to hear your opinions about it. You have every right to talk about these things." Kate sighs and looks down to the ground. "I know that some women would be frightened of the things you said. Honestly, I'm not sure what I feel about all of it just yet. But I want you to know that you can trust me." She looks back up to meet Rhia's questioning gaze. "If you ever want to talk about it some more, I'd be honored if you'd confide in me. I won't tell anyone."

With an expression conveying both surprise and relief, Rhia hesitates before saying, "Okay. Well, thanks, Kate."

"You're welcome."

Rhia stands in place, looking at Kate, and throws her arms around her in a warm embrace. Kate hugs her back tightly as she says, "Thank you, Rhia."

The two women pull apart and smile. "Well," Rhia says, "I do really need to get back to my boat. I guess I'll see you at the market this weekend?"

"Of course," Kate answers. "I'm going to head home, too. Have a safe walk back."

"You, too."

Kate watches Rhia walk away before turning onto a side street that will lead to her path home. She chews on her bottom lip, trying to digest all this new information, happy to have a new confidant, hopeful to have found another woman who might be on her side.

~ Fourteen ~

THE SUN RISES LATE this time of year, and Kate sits alone in the quiet, dark kitchen, holding her steaming mug of peppermint tea. It always surprises her how much more sleep the children seem to need during the winter months. Their bodies, so attuned to the diurnal rhythms of the changing seasons, have never lived in a time of alarm clocks or rushed morning schedules. Like so many creatures of the earth, they somehow modify their sleep patterns instinctively, spending more time awake and working during the long summer days, and sleeping through much of the darkness of winter. She tucks her chin deeper into the collar of her thin, worn robe, snuggling down into it as she waits for the fire to warm the room.

There is a quiet knock on the front door, and then Kate hears a key turning in the lock. She strains her ears to listen as Michael ushers Evan into the house, eavesdropping on the gentle words he mutters over the soft scuffling of their boots and coats.

"Go on in the kitchen, and warm up," he says.

When Kate sees Evan round the corner in the soft glow

of morning light, she lifts her chin and smiles brightly. "Good morning. Here, you can have my chair by the stove." She steps to the cupboard, pulling down two more mugs from the shelf and setting them on the counter. Evan shuffles forward and sits on the warm wooden chair, tucking his legs under himself and rubbing his arms.

Michael crosses to the counter and picks up a small metal tin. He opens the lid and scoops out some of the dry, pungent leaves, putting them into the mugs Kate selected. "Good morning, Kate," he says groggily as he turns toward the stove to fill them with hot water from the kettle.

"Good morning."

Michael hands a mug to Evan. "Careful, buddy, it's hot."

Evan takes the mug without speaking, and Michael looks up to Kate. "He's pretty tired this morning."

"My kids are still asleep. If he's tired, don't feel like you need to get him up. He can sleep as long as his body needs," she says. Even as she speaks, she can hear muffled sounds coming from the bedroom as her children begin to stir. Within minutes, they have emerged, shuffling to the kitchen in stocking feet, slowly making the transition into the waking day.

"Good morning," Michael says to them as they enter. He moves to the edge of the room to make space for them as they fumble around for mugs and hot water, watching as they each step to their mother for a hug. For each child, she has a special touch and a special look that she greets them with—a unique bit of kindness that is their very own.

When they all have tea in hand, they circle around the kitchen, trying to warm up in the one room with heat this early in the day. As the day progresses, the stove will pump air to the other sections of the house, making it more comfortable, but winter mornings mean breakfasts in this small space. Jonah and

Evan begin working on breakfast, warming goat milk and cornmeal on the stove, adding a drizzle of honey as the mush begins to thicken. They scoop the food into bowls and offer it to the others with a selection of dried fruits, talking more and more as the fresh energy begins to fuel their bodies.

"The sky looks pretty clear today," Michael tells Kate. "I bet I could get up on the roof to fix that leak if you want."

"That would be great. Thank you." Kate looks at Margaret and Laura. "Girls, I'd like you to help Michael with that project. You can go with him to get new shingles, too."

"Sure. Okay," they both say.

"Take Kiko and Ruby with you," Kate adds.

"Jonah, you and Evan need to clean out the coop this morning after you check the traps and collect the eggs. And I want you to pull weeds in the field. I'll come out and help you after I clean the leaves out of the gutters." Kate moves to the kitchen sink to wash her bowl and spoon. She sets them on the drying rack and turns to leave the room. "I'm going to get dressed. The sun is starting to come up now, so let's get going. If it really is going to be sunny today, we should try to get as much done outside as possible."

~

Kate leans against the bamboo ladder angled into the edge of the roof, scooping a wet, decomposing mass from the metal gutter. From her perch, she can see Michael standing on the Schumers' roof several houses away, pulling shingles off what's left of their house. The clarity of the air allows the sound of his heavy steps across their empty attic to carry all the way to Kate. Every few minutes, she notices him drop a load of shingles to the ground, where Margaret and Laura wait unseen by Kate. After a while, he joins the girls on the ground, and Kate hears his voice directing them.

A few minutes later, Kate sees the crew walking across the front yard, the two dogs loping happily beside them. Michael is pushing the wheelbarrow full of shingles they have scavenged, and the girls walk in front of him, talking and laughing as they carry the ladder. Kate scoops the last of the leaves from the gutter and lets them slop down onto the ground below. She carefully descends, her feet touching the grass as her daughters reach the house.

"Were you able to find some shingles?" Kate asks as they walk to her.

"Yes, we found plenty," Laura replies.

"Everything on the far side of the street is too burned up, but the Schumers' house still has a lot left," Margaret adds.

"That house has helped us a lot over the years," Kate says, and smiles at Michael as he pushes the wheelbarrow up to them. "Looks like you had some success," she says to him.

"Yep. No problem. Parts of that house have sunk in, but enough is left," he says. "Are you done with this ladder?"

"It all yours," she answers. "I'm just going to rake up these leaves, then I'll go check on the boys."

"Do you want us to rake, Mom?" Margaret asks.

"No. I want you two to help Michael. One person should hold the ladder. You can take turns being up on the roof with him." She turns to Michael and asks, "Are you okay teaching them to do this?"

"Sure. I'm happy to have some help," Michael says.

"That's for sure," Laura says, and the girls and Michael laugh.

Kate notices the secret that seems to have passed between them, and asks, "What do you mean?"

"Nothing, Mom," Laura says. "I'll go get the bucket of nails and the hammer from the shed."

Though she is uncomfortable with the idea of secrets between her daughters and Michael, Kate tries to let it go. I'm just feeling jealous, she thinks. I need to accept that they don't tell me everything anymore. She hesitates, then follows Laura to the shed to get the rake.

Later, after pulling the wet leaves away from the house, Kate adds them to the large mulch pile by the edge of the forest. She sweeps the pile around, aerating it, to help it evolve into next year's compost. She can hear Michael's voice from on top of the roof, talking to Laura, instructing her, guiding her as she rips off the old shingles with the forked back of the hammer. From time to time, Laura and Margaret laugh at something Michael says. The rasp of the metal tines of Kate's rake ring out over the yard with each pull, and she falls into an easy rhythm with her work.

It takes a few seconds for Kate to realize the silence that suddenly descends. She stops and leans against the rake before turning to look up at the roof, sensing that something has gone wrong. Even from this distance, she can see that Laura's face has gone white as she sits silently staring at Michael. He is sitting on the roof next to her, holding his left arm close to his body.

Kate drops the rake and runs. Margaret stands on the ground, holding tight to the ladder, fear in her eyes.

"What happened?" Kate asks.

"I don't know," Margaret says quietly. "But I think he's hurt."

Kate is already climbing the ladder as she calls out. "Michael? Laura?"

"I'm okay," he says.

Kate steps carefully onto the roof and walks to where they sit. Out of breath, she repeats, "What happened?"

Laura looks up at her mother, and tears begin to fill her eyes. "I didn't mean to," she says. "I'm so sorry."

"It's okay," Michael says. "It's just a cut, Laura. Don't worry about it." He is smiling at her, trying to console her.

Kate can see the dark blossom of blood spreading over the sleeve of his sweatshirt, and notices that he is still gripping his arm tightly. "Let me see," she says, bending to his side.

"Shit," Michael says under his breath.

"Mom, I didn't mean to. I was just trying to rip up the shingles."

"It's okay, honey," Kate says, turning to make eye contact with her daughter. She reaches out to touch her arm. "It's okay." Turning back to Michael, she asks, "Can you make it down the ladder?"

"Yes, it's really not a big deal." He looks at Laura and adds, "Can she make it down, though? She's pretty white."

"Hey, Margaret?" Kate hollers.

"Yeah?"

"Michael has a cut on his arm, and Laura's pretty upset. I'm going to help her down. Hold the ladder, okay?"

"Okay, Mom."

Kate helps Laura stand and gently guides her to the edge of the roof. "Take a breath, honey. It's okay. I'll be right behind you," she cajoles. Slowly, she guides Laura down the ladder, standing close behind her with each step until they finally touch the ground. As soon as Laura sees Margaret, tears spring from her eyes, and she falls into her sister's waiting arms.

"There's a lot of blood," Laura whispers into Margaret's ear.

"Mom will help him," Margaret replies, barely audible.

Kate turns to climb back up the ladder, but Michael is

already at the top, beginning his descent.

Once on the ground, Kate rushes him into the house, where she helps him pull off his sweatshirt. The blood has also seeped through the left arm of the shirt he wears underneath. She stands in front of him, and begins to unbutton the top button. Their hands bump as he also fumbles for the buttons, and she wordlessly moves his hands to his side with her own. She sees the rise and fall of his chest as her fingers work their way down to the bottom of his shirt. She softly glides her hands over his shoulders, sliding the fabric off his body, and lets it fall to the floor behind him.

The cut is long but shallow. "Come to the sink and let me wash it for you." She takes him by his good arm and leads him to the basin. As she turns on the faucet, the water streams over his arm, and he winces with the sting of it.

"It's not too bad," she says, pooling water in her palm near the wound to flush it out. "What happened?"

"It was just an accident. She was pulling up the shingles and slipped a bit. It was my fault, really. I was too close, and she caught me with the claw of the hammer as she fell backward. It's no big deal."

"Well, we'll get this cut cleaned up and bandaged. I think it will be fine. Keep running it under the water for a minute." Kate steps away from him and takes off her own coat and hat, throwing them onto the dining room table. She sees Margaret and Laura standing in the front room, obviously waiting for her.

"Is he okay?" Margaret asks.

"He's fine." She crosses to them and wraps her arms around Laura. "Honey, it's just a cut."

"I'm so sorry, Mom," Laura says quietly.

"Laura, I know it was an accident. Don't worry. He's

fine." She pulls away and holds Laura at arm's length. "I'm just glad you're okay. He said you almost fell."

"I'm fine. He caught me."

Seeing the color returning to Laura's face, Kate pats her arm and heads back to the kitchen. As she rounds the corner, she catches her breath at the sight of Michael. He has turned off the faucet and is leaning against the sink, his body angled toward her. He is looking down at his torn arm, pressing a small towel against the cut. Kate's eyes involuntarily trace the curves of his naked torso, from the top of his strong, broad shoulders down over his bare chest, and to the slight ripples of the muscles in his thin, firm stomach. She forces herself to stop there, unwilling to allow her eyes or her mind to drift any lower.

Michael looks up when he hears Kate enter, and watches the course her eyes take over his body. For a split second, his body shrinks; he looks embarrassed and begins to turn away. But the feeling seems to pass as swiftly as it arrived. Instead, he lifts himself away from the sink, standing to his full height. He lowers his hand away from the wound, and drops his arms to his sides, standing still.

When Kate pulls her gaze back up to meet his, she feels the flush of color flood into her cheeks, and forces herself to look away. Scanning the kitchen for anything else to focus on, she spots the jar of honey on the far edge of the counter. She crosses the floor, picks up the jar, and carries it to where Michael stands. She is unable to look him in the face, now thinking that she is the one who should feel exposed and embarrassed. Instead, she puts the honey on the counter next to him and says, "I'll go get a bandage. Stay here."

In a minute, she returns, several long strips of cloth in her hand. She goes to Michael's side and takes the small towel from him. She wipes away the water still dripping from his arm, careful not to hurt him. The cut is jagged, but the bleeding has slowed. "It's already coagulating," she says. "You'll be fine."

Kate opens the jar of honey and pours a thick line of the sticky stuff over the top edge of the wound. Setting the jar back on the counter, she picks up the first strip of cloth and gently wraps it around his arm. As she works, she can feel his eyes on her, watching her silently. She stands close, and his injured arm is outstretched just enough for his hand to be hanging in the air beside her waist. When she tugs on the bandage to make the first knot, his hand is pulled to her, lightly brushing the side of her body with the tips of his fingers. When she tugs again to make the second knot, he presses his hand to her waist, and she feels the subtle constriction of his fingertips.

She steps away from him to survey her work. She looks only at his arm, only at the bandage, though she feels that his eyes are still on her. She clears her throat and puts her hands on her hips, saying, "Okay, you're all set. You can go get dressed." Without looking at his face, she turns to leave the room. Over her shoulder, she says, "Toss your clothes in the wash. Then go let Laura know you're okay."

Kate scoops up her coat and hat and puts them on as she passes through the front room. "Girls, I'm going to go check on the boys. I'll be back in a bit." Without waiting for their answer, she opens the front door and rushes out into the cold afternoon air.

~ Fifteen ~

THEY SIT TOGETHER at the table, finishing up the last bits of dinner. The children chatter away, joking and laughing with each other. Kate managed to avoid Michael's eyes for the rest of the day by swimming slowly on her knees through the sea of long brilliant-green blades poking out of the rough dirt of the wheat field. Although she was able to keep her body busy weeding throughout the afternoon, her mind would not forget the way he had touched her. When the sun began to set, she was finally forced back into the house.

As the children clear the dishes, Kate says, "It's bath night tonight. Laura, can you start heating up the pots of water?"

"Sure, Mom," Laura answers.

Kate is happy to see that Laura is fully recovered from the events of the day. She had pulled her aside before dinner to check in with her, and was pleased to hear that Michael had, indeed, sat down with her to talk about the accident.

"I'll go wash up now, then you can take turns after the dishes are done," Kate tells the children busy in the kitchen.

"I go first today!" shouts Jonah, happy to have his turn in the rotation.

Each week they heat several large pots of water on the stove, and pour the boiling water into the cold tub in the bathroom. Years ago, Kate rigged the outflow pipe of the tub to flow outside into a channel that irrigates the garden, hacking away at the outside wall of the house to replumb the system. Now, to be first in line for the weekly bath is a coveted position, and the children take turns having the honor.

Kate steps to the stove and picks up a pot of hot water. "Jonah, you need a haircut, too. After bath we'll do that, so please set up the stuff, okay?" As she steps into the hallway between the kitchen and the bathroom, she stops and turns back to them. "Evan," she says, "Why don't you take a bath tonight, too?"

Evan stops washing the plate he is holding and looks first to Kate, then to his father. "Can I?" he asks.

Michael shrugs. "Sure, if that's okay with Kate, that's fine by me."

"Great," Kate says, smiling at Evan. "You can go after the girls. And I'll cut your hair, too, if you want." She sees his eyes light up as he giggles, nudging Jonah in the side. Kate closes the door to the bathroom behind her.

She takes off her warm clothes, feeling the chill of the cold air as it hits her skin. As she steps into the tub, she pulls a thin washcloth from the small shelf on the wall. She bends over to stop up the tub with a thick, round piece of black rubber, and sits down on the icy tub floor. After dipping the washcloth into the pot of warm water, she rubs it around the hard rectangle of homemade soap, releasing the subtle scent of lavender.

Starting at her face, Kate begins to wipe away a week's worth of dirt and grime. She works her way down over her neck and shoulders, then slides the cloth over each of her long arms. After a few swipes, she wrings out the cloth, watching the dirty gray water swirl among the clean water in the pot. She washes her chest, and gently glides the soft cloth over her breasts, her nipples growing hard as the warmth quickly fades in the cold air.

It takes only a few minutes for Kate to work her way down to her toes, scrubbing each one as she holds her foot in her hand, her knees bent up to her chest. A small pool of dirty water sits at the bottom of the tub now, already cold. She rinses and squeezes out the washcloth, and hangs it over the edge of the tub to dry. Then, standing up, she allows herself the luxury of pouring the last of the warm water from the pot over the tops of her shoulders, feeling the heat as it slides over the length of her body.

Stepping out of the tub, Kate quickly wraps her thin robe around herself. Then she kneels down next to the tub and, reaching into the gray water, she pulls the plug and listens to the quiet gurgle as it circles down the drain. Turning on the faucet, she bends her head upside down into the tub, and washes her hair with the icy water from the tap.

When Kate comes back into the warm kitchen, she is dressed in clean pajama pants, with the drawstring tied in a bow just below her navel. Her long-sleeved shirt is old and worn, but soft from the many washings it has endured. Her damp, combed hair hangs long in a loose ponytail over her back.

Jonah quickly begins his bath, hauling the next pot of hot water to the tub. Kate refills her pot and sets it on the stove, noticing at the same time that the dinner dishes have all been cleaned and put away. A stool stands nearby, and a pair of sharp scissors is waiting on the counter. Michael is leaning at one corner, holding a mug of hot tea in his hands, and talking with Evan and the girls.

"Margaret, you're next in the tub, so please get your things ready," Kate says.

"Okay."

Both girls leave the kitchen, heading into the hallway to gather fresh clothes and towels.

"Evan, do you have some clean clothes in the shed? Do you want to go get them so they can start to warm up?" Kate asks.

"Sure. I'll go now," Evan replies, and heads toward the front door.

Michael and Kate are left alone, and they stand awkwardly. Finally, he says, "Thanks for letting Evan take a bath."

"No problem," Kate says. "In fact, you can take one after the kids. If you want to."

"That would be great. Thank you."

Kate goes to the cupboard and pulls a cup from the shelf, beginning to prepare tea for herself. "In fact," she adds, "I have a razor if you want to shave."

He doesn't say anything as he slowly sips the steaming tea from his cup.

"You don't have to," Kate adds. "I just thought I'd offer. I don't care."

"No, that would be nice. Thanks again."

She crosses to the dresser pushed against the far wall of the kitchen, and pulls open the top drawer. "Here you go," she says as she walks toward Michael, a sharp blade still wrapped in cloth in her outstretched hand. "It's sort of a straight-edge razor. It used to be a knife, really, but it's very sharp. Do you know how to shave with something like this?"

Michael smiles and takes the wrapped blade from her.

"Yes, I think I can handle it." He pulls one hand through his scraggly beard, rubbing his chin and scratching his neck below the grizzled dark hair.

"There's a mirror in the bathroom."

"Okay."

She hears the front door open, and soon Evan returns, carrying a small bundle of clothes. Before long, Jonah is back in the kitchen, too, clean and freshly dressed. The room begins to buzz with activity again as he sits on the stool with Kate behind him, cutting his hair. Evan and Laura watch, and they all talk about books they are reading, their friends, and plans for tomorrow.

"I'll go get myself some fresh clothes," Michael says, and leaves through the back door to go to the shed. After a few minutes more, Margaret returns, and Laura heads to the bath, carrying a fresh pot of hot water.

Kate is just finishing Jonah's hair, squatting in front of him to check the length of the sides with gentle tugs of her fingers, when she hears the door open and close behind her. She concentrates hard on Jonah's head, actively trying to keep her eyes on her son, trying so hard not to turn around.

"Wow!" Margaret says, looking at Michael. "Is it snowing?"

Kate spins around on her heels and sees that Michael has a thin layer of white snow covering his shoulders. He meets her gaze briefly before turning his head in Margaret's direction. "It is!"

"That's great!" Jonah says, grinning at Evan.

Kate turns quickly back to Jonah and lifts her hands to his hair again. "You're all set, honey." She stands and unclips the sheet from around his neck, letting the cut hair drop onto the floor.

"Okay, Evan, I'll cut yours when you've finished your bath," Kate says as she sweeps the fallen hair into a pile and scoops it into a large bowl near the back door. Jonah leaps off the stool, and the two boys run to the front room to look out the window at the falling snow.

"Mom! Come see!" Jonah shouts.

Kate leans the broom in the corner before quickly walking out of the kitchen, passing close to Michael without looking at him.

A while later, Kate is finishing Evan's haircut when Michael comes back, dressed in clean clothes, fresh from his bath. Standing behind Evan, her comb and scissors working through his shaggy reddish-brown curls, she glances up at Michael in the doorway. He is looking right at her, as if waiting for her reaction. She stops moving, the scissors and comb hanging frozen from her hands, and soaks up the sight of him.

His face, clean-shaven, is more handsome than she imagined. His blue eyes shine in the soft light, somehow even more brilliant now above the strong curve of his cheekbones, the soft skin of his cheek. She exhales slowly, and her lips drop slightly apart. He drops his gaze to the floor.

"Well, what do you think?" he says, sliding his hand over his cheek and tugging on his chin.

"Um . . . I think . . ." Kate stammers, then rips her eyes away from him to collect herself. "I think I'm about done with Evan's hair. Does it look okay to you?"

"Fine."

She unclips the sheet from around Evan's neck. He hops off the stool and walks to his father's side. Margaret walks into the kitchen to put an empty mug into the sink. "Hey!" she says, tilting her head to look up at Michael. "You shaved! Very handsome."

Michael gives her a small laugh and says, "Thanks, Mags."

"Mom, since it's snowing out, can Evan sleep over?" Jonah asks, following Margaret into the room.

"What?"

"I mean, it's snowing, so it's really cold. Could we have a sleepover?"

"Where?" she asks.

"In my room. He can share my bed," Jonah says.

"I don't think so, honey. I mean, your sisters are in there, too, and—"

"We don't mind," Laura cuts in, close behind on Jonah's heels. "We already talked about it."

Kate looks at each of the children, slightly amused and slightly annoyed by the way they have been planning things behind her back lately. "Well, you'll have to ask his father," Kate says.

"Dad, can I?" Evan pleads, moving close to his father, tugging on Michael's arm with his small hands.

"Ow! Buddy, that's my sore arm," Michael says gently, and Evan releases him for a moment before beginning to tug on the other arm.

"Please?"

"I suppose so. As long as it's really okay with Kate," Michael says, looking over at her to confirm.

Kate sighs. "Sure, it's fine by me."

The children hurry into the bedroom, excited by the novelty. Kate and Michael smile as they watch them disappear around the corner, then turn to look at each other. They stand silently before he says, "Thanks for the bath."

"No problem. Did you pull the plug after?"

"Yes. And cleaned out the tub, too. Sheesh, we're a filthy crew," he says as he moves to the edge of the sink to wash out the few mugs that have gathered.

Kate sweeps the last of the hair from the floor and dumps it in the bowl. Looking out the small kitchen window, she says, "It looks like it's snowing harder now."

Michael sets down the last mug on the drying rack and crosses to Kate. He stands close behind her and looks out the window. She can see his reflection in the glass and feels the beat of her heart increase as she secretly watches his face. They stand this way for nearly a minute before their eyes lock in the reflection and she feels him move just a little bit closer.

"I'm going to go dump this in the compost," Kate says as she steps away from him, reaching to take her sweater off the hook by the back door. She slips on her boots and bends low to pick up the bowl full of hair clippings.

"I'll take it for you," Michael says.

"No, that's okay. I'll do it." As she opens the back door to the garden, she says, "I can cut your hair, too. If you want." And before waiting for an answer, she escapes into the softly falling snow.

When she returns, Michael is gone, and part of her hopes that he has gone to the shed, avoiding her offer, avoiding her. She tidies up the last of the kitchen clutter, and then goes to the bedroom, where the children are already tucked into their beds.

Margaret and Laura are snuggled together, trying to warm the cold sheets. Jonah and Evan are on their stomachs in the other bed, propped up on their elbows, reading a book by the dim light of the small lamp next to them. Jonah is reading quietly to Evan, who watches the words, following along with the story.

"Boys, it's time for lights out. It's getting late." Kate leans over and tucks the blankets closer around each of their bodies.

"Okay," Jonah says as he sets the book on the floor beside the bed.

"How much do you think it will snow?" Evan asks.

"I don't know. It's still early in the season, but it is coming down pretty hard. We'll see in the morning, I guess."

"If it keeps snowing, we can go sledding tomorrow!" Jonah says to Evan, and they both twitter with excitement.

Kate gives them each a quick kiss on the top of their heads and ruffles their freshly cut hair with the palm of her hand. "I know that's exciting, but try to get to sleep. You'll need lots of energy if you do go sledding tomorrow." She moves to the girls' bed and leans over to kiss each of them on the cheek. "Good night, my sweet loves," she says. She turns off the lamp and walks to the doorway. As she closes the bedroom door, she looks back at the four children tucked snug and safe, and she smiles.

When Kate walks into the front room, she is surprised to see Michael sitting in a chair in front of the piano. She says nothing but crosses the room and stands next to him.

"I've been sitting here for a long time," Michael says, looking down at the keys. "I guess I've been waiting for you to find me." He chuckles a bit and rubs his hands together to warm them.

"I thought you said you can't play?"

"I said I don't play. I didn't say I can't play." He shifts uncomfortably in the chair, then finally asks, "Would you like me to play something?" He looks up at her with a smile in his eyes, and she gives a quick small nod.

Michael raises his right hand to the piano and glides it over the keys in a gentle caress. Then, he slowly places both hands in position and waits, as if gathering his courage, focusing his mind and his body to the task. He takes a deep breath, and begins.

His left hand plays the first low notes, quietly separating out a chord into three soft tones, his fingers rising and falling slowly several times before his right hand joins. The light, warm notes float above the steady beat, which rocks like a small ship on a gentle ocean.

As she watches him, Kate begins to feel the rhythm of the music pulse through her body. Her mind floats on the waves of harmony his fingers create, and slides back to a time long past. She imagines sitting in a rocking chair, moving back and forth to the beat. Cradling baby Jonah in her arms, she snuggles him as moonlight filters in through lace curtains. It is a made-up memory, the mother and child in her mind dressed in fine clothes, sitting in a fine home. A home in a world free of the sting of hunger and free of the stench of death. It is a memory evoked by the beauty of the song and the honesty of its playing, and she surrenders herself to it, believing that it could have happened that way, somewhere, sometime.

The soft and easy crescendo and decrescendo of the melody is like a lullaby, the notes like the whispered words she would have cooed to her child on a cold winter night. Words so full of love they could banish all the darkness and fear from the night, lulling the peaceful baby in her arms. Lulling her, too, as she imagines looking down at the small, perfect face lying on her breast.

She feels the familiar sway again, the years of holding babies never as far from her body as they seem from her mind. The melancholy sweetness of it spreads through her, and a soft glimmer shines in her eyes.

Next to her, Michael plays on, his hands effortlessly moving over the keys, his fingers in a relaxed curve above each note. Kate pulls herself from her thoughts to watch the smooth movement of his body, swaying to the rhythm, pulsing with the beat, and she purposely moves her body in time with his. She studies the side of his face, his neck, his arms, and with each subtle movement they make together, she feels more connected to him, even through the air and space that separate their bodies.

Several minutes later, the song fades to its finale, ending as it began, with the quiet simplicity of a separated chord. Michael's hands hover over the keys for a second before he sets them in his lap. He turns his head to look up at her, and waits.

"That was beautiful," she says.

"The piano's a little out of tune, but that's okay."

"What's the name of that song?"

He shifts in his seat. "It's one of Beethoven's piano sonatas. Number nine, I think. I might be wrong. I haven't played in a long time."

"I loved it. Thank you."

He looks back up at her and smiles again. "You're welcome. It's not a difficult piece. I was never a great pianist or anything. I just liked to play."

"Well, I thought it was wonderful. You can play our piano anytime."

"Thanks," he says, standing and lifting the chair to move it back to the dining room. When he has set it back in place, he turns to her and asks, "Are you still up for giving me a haircut?"

"Um, sure," Kate answers, trying to regain her composure, trying to ignore the warm feeling that has spread through the bottom of her belly. "Come in the kitchen."

Michael sits on the stool, his feet resting lightly on the floor. Kate steps behind him and shakes the sheet open. She wraps it around his neck, clipping it behind him to keep hair from falling on his clothes, then lifts the comb and scissors off the counter behind her. She pauses, studying the back of his head, trying to focus on the job at hand. His hair falls just above his shoulders, tangled and uneven, and she pauses before she begins.

"How short do you want it?" she asks.

"Not too short," he replies. "Whatever you think is best. I mean, anything would be an improvement."

They both smile, and Michael gives a small nervous laugh that is cut short when Kate runs her right hand along the side of his head, her fingertips brushing the top of his ear as she combs through his damp hair with her fingers. She slowly lifts her hand to the top of his head and drags her fingers over his scalp from the top of his forehead all the way to the base of his neck.

Michael closes his eyes as Kate touches him, and his shoulders release as the muscles in his neck begin to melt. She can feel the warmth of his body in front of her, and has to struggle against the urge to lean into him.

Kate pulls the comb through his hair and pinches a section between two of her fingers as she makes the first snip. When she has worked her way around the right side of his head, she steps behind him and starts again at the back. She works slowly, trying to savor the closeness, this justifiable reason to be touching him. Long locks of soft brown waves drop down to the floor below.

She moves her body to his left side as she cuts, her arms raised to hold the tools. Out of the corner of her eye, she sees Michael watching the deep rise and fall of her chest as she breathes. When her hip gently brushes against the side of his thigh, his eyes shut again. She stops fighting the feeling growing inside of herself, and allows it to swell and rise.

Kate lowers the scissors and steps to the front of him. She can feel him watching her, and forces herself to look only at his hair. His legs are spread slightly apart as he sits on the stool, and she slides her body between his knees as she lifts the scissors to his head again. She can feel the inside of his legs slightly squeeze around her and, in the silence of the room, she hears the change in his breath, each inhale and exhale deeper now than before.

With her this close, he has nowhere to look but her chest. His eyes are at the perfect level to trace the curve of her breasts under her thin shirt. He slowly drops his chin to his chest. His hands lie heavy on top of his thighs, below the bottom of the sheet encircling him. She sees his fingers lift ever so slightly in her direction, close to touching her hips. The sheet draped around him has tented between his legs, and the sight of it forces her to pause. She closes her eyes few seconds in an effort to keep control.

"Keep your head up, please," she whispers, and he complies, slowly raising his chin back to level.

A few minutes more, and she is finished. She pulls her body out from between his legs, circles around to his back, and unclips the sheet, shaking the last of his locks to the floor. She folds the sheet loosely and sets in on the counter, then steps in front of him again.

She tilts her head from side to side as she inspects her work, and reaches up to run her fingers through the front of his hair, checking the length around the curve of his brow, over the tops of his ears. Finally, she drops her eyes to his and smiles.

He does not smile back, and his eyes burn so brightly, the blood rushes to her cheeks.

Kate slides her body forward, between his knees, reaching her right arm up over Michael's shoulder, to set the comb and scissors on the counter behind him. As she sets them down, she feels the tips of his fingers touch the outside of her thighs, and she stops, frozen in place, suddenly unable to breathe.

He moves his head toward her, touching his cheek to the side of her left arm, and her eyes close. Slowly, inch by inch, she slides her body down over his chest, until her cheek grazes his. Kate moves her right hand to the back of his neck and touches him, her warm palm resting lightly against the top of his spine.

She presses her cheek to his, feeling the smoothness of his freshly shaved skin against hers, and listens as a barely audible moan rumbles from his throat. She slides her cheek down and tilts her head to his, her lips parting in anticipation. There they hesitate for the slightest moment, before his lips graze hers.

She feels the full strength of his hands around her hips as he pulls her close, pressing her against his belly as he presses his mouth to hers. She wraps her arms tightly around him, trying to get even closer as he thrusts his tongue deep into her mouth. Together, they stand, and he moves her backward to the edge of the counter as they kiss. His hands reach down to the backs of her legs, and he lifts her to the counter, pulling her legs apart, pushing himself close to her.

Michael's strong hands slide up the side of her body, gliding underneath her shirt and up to her ribs. As he slips one hand behind her back, the other moves up to hold one of her breasts, cupping the side of it as his thumb slides over her nipple. She pulls her mouth from his and tilts her head back with a quiet moan, and his mouth moves down to her neck, kissing her hard, biting her gently as he grinds his hips deeper into her. As tightly as they hold each other, they do not get close enough to satisfy the need that consumes them both.

Michael pulls his face away from her suddenly and reaches up with his right hand to hold the back of her head. He kneads the back of her neck and jaw roughly, looking forcefully into her eyes as his left hand brushes down her spine. She feels the way his body is throbbing, and despises the thin clothes that separate them.

"Come out to the shed with me," he says, with no hint of a question in his voice.

Kate falters slightly, and her brow furrows as she bites her bottom lip. "I . . ." she begins, struggling to regain control, terrified of losing it. Michael must see the fear in her face, and his eyes soften, though his touch does not. Her eyes drop to his lips, his jaw, and she searches for a way to stop. "But," she whispers, closing her eyes. "But it's so cold out there."

He softly slides his hand to the side of her face, lifting her chin with his palm, and her eyes look directly into his. In a voice barely over a whisper, he says, "I'll keep you warm."

She surrenders. Kate moves down off the countertop and into his arms. They turn and hurry toward the back door. As she slips on her boots, Michael lifts her sweater from its hook and drapes it over her shoulders, pulling it together across her chest. Then he holds the door for her as she steps out into the silently falling snow.

~ Sixteen ~

"TIGHTEN UP THE LAST BOLTS," Rhia says, leaning heavier onto the top of the metal frame.

Kate gives a dozen tugs on the ratchet wrench, securing the frame around the lever, then stands to survey their work. Six other women surround them, watching and giving encouragement as Rhia and Kate perform the final assembly. They've made the journey to New Hope today, along with Iris and Patrice, hoping the bits and pieces they have scavenged will come together to complete the siren.

They left as early as possible, forced to wait until the sun came up before beginning the walk. Taking turns pushing and pulling the cart, they lugged sections of ductwork, a fan harvested from an old air conditioner, a cone banged into shape from a dented ferryboat horn, and as many bolts and bits as they could find.

Crossing the ridges had been the most treacherous part. The week-old snow that had melted in the valleys below still remained in thick patches on the path. The two-hour trip had taken them half again as long, and they were cold and wet from the constant drizzle of the day, but they had finally arrived.

And the welcome from the women of New Hope was filled with such warmth and affection, it made the journey worth every slip and skid.

"I think that might do it," Kate says. She turns to the crowd and, finding Joy's eyes, asks, "Where do you think we should test it?"

Joy is wiping the grease from her hands with an old rag, her gray hair disheveled and hanging over one side of her face. With the back of her hand, she sweeps it behind her ear and then says, "Well, let's try it here in the garage first to see if it makes any sound. If it does, we can take it outside and really see how loud it gets."

Nervously, they all move to the back of the siren and look to Rhia. It looks as if she doesn't realize they expect her to be the first to try the crank.

"Go ahead," Kate says, nudging her gently toward the siren. "This is your baby. You get to do it."

Rhia steps to the back of the siren and grasps the handle. She looks back at the women once, then widens her stance, balancing her feet on the floor. She pulls the handle up toward her body and circles it around to the other side, pushing it back down again. The crank moves slowly at first, but after a few turns, the momentum helps it pick up speed. They hear the whir of the fan inside the casing as Rhia turns the crank faster and faster.

Suddenly, a low moan begins to sound throughout the room, and the women take an involuntary step back. The pitch changes as Rhia spins the crank, rising slightly, and she releases the handle. As it slows, the sound quickly drops to silence. When she turns to look again at the women, a smile shines on her face, and they all burst into a cheer that fills the small space.

"I can't believe it!" shouts Joy. "I mean, of course I *can* believe it," she says, stepping to Rhia and throwing her arms around her shoulders with a laugh. "Rhia, you're a genius!"

"It wasn't all me," Rhia insists. "Kate helped find all the parts, and you all helped put it together."

Kate beams at her friend, relishing their accomplishment. A hand touches her shoulder, and Kate turns to see Iris standing beside her, a smile on her face. She hesitates, looking into Iris's eyes, afraid to see the same coolness she has seen over the past month. But there is nothing but friendship and pride. Kate smiles warmly, and the two embrace, letting go of the distance that has separated them for too long.

"Let's get it loaded onto the cart and move it outside. We'll try it out there next," Joy says. "Let's see what this thing can really do."

Together the women lift the heavy siren onto the large metal cart and push it over the cement floor, through the overhead door, and into the late afternoon light. Rain drips onto their heads and shoulders as they gather behind the cart, ready to perform the real test of the siren's power.

More confident this time, Rhia grabs the handle. "Okay, here goes!" she says, and begins to turn the crank. Faster and faster she spins it, the low moan revving up into higher and higher pitches, flying through several octaves in less than ten seconds. A deafening sound erupts from the siren, as chilling as a hundred terrified women screaming in unison. Even behind the cone that amplifies the sound, they are forced to push their hands to their ears to try to block the scream.

Rhia continues turning the crank for a few seconds longer before releasing it to let the sound fall and fade, finally becoming quiet again. They can hear the remnants of the scream floating over the town, echoing off the houses and rocks of the surrounding hills. The women stand in stillness for a minute, amazed at the power and volume of the device.

When they finally recover, lowering their hands from their ears, dozens of women spill out of the neighborhood houses, some standing in their yards or on their porches to look in the direction of the sound, some walking quickly toward the group to congratulate them.

"Wow," Rhia says. "Well, I guess that will work." She steps close to Kate, and takes her trembling hand. Rhia turns to Kate and gives her hand a small squeeze.

~

The house is full of happy women. They come and go throughout the evening, stopping by Joy's house with bits of food to help celebrate their success. They open and share jars of homemade jams, smearing thin layers on thin slices of bread. Some women have brought preserved vegetables: pickled beets and cucumbers. One comes with a pot of chicken and vegetable stew, thick with tomatoes and potatoes.

Kate notices Joy pull aside one of her children and whisper something in his ear. A few minutes later, the boy is back, carrying two large jugs. He hands them to his mother, and she lifts them high. Shouts ring out around the room, and women move close to her, their cups and mugs held out.

Iris is one of the first in line. She gets two cups, and makes her way through the crowd to Kate. "Here you go, my dear."

"What is it?"

"I don't know yet, but I'm hoping it's alcohol." Above her wide smile, her cheeks are red from the heat of the crowd and the noise of the celebration.

There is a knock on the front door, and someone moves to open it. Outside, a tall man stands behind a young girl. His skin is darker than the girl's, but Kate can see the resemblance. One sleeve of his coat is folded up and tied in a knot, hanging loosely where his arm used to be. The girl is holding a pie plate in her hands, covered by a thin terry-cloth towel.

They step cautiously into the room, and Kate notices every head turn in their direction. The festive noise from the group fades away. Out of the corner of her eye, Kate sees Iris quickly move her cup behind her back. The man stays close to the girl, his hand on her shoulder. Joy pushes through the group of women and stands in front of the pair.

"Hello, Jacob. How are you this evening?" she says.

"Very well, thank you. You remember my daughter, Ondine?"

"Of course." Joy looks down at the girl and smiles warmly. "What have you got there?"

"It's an apple pie," the father says. "I heard about your success today, and that you have visitors, so we wanted to bring something over." His hand is still resting on the girl's shoulder. He speaks quietly.

Joy takes a deep breath and looks down at the floor. "You could have just sent Ondine," she says, looking back up at the man. "You didn't have to come out after dark."

He doesn't answer at first, and Kate struggles to read his expression. Everyone in the room can feel the tension between Joy and this man. "It's late," he finally says. "I thought it was best to come out with her."

To her own surprise, Kate takes the few steps to Joy's side. The man looks at her, and she tries to smile. "Did you say this is apple pie?"

He nods, a puzzled look on his face as a strange woman speaks to him.

"That is quite a treat!" Kate reaches to take the pie from

the girl. She feels the warmth of it in her hands, and smells the sweetness of the baked apples rising out of the dish. "Would you join us for a slice?" Several women exchange glances, and Kate watches the man's expression turn from puzzled to apprehensive. Silently, Rhia slips in behind Kate and stands close to her.

"No, thank you," he says. "I just wanted to drop this off."

"Well, thank you, Jacob," Joy says, angling her body between Kate and the man. "We appreciate it."

"Good night, then." He drops his eyes to the top of his daughter's head and gently squeezes her shoulder. His eyes dart to Rhia for a split second before he and the girl turn to leave.

When the door closes, Joy turns to Kate. "I want to apologize. Jacob's wife and baby died in childbirth this spring, and it's just him and the little girl. Of course, several women have offered to take them in, but he just keeps saying he's not ready. We've been trying to be patient with him."

"You don't have to apologize," Kate replies.

"We've even been letting him speak at the meetings, since he's the only parent that girl's got, but I didn't expect him to come here. He knows he's not supposed to be out walking alone after dark."

"It's okay."

"His arm," Rhia says. "Did he loose that in the war?"

Joy nods. "He was one of the fifteen-year-olds they drafted near the end." She takes the pie from Kate and walks back to the kitchen to slice it.

When Kate turns to follow, she sees Iris watching.

~

Iris and Kate sit together on the floor of Joy's front room. After the last woman left about an hour earlier, they had worked with Joy's family to clean up the house before getting ready for bed.

Kate runs a brush through her long hair, teasing out the tangles and snarls. When she is done, her hair shines in the dim light from the lamp in the corner, and she drops the brush into her backpack. With both hands, she sweeps her hair back into a loose ponytail and holds it with one hand while she pulls the thick elastic band out from between her lips. Two quick twists of the band, and she is ready for bed. They both look up to see Joy entering the room, a pile of blankets and two pillows in her arms.

"Joy, we don't need pillows," Iris says, knowing that Joy has probably taken these from her own family for the comfort of her guests.

"No, no," Joy replies. "Don't worry about it. These are extras."

"Well, thank you."

"Yes, thanks, Joy," Kate adds. "For everything."

"My pleasure. Good night, ladies."

The two women pull the scratchy wool blankets around themselves, maneuvering their bodies onto the floor. Iris sighs deeply, and says, "Good work today."

"You too. I'm exhausted."

"Good night, Kate."

"Good night."

Kate lies quietly in the dark for several minutes, waiting for sleep to drift over her.

"I bet I know who you're thinking about," Iris whispers.

At first, Kate says nothing, pulled so suddenly from her silent reverie. Then she asks, "Who?"

"Isn't this the first time you've ever been away from your kids for the night?"

"Oh, yes."

"Don't worry. They are probably having a great time at Sarah's house."

"You're right," Kate says. "They're very comfortable with Sarah's family. I guess I shouldn't worry so much about them."

"And think about how excited they'll be when we come back tomorrow with the siren. Maybe before you go home, you can help us mount it in the watchtower. We can do a trial to see how the sound carries in our neighborhood."

"Perhaps. I guess it just depends what time we get back. I need to get home before dark."

"Of course. Otherwise, we can schedule a time to test it when you are home. I think you might be able to hear it all the way out there!"

"Do you really think so?"

"Sure. Though it might depend on the weather. The sound will carry better on a clear day, I suppose. We'll have to see." Iris yawns and rolls onto her side, away from Kate.

Kate lies in the dark for several minutes more, listening to Iris's breath as it slows and deepens. She smiles a little at the thought of her children, knowing they are happy and safe, imagining them still awake, too excited by their sleepover to fall asleep. Then her thoughts turn to Michael.

She had insisted that he sleep in her house tonight with Evan. It didn't make sense for them to stay in the shed with the house empty and beds available. Evan had stayed with them every night for the past week, happy to be warm, happy to grow closer to the family he was beginning to think of as his own.

Though she had tried to hide the evidence, Kate knew that the children suspected she was staying with Michael at night, and was grateful they were pretending not to know. She couldn't begin to imagine the conversation they would eventually have to have about it, but she hoped her children would understand.—hoped they would be able to forgive her for this deception.

She thinks of Michael lying in her bed, with Evan asleep nearby on Jonah's mattress. She thinks of the shape of his body as it must look below her blankets, lying on his side, his knees curved up, one arm tucked under her pillow. Closing her eyes, she imagines herself next to him in the bed.

In her mind, she moves her body closer to his, sharing his warmth, her belly pressed against his back, her thighs curving up to meet the back of his own. Slowly, she reaches up to caress the top of his shoulder with her fingertips. Her hand slides over his arm, following the bend of his elbow, tracing down to his hand. He sighs in his sleep and turns his hand to hold hers.

Feeling full and warm, she falls asleep on this strange floor, ready for the sweet torture of the dreams that will soothe her through the night but leave her unsatisfied in the morning.

~

Laura and Jonah reach the top of the hill first, anxious to return home after being away nearly two days. Kate climbs behind them with Margaret at her side.

"Mom, come on!" Jonah shouts down to her. "I can see the smoke from the stove coming out the chimney. They have a fire waiting for us."

Kate quickens her step. Margaret pulls up close to her as they summit the hill, sliding her mittened hand into her mother's as they look down to the valley below.

"It's good to be home, isn't it?" Margaret says quietly.

Kate smiles at her, and answers, "Yes, it is. Let's keep going."

As they approach the house, Kiko and Ruby burst out the

front door. The dogs fly across the front yard, nearly knocking the children over with excitement. Kate rubs their backs in greeting, pushing them and tugging them with both hands as they leap and spin around her.

When she looks up, Evan and Michael are standing on the porch. She crosses the yard quickly, her eyes fixed on Michael, and has to stop herself from hugging him when she gets to the top of the steps. He smiles at her as his fingers brush her sleeve. Jonah pushes past them both to get to Evan, and the two boys walk into the house together, already catching up on the events of the last two days.

"Hi, girls," Michael says as Margaret and Laura reach the porch. "How was the sleepover?"

"Good," they both answer.

"You all look pretty wet and cold," he says, glancing up to catch Kate's eye. He puts out one arm to usher the children into the house, and Kate follows behind, calling the dogs in with her.

As they peel off the wet coats, boots, and hats, Kate breathes in the scent of food cooking in the kitchen. "Did you make dinner?" she asks, unhooking the belt that holds her knife and hanging it by the door. "It smells wonderful."

"I did," Michael answers. "Actually, it's a special dinner." He takes the wet coats from them, piling them into his arms.

As she unwraps the scarf around her neck, Kate says, "Special? Why special?"

"Come see."

She pads to the dining room in her stocking feet, and stops to look at the table before her. There are plates at each spot, with a soup bowl set in the center of each one. Mismatched cloth napkins are folded neatly next to the plates, with forks, spoons, and knives positioned on top. Mugs wait above each setting, and in the center of the table, several sprigs of light-green rosemary are woven among a bough of dark-green evergreen.

"What's all this?" Kate asks.

Michael begins to fill each glass with a pitcher of water. "I told you, it's a special dinner."

"I can see that, but what's the occasion?"

"Well, this week is Thanksgiving, and Laura and Margaret told me you guys always have a big dinner with Iris's family. So I thought we could have our own dinner here tonight."

"Um, yeah, we do go to Iris's. I guess I hadn't really thought about it yet." Kate watches him as he makes his way around the table. "If that's a problem, we can try to work something out."

"No. It's not a problem." Michael walks back into the kitchen, and Kate hesitates before following him in.

"I guess I didn't say anything because I figured you wouldn't want to come anyway," she mumbles. "I mean, obviously . . ."

As he turns to look at her, a sincere smile graces his lips. "Kate, really. Don't worry about it. I understand."

Jonah and Evan nearly knock into Kate as they run through the doorway. "Dad, do you want me to flip the fish?" Evan asks.

"It's got a couple more minutes," Michael replies.

"You made fish? Is that what smells so good?" Kate asks, moving deeper into the kitchen, toward the stove. As she reaches her hand out to open the oven, Michael takes three quick strides to her and pulls her arm away.

"Nope. No peeking. Evan and I have everything taken care of. You can go relax for a few minutes until it's all done." He looks back at Jonah. "You, too, Jonah. We're doing all the work tonight."

A smile breaks over Jonah's face. "Great!" he says, and runs out of the room. Kate laughs and shakes her head, stepping away from the stove. She crosses her arms and leans against the counter before she says, "You two don't have to do all the work. We are happy to help."

"Forget it," Michael responds. "This is our gift to you. To your family."

She stands there a minute more before he stops his work and looks at her. He points his index finger at her, then quickly jerks his thumb in the direction of the dining room. Kate raises her eyebrows and, with an exaggerated sigh, leaves the room.

~

Twenty minutes later, they are all seated around the table, feasting on the meal Michael and Evan have prepared. A fresh roll with butter, soup made from baked sweet potatoes, pumpkin and onions, and a warm kale-and-apple salad surround a flaky white serving of broiled fish on each of their plates. When Evan carries the fish out to the table, each of the children cheer at the sight of the beautifully butterflied animal, its meat lightly sprinkled with salt and garnished with a sprig of sage.

"We went fishing right after you left yesterday," Evan tells Jonah as he sets down the platter. "I can show you the place we caught this. It was perfect."

As they eat, the boys talk about the best bait to use in the stream, and Margaret and Laura talk about the Shakespeare play they are studying at school. Both Kate and Michael have read the story, and remember enough about it to chime in from time to time with questions about the main characters and plotlines.

Suddenly, a sound makes them all stop and look toward

the front room. It is a mournful sound, high-pitched and faraway, quiet enough to invoke the image of a ghost in the darkness. It seems to bounce around the valley, and it makes the hair on the top of Kate's arms rise. The sound continues for twenty seconds before fading away, the echoes of it still hanging over the hills.

"Oh . . . that must be the siren. They were testing it," Margaret says in epiphany, and the children are instantly freed from the spell. They laugh, uncomfortably at first, trying to hide the fact that they had been frightened. Then their laughter comes more easily, and they joke with each other about their fear. Only Kate and Michael are unable to let go of the uneasy feeling the siren conjured up in them.

~ Seventeen ~

THEY LIE TOGETHER under the blankets late that night, her naked body draped over his in the cold darkness of the shed. He is on his stomach, his arms tucked under the pillow, and she breathes in the scent of the back of his neck and his shoulder as her belly molds around the firm curve at the bottom of his spine.

"What do you miss the most?" Michael asks.

"You mean, from before the war?"

"Yes."

She shifts her body a bit, trying to decide what sort of answer to give. "Besides people?"

"Of course. I mean the little things."

"I don't know. It's different now than it was at first." After a long pause, she adds, "In the beginning, I remember missing my phone, and computers, and ridiculous things like that. But those things faded out of my mind so quickly. During the worst of it, we were just so hungry all the time. Now we're doing okay. We could use some new clothes, I suppose. And I'm out of cinnamon. But as long as I have a warm house and my family is healthy, what more do I really need?" A moment later, she asks, "What about you? What do you miss?"

"Pomegranates."

Her laughter rings out in the small shed, and Michael smiles beneath her warm body.

"Pomegranates?" she asks at last.

"Yep. When I was a kid, we used to get pomegranates every December. And you could get oranges and pineapples, and lemons any time of the year. You want a fresh blueberry in January? Here you go. Coffee? Chocolate cake? Whatever you want." He moans and shakes his head. "Now I want a pomegranate. Thanks a lot, Kate."

"Hey, you started this!" she says as she lightly pinches his shoulder. "Maybe you should migrate to California. There's plenty of fresh fruit there."

They snuggle back down under the warm blankets. The cold night air is still and silent outside the shed.

"MacGregor," Kate says, and traces her fingertips down the side of his arm. The wound from Laura's hammer has healed well, and she delicately skims over the jagged, fresh scar. "Are you Scottish?"

"My grandfather was," he answers sleepily. "Big guy. Great laugh. My parents always used to say we'd go back there someday, but somehow it never happened."

Trying to remember the sound of a thick Scottish brogue, she whispers, "MacGregor. Michael MacGregor."

He draws in a deep breath. "Mmm," he growls, raising his chest and tipping her off to the side. He turns to her, now next to him, and pulls the blankets up to cover her shoulder. Then he wraps his hand behind her back and says, "I like the way you say that." A sultry smile graces his face, a fresh fire awakened in his body.

As he tugs her close and bends toward her to kiss her

neck, Kate laughs.

"Shh," he mumbles. "Don't wake up the kids."

"You're right. Sorry."

Between kisses, he mumbles, "What about you? What was your family like?"

"My parents were great. They were always telling my sister and me we could do anything we set our minds to. Maybe that's why I was so surprised when everything started being taken away." She scoots back a few inches to look into his eyes, which sparkle in the dim light of the lantern hanging above. "But, sometimes I think it was harder on them than it was on me. Especially my mom. She was really intelligent and accomplished, even though her own parents weren't at all supportive. I remember a story she used to tell us about when she was in high school. She was starting to look into colleges and her father told her, 'You can go to a school for nurses and teachers. That's what smart girls are supposed to be.'"

"And she didn't buy that?"

"No. Those are great jobs, but she had other things in mind. And, by then she already realized that she was different from her parents. She told me her father used to sit around the house while her mother cooked, and cleaned, and took care of the kids. And if she asked for his help, he would scoff and say, 'That's women's work.'"

Michael shifts his weight on the bed, and Kate watches his eyes scan the wall behind her, as if looking for the right words to say. After a few seconds, she says, "Can I ask you something?"

"Sure."

"What did you do before the war?"

"Do you mean, like, for work?" He begins to watch the tips of his fingers as they play across the bow of her collarbone.

"Yes."

"Well," he says, a smile spreading across his face. "I was a chef."

Kate's jaw drops just a little, and her eyes squint slightly at the answer. "What? What kind of chef?"

"A pretty good one, actually," he replies, rolling over onto his back as he pushes up to lean against the pillow. "I was the head chef in a very nice restaurant in Portland. In the Rose Quarter." He looks down at her and smiles as her face evolves from surprised to perturbed.

"You jerk!" she says, grabbing his arm with her hand and giving it a shake. "You mean that all this time I thought I was torturing you by asking you to cook for us, and you were enjoying it the whole time?"

He leans his head back against the wall, his grin growing wider. "Yeah, I guess so."

"Ugh! Well that . . ." she stammers, shaking her head. "You asshole." He laughs as he rolls back to face her, and wraps his arm around her waist. Kate stiffens her body against it, and says, "Now you need to tell me something you hate so I can make you do it."

Michael says, "The question is, do you still feel the need to torture me?"

Kate looks at him sideways and sighs. "Well, maybe just a little."

"In that case," Michael says, propping himself up on his elbow, his face growing very serious. "You should know that there is one thing I hate."

Her face softens a bit, a concerned and curious look in her eyes. Michael takes a deep breath and says, "It would be really terrible if you keep making me have sex with you every night. That would just be the worst."

She rolls her eyes and laughs. "Right."

He laughs with her, but then his smile fades just a little. Kate notices the change and reaches up to touch his cheek.

"What's wrong?" she asks.

"Nothing."

"Are you sure?"

"I guess I was just thinking about the past. It's nothing." He tries to smile again, but she is unconvinced.

Kate slides her hand down over his neck, then rests it on his chest. She can feel the beat of his heart below her hand. "Is that where Evan was born? Portland?"

Michael drops his eyes and shrugs. "No."

"Then where?"

"South of there. After I came back from the war, there wasn't much left in Portland. The ground forces hit it pretty heavily. It had been a year since the fighting stopped, but it was still a mess."

She hadn't known he'd been in the war, and Kate has to stop herself from pulling away. She quickly realizes how naive her ideas about him had been. Of course he had been in the war. They all had. Some had volunteered, but most were forced into it, forced to fight. Even her husband had been pulled into the war machine. She suddenly feels foolish for assuming Michael could have avoided it.

"I grew up in Cantonis, so I made my way down there, hoping . . ." His voice trails off, and Kate moves the slightest bit closer. "I don't know. My parents were dead by then, so there wasn't anything for me there either. But at least some of the people remembered me. They had a big meeting to try to figure out what to do with me. Claire was there. We'd known each other in grade school." A small smile flickers to the corner of his mouth, though he is still looking down, avoiding Kate's eyes. "She agreed to take me in."

With this, he shrugs and sits up in the bed again. She watches him silently, hoping for more. When he doesn't offer anything further, she asks, "Did you love her?"

He hesitates a long time, weighing his answer, trying to find the right words. At last, he says, "Love is different in a time of destruction. It's not like a Shakespeare play, or a Hollywood movie. After all the things I'd seen, all the things I'd done . . . I loved that I was still alive. I loved that she was alive, and that she had managed to stay whole. After being surrounded by blood and death for so long, I loved being able to wake up in the morning and know that I didn't have to kill anyone that day." He adjusts his shoulders a little, and pauses as he swallows.

"And, there is something defiant in that kind of love. Like, no matter what we've been through, no matter how terrible it was, they can't stop us from living again. Yes, I loved Claire. She was like a beacon for me. She helped bring me back from all that death. And when Evan was born, well, you know. Suddenly there was someone on this earth actually worth dying for."

Michael looks down to meet Kate's eyes. She nods just a little, a small knot of sadness forming in her throat, understanding full well the depth of that kind of love.

"What happened?" she asks in a quiet voice.

He takes a deep breath before continuing, as if steeling himself for the words he'll have to say. "A few years ago, Claire found a lump in her breast. The doctor cut it out." He stops speaking and looks down at his hands. "I remember just staring at my hands during the surgery. I felt so powerless sitting there alone in the kitchen. There wasn't any sort of anesthesia. It took five women to hold her down. Her screams echoed through the house." He slowly flips his hands over, his palms open to the ceiling. "When the lump grew back, she didn't tell anyone. She said she would rather die than feel the knife cut into her again. And by the time she was too sick to hide it, it was too late."

Kate stares at him, speechless. Her eyes well up as she imagines the fear the woman must have felt discovering her illness, the horror of the treatment, and the sadness when she knew she was going to die. The thought of leaving behind her son, and being the cause of his unfathomable grief, must have been incredibly hard to bear. It was certainly difficult for Kate to comprehend.

"I'm so sorry," she says at last.

Michael looks blankly at Kate. "I heard those words a lot. It seemed to be the only thing anyone ever said to me in the end." He shakes his head. "It always felt like those people said it just to make themselves feel better."

"Do you think that's why I said it?" She sees the sadness in his eyes. "I've known some loss, too. I know how hard it is to lose part of a family."

"Thank you," he says without emotion, and looks away.

Kate's brow furrows as she watches him. After a minute, she asks, "Why did you leave?"

Michael adjusts his body, straightening his spine, then says, "Don't you know?"

"What do you mean?"

"Think about it. They weren't going to let me keep Evan. I had no choice."

She pushes herself up onto her elbow and says, "That can't be right. You were there. You're his father. They couldn't just take him away from you."

Michael looks at Kate, and she sees anger flash in his eyes. "Why not? I don't have any say in it. And don't act like that neighborhood was any different from this one. Do you think I don't realize you could take Evan from me anytime you want to?"

"I wouldn't do that."

"Bullshit, Kate. You've thought about it."

"No. Not since the beginning. Not since I got to know you. I thought we were working toward something here, Michael. I've been working on some of the women, trying to get them on our side. I thought you wanted to be a part of this neighborhood, you wanted Evan to be a part of this neighborhood."

"I could really feel the love tonight when that siren screamed out at us," he says sarcastically. "I could tell how warmly I'd be welcomed by the women in your neighborhood."

Kate sits up fully, pulling the covers around her body as she moves to the edge of the bed farthest from him. "I told you that siren is for emergencies."

"Right. What kind of emergencies?"

"Any kind. For fires and storms, and danger." Seeing him shake his head and look away from her, Kate says, "And yes, for raiders. What's wrong with that? Do you expect us to not want to defend ourselves?"

"Raiders? It's to warn your neighbors if a man comes into town! You're so scared of men, you truly believe they're all just out to get you. You think if a man comes within a mile of you, you have to gather all your troops so you can go kill him! Jesus, Kate. And you helped build it!" He throws his legs over the edge of the bed and pulls himself to standing. With quick, jerky movements, he grabs his pants and tugs them onto his body.

"I can't believe I ever came here. I can't believe I thought you might be different."

"Fine!" she hisses. "I'm not different. I'm just as scared as the rest of them," she says, sweeping her arm in the direction of the town.

"What are you scared of?" he yells. "We're not all violent!"

"Well, you men have done a shitty job proving that to us. There's a big difference between men and women," she says. "You have to admit there is a difference."

"Of course there's a difference, Kate. And there always will be. No matter how much you try to change it. But guess what? Women are not all goodness and light, and men are not all violence and darkness."

"I'm not saying that," she says. "I'm not saying women are perfect. I'm just saying throughout history men have proven time and time again that they are more aggressive, more likely to fight over a problem instead of compromise. There's light and dark in all of us, but we were made to work together and balance each other out. And when you pushed women into a submissive role, the balance was lost. We are trying to save us all. We are just trying to help."

"Then why the fuck are you treating men like shit? Why are you building sirens to keep men out of your neighborhood?"

"I don't want raiders to come here and kill my children. I just want to feel safe for once."

"And do you feel safe now?"

"No! I haven't felt safe in years!"

"But I'm not a raider!" he says, throwing his hands up in exasperation. "And neither are most of the men out there. But they're not going to let you tell them they can't think and speak for themselves. They're not going to just sit back and let you turn them into second-class citizens. Kate, seriously—what are you so scared of?"

"I'm scared of men who thought it was okay to take away everything I had. Who thought it was right to lock me up inside a house and take away my voice. Who told me I had no right to learn, to travel, to think for myself." Kate stands up, too, her blanket held tightly around her chest. "Oh, poor you," she says, mocking him. "You poor man. You only had control of the world your whole fucking life. You only got to beat us and rape us for a million years. How terrible it must be for you to have to listen to what a woman thinks for a change."

"How can you even say that to me? Do you really think I just went around raping women? Do you really think I want to dominate you and own you?" He takes a step closer to her, and points his finger at her. "The problem began when you started assuming we were all like that. That all men were just evil woman-haters. And that's bullshit."

"Well, what do you expect us to think? Christ, they held down Patrice as they raped her two daughters right next to her. Then they slit their throats from ear to ear and walked their big fucking boots right through the blood as it drained from their bodies. They bombed us, and beat us, and nearly exterminated us before we finally stood up and forced them to stop."

"That was the war! Can't you understand that? It wasn't just women who died. Everyone died! You can't say that things were like that before the war. Nobody did that stuff before. Things weren't so bad back then."

Her jaw drops as she hears his words. She shakes her head. "Are you kidding me? Yes, things were a lot worse during the war. You're right. Before that, a group of men couldn't just storm through a town slashing women with no repercussions. At least not in this country. But what about all the places where women were treated like cattle? What about all the places where women's bodies were so hated and feared they were forced to cover up everything but their eyes? And even here, men were working on silencing us for years before the war. Little by little you were taking away our freedom."

"Kate, I wasn't taking away anything! I wasn't the one doing it! Assholes in politics and government were doing that, but I wasn't. Maybe men in other countries were doing that, but I wasn't."

"And what did you do to stop them?"

At this, his arms drop to his side and he looks down at the floor. Slowly, he shakes his head and then closes his eyes. "I don't know," he says quietly. "I don't know." They stand in cold silence for a minute before he adds, "I just think there has to be a middle ground. There has to be a way for you to admit that we aren't all bad. We aren't all trying to hurt you. And, even though we aren't all heroes, maybe we don't all deserve to be punished."

"We're not trying to punish you," Kate says more gently, trying to let go of her anger. "We're trying to fix it all. Can you see that maybe we had to do all this just to stop the war and to survive after it? I didn't want Jonah to grow up in a world where women had no rights. I didn't want him to think that violence and oppression were the only ways to control a society."

"But Kate," he says as he looks up at her again. "Now he's growing up in a world where he has no rights. How is that better?"

She sighs and sits down on the edge of the bed. "I don't know," she says. "I'm just trying to do my best."

Michael puts his hands on his hips and watches her for a

long time. Silent tears of frustration and sadness spill from her eyes, and she turns her face away, trying to hide those tears. Finally, he sits down next to her and sets his hands in his lap.

"I know you're not one of the bad men," Kate says.

"And I know you're not one of the bad women."

She smiles a little and looks down at his hands. She rotates her wrist, flipping her palm toward the ceiling and extends her hand halfway to his. He raises his hand to meet hers and clasps it tightly.

He sighs. "So, where do we go from here?"

"I know we have more work to do, Michael. I know the world's not perfect yet. But please try to understand that I'm trying. I am truly trying to make it all better."

Michael sets her hand in his lap and strokes it gently with his fingertips. "I know you are. I understand some of what you said, but you have to try to understand where I'm coming from, too."

"I think I do."

They sit together quietly for a while until Kate asks, "What can I do to help right now? How can I help you and Evan? I feel like, if we could introduce Evan to some of the women, then maybe they would have an easier time meeting you."

"I won't put him in danger," Michael says decisively.

"I understand that. I do. But what if he can meet someone right here, in my house? Maybe it's time to let Sarah meet him."

Kate raises her head to look at his face. She can see the doubt in his eyes but thinks there is the faintest light of hope behind it. She has asked so much of him, working to convince him to let Evan stay with her, trying to build up his comfort level slowly over time so that he will eventually trust her. She knows if she can get Sarah fully on her side, she will have an ally in her fight to get Evan and Michael established in the neighborhood.

"Let me think about it," he says. "Maybe if it was just her, and I'm close by . . ."

She smiles as she turns toward him. "I'll talk to her on Friday."

"Not yet. Give me a little more time."

He lets go of her hand and raises his hand to her cheek, caressing it softly as he looks into her eyes. Slowly, he leans toward her and kisses her mouth, parting her lips with his as he pulls himself closer. They move back onto the bed together, drawing the blankets around themselves.

~ Eighteen ~

"THIS IS EVAN."

Kate is standing behind him, her hands on his shoulders as they face Sarah, who is standing next to the dining room table. She had been nervous when Michael said that he was finally willing to let Evan meet the teacher, but Sarah's excitement about meeting the boy put her mind at ease.

Sarah takes three steps to him and extends her hand with warmth and kindness. "It's nice to meet you, Evan. Peace to you."

"Peace to you, too," Evan replies confidently.

Kate meets Sarah's eyes, and the two women smile at each other. Then she looks at her children sitting around the table and says, "Jonah, why don't you go outside and find Michael. You can ask him to come in, too."

"I'm busy," Jonah mumbles, not looking at his mother.

"Jonah, please go outside and get Michael. Now."

When he stands up and leaves the room, she looks at Sarah and says, "Sorry about that. He's been grumpy the last couple days."

"No problem," Sarah says. "Evan, why don't you come sit

down with us. I'd love to talk with you about what you've been learning so far, and where we might go from there."

A few minutes later, the back door swings open, and Jonah stomps back inside. Kate turns and takes a step toward the kitchen, where Michael is hanging up his coat and hat on the hook by the door.

"Hi," she says. "Come on in."

Michael hesitates, searching Kate's eyes. She nods, and tries to mentally send him the boost of confidence he needs. He takes a deep breath. "Okay."

As they walk into the dining room, Sarah looks up from the workbook she has been paging through with Evan, and Kate notices her shift uncomfortably in her seat. She smiles awkwardly, rises, and takes a step toward Michael.

"Sarah, I'd like you to meet Michael MacGregor. He's Evan's dad."

"It's nice to meet you," Michael says, trying to smile as he extends his hand. Instead of shaking it, she folds her arms, and he lets his hand fall back to his side, though he holds her gaze.

Sarah clears her throat and says, "Nice to meet you, too." Then, as an afterthought, she says, "Peace to you, and good morning."

Trying to bridge the gap between them, Kate says, "Sarah was just going over some lessons with Evan. She says she's impressed at how well he can read already."

Michael gives a small nods and looks at Kate. "Great."

"Um . . . that's true," Sarah says. "It looks like you've been doing a good job." Michael glances at her, as if waiting for the rest of that sentence—the part where Sarah belittles him or explains why Evan would know even more if he'd been allowed to attend school before this. But Sarah says nothing more.

"Thank you," he says.

Kate looks desperately back and forth between the two of them, feeling the hope she had for this meeting slipping away from her.

Sarah's shoulders slump, and she looks up at the ceiling, as if looking for a secret message embedded in the cracks of the white plaster. Apparently finding no help there, she looks back to Michael. "Please forgive me," she says. "It's just been a long time since I've had to meet anyone new, and I guess I'm a little nervous. But Kate has told me all about you and Evan, and I was truly honored that you agreed to meet me today."

Michael's eyebrows knit together, and he stares at Sarah. He seems to be trying to soak in what she has said. Then Kate sees something unexpected in Sarah's expression. Kate feels confused, until she realizes that the odd look in Sarah's eyes is simply a complete lack of fear. She has become so used to being on guard, has been stuck in survival mode for so long, that it feels foreign to see someone looking so open, so free of malice.

Sarah's honesty seems to disarm Michael. His guarded countenance changes, and his eyes soften into a smile. "I guess I'm nervous, too," he says. "I really appreciate you meeting us. It's would be great for Evan to take lessons with you."

Kate watches with relief as the two of them smile at each other, though a small knot of jealousy forms in her belly. What took her weeks to accomplish, Sarah has done in minutes. Kate squints at Sarah, wondering how she can be so decent, so good. She wishes she could be more like Sarah and dislikes her for highlighting her own inadequacies.

"Well," Sarah says. "Do you want to stay while we do some work? You're welcome to sit down and join us if you'd like."

"I'd like that." He pulls out a chair next to Evan. For twenty minutes he watches and listens. Sarah is gentle and patient. She somehow includes all four children in the lesson of the day, working with each of them at their own level. They discuss the idea of an estimate versus an exact measurement, and each child is encouraged to come up with examples to illustrate the differences between them. Occasionally, she asks Michael a question about Evan's schooling, but mostly gleans what information she needs from talking with the boy.

Kate busies herself in the kitchen for a while, glancing from time to time into the dining room. She notices the way Michael watches Sarah, seeing him grow more comfortable in her presence with each passing minute. When Kate has finished kneading a ball of bread dough, she sets it in a lightly buttered bowl and covers it with a clean, damp towel. She places the bowl in a nice warm spot near the back of the stove top, to help it rise.

Kate slaps her hands together a few times, sending the last of the flour on them into a small cloud of white dust. Michael looks up to see her standing in the doorway as she says, "I'm done with the bread. Michael, maybe we should get back to the fence."

He pushes back his chair. "Thanks for letting me watch for a while, Sarah. If you don't mind, Kate and I need to go out and work on the new fence. Since it's not raining today, we're going to try to get as much done as possible."

Sarah laughs lightly and says, "I understand. We have to really make the best of these clear days, don't we?"

"You'll be here until about noon, right?" he asks.

"Right."

He looks at Evan and says, "Maybe I can come back in later and see what you've been working on, okay?"

"Okay, Dad."

Michael steps to Kate and touches her arm, and they walk together into the kitchen. After pulling on their coats, hats, and gloves, they walk around to the side of the yard where they have been slowly building a fence that will hold the young goats Kate hopes to get next year. It is tedious work finding sufficient flat boards in the rubble of the neighborhood, and they have had to chop down several small trees already to use as posts.

Michael lifts the heavy wooden box of assorted nails from the ground where they had worked earlier, and moves it several feet down the line to the next empty post. Kate picks up a board from the nearby pile, a faded yellow section of siding torn from a neighbor's dilapidated house. She holds it flat against the posts as Michael bangs several nails into position. As she turns to pick up the next board, she says, "So, are you okay?"

"You mean because of Sarah?"

"Yes."

"Yeah, I think so."

"She's great, isn't she?"

"Yeah. You were right—she's different."

Kate hesitates. "Well, maybe she's not so different. I think she was pretty scared at first."

Michael looks sideways at Kate. "No, I think she is different. She seems so smart and kind. And she's so young. And beautiful. Did you see her smile? Wow!"

"Okay, okay. You can shut up now," Kate says, rolling her eyes. "I'm too old to be jealous of my female friends."

Michael leans in to give her a quick peck on the cheek as he passes behind her to the post. "I'm glad, because you have nothing to be jealous of. I'm all yours, baby."

Kate can't help but laugh at him, his easy manner, his goofy phrase. "Seriously, though," she says, looking over her shoulder at him. "I'll understand if you want to be in the house today. I know it must be hard for you to leave him alone in there with a stranger. A strange woman."

"Well, he's not alone. He's with Jonah, Laura, and Margaret. And maybe I have to just make this leap, you know? I can't hide Evan forever. Maybe I just have to try to really trust . . . well . . . you. You keep telling me that Sarah isn't going to hurt Evan. Maybe I need to trust in your instincts. Maybe you have some of that female intuition I've heard so much about."

Kate watches him, the way he pauses at times, as if trying to convince himself of the words he's saying. She watches the way he bangs the hammer hard onto the head of each nail, as if trying to solidify his conviction, solidify his trust. When he looks up at her, she can see the effort it takes. She can see the mixture of hope and fear that flicker in his eyes.

"If it's any help, I think you're doing the right thing," she says, looking back down at the board in her hands. "I really think this is going to work out."

"Before you get too excited," Michael says, "remember this is just an experiment." His smile drops away, and Kate sees a cloud pass over his countenance. "I still don't plan on marching into town anytime soon. And, you should know, I'm still keeping my eyes on the yard. I'd know if anyone tried to leave the house. And I'd know if anyone was coming."

"That's fair." Kate smiles, actually a little more comfortable knowing that he hasn't given up all his mistrust.

They work together until midmorning, securing several sections of fence before the cold December air permeates their gloves, leaving their fingers numb. When Michael's hammer strokes begin to miss more times than land, Kate suggests they take a break to warm up.

As they walk through the back door, they can hear the children talking, though they are not sitting at the table as before. Michael follows Kate to the front room, and a smile breaks over his face when he sees Kate's three children, standing straight, their arms hanging by their sides. Sarah is next to Evan, helping him hold a small ruler along the side of Laura's leg, talking him through the exercise.

"Two feet to here. Then move it up. Three feet. You can set your finger at the top to remember where to put the ruler. Go ahead and step on the stool. Four feet. Five feet to here. Plus ten inches. Good job. Now let's compare that curvy measurement—our estimate in this case—with the straight line measurement we got when Laura stood against the wall and see how they differ."

Sarah looks up at Kate and Michael. "We're working on measurements right now."

"Dad!" Evan says. "Did you know that I'm four feet and six inches tall?"

Michael's smile falters, and he looks embarrassed that he didn't know such a basic fact about his son. "That's great, buddy."

"We won't get in your way, Sarah," Kate says. "We're just going to make some tea and warm up. Can I bring you a cup?"

"Sure, thanks," Sarah says. "If you don't mind, I'll sit down and join you in a minute. I brought along an outdoor lesson today, too. It's a scavenger hunt about what we've been working on this morning." She turns to the children. "I'll put you into teams. Jonah and Evan against Margaret and Laura."

"Why am I always on Evan's team?" Jonah asks bitterly.

Kate says, "Jonah! Be polite."

"That's okay," Sarah says. "You're probably right, Jonah. It will be more fair if we split you up differently. Laura, you go with Jonah. Margaret and Evan will work together." She holds out her arm to lead Evan toward the wall where Laura's height is marked.

Michael fills the kettle with water before setting it back onto the stove. Kate busies herself taking down three mugs and measuring tea into each. "Sorry about that," she quietly says to Michael. "I don't know what's gotten into him. Maybe they had a fight or something."

"Maybe."

When he doesn't say anything more, she turns to look at him. He's leaning against the stove, his arms crossed and his chin angled to the floor. He seems lost in a thought. "You think it's something else?" she asks.

"I don't know," he says. "I'm just thinking about how I'd feel if some guy started sleeping with my mom." Michael looks up at Kate and offers a gentle smile.

"What? No . . . I don't think that has anything to do . . . I mean, we've been careful. I don't think they know . . ." Even as she says the words, she knows they're not true. She lifts her hand to her face and rubs her forehead. "Ugh. Well, that stinks."

"Aw, come on," Michael says, moving to her and touching her arm. "They're smart kids. They were bound to figure it out." Seeming to sense that this is little consolation to Kate, he adds, "Don't worry about it. Give him a few days. He'll be back to normal soon."

Steam begins to erupt from the nozzle of the teakettle. Michael turns to the stove and pours the water carefully into the three mugs. He glances at Kate, picks up two of the mugs, and silently walks into the dining room. She stays where she is for a moment and then, with a deep sigh, Kate lifts the third cup and follows him.

Sarah closes the front door as the last of the children exit the house. She pulls her sweater tightly around herself as she walks to the dining room, to join Michael and Kate. Michael rises slightly from his seat as she nears the table, and she gives him a strange look, probably not understanding the hint of chivalry in this foreign gesture.

"Thank you for the tea," Sarah says as she sits. "It's pretty cold out there today. Did you get a lot done on the fence?"

"We did," Kate says. "There's still a lot to go, of course, but there's time."

The three sip quietly for a minute, uncomfortably looking down into their mugs. Kate finally breaks the silence when she says to Sarah, "So, how do you think Evan is doing so far?"

"He seems to be catching on pretty quickly with the reading and math," Sarah says. "And, we talked just a little bit about the seven Habits of Humanity. He obviously doesn't know the details yet, but the core concepts are already there. That's a tribute to you, Michael."

"Um, thanks, I think," Michael replies. "I'm not really sure what that means, but it sounds good." He looks questioningly across the table to Kate.

"Don't worry," Kate says. "It's a good thing. In school now, kids are taught about the seven basic concepts of being a good person. Remember the seven deadly sins?"

Michael nods. "Jealousy, greed, anger . . . I can't remember the others."

"Close. Anger, greed, laziness, pride, lust, envy, and gluttony," Kate says. "The Habits of Humanity are essentially the opposite of those—kindness, sharing, hard work, humility, control, patience, and moderation. They're the recipe for how to be a good human. How to live in peace and harmony with the rest of the planet."

"Oh, okay."

Kate rotates the mug in her hands and then twists it back to center. "So, do you think he could join the lessons every week?" She asks it to her mug, unsure herself if the question for Michael or Sarah.

Sarah leans back in her chair and looks back and forth between Kate and Michael. "I'm happy to have Evan join us here on Fridays. I think it's good for him to have some formal lessons. But I'm a teacher, so of course I think that. I guess it's up to you, Michael."

Michael takes a deep breath before speaking. "Well, I can see that he likes it. I try to teach him, but it's probably good for him to get another point of view, too."

Sarah smiles encouragingly and asks, "And do you think he might start coming into the neighborhood for school on Wednesdays?"

At this, Michael lets go of his cup and sits up straight. His cheek twitches, just a little, near his left eye. The movement borders between a nervous tic and a wince of pain.

"I don't know if he's quite ready for that, Sarah," Kate says. "And I'm not really sure how that would work."

Sarah's smile fades, and she says, "I understand."

They sit in silence until Kate says, "I think we would all like Evan to eventually be able to do that, though. Am I right, Michael?"

"Kate," he begins, but then simply shrugs and shakes his head.

"Okay, we don't have to make a decision right now," Kate says as she lifts her hand to the back of her neck. She squeezes the muscles there, then slides her fingers over the bony edges of the base of her skull. "Sarah, what do you think? I've been trying to figure out how to make this work. I've been trying to figure out how to help, and I have no idea what to do. At this point, I could really use some input. I'm open to any ideas you might have."

Sarah hesitates before speaking. "I don't know. Obviously, it would cause quite a stir if Michael and Evan just walked into town one day, but I think if you told people about them first, maybe that would help. What does Iris think?"

Kate tilts her head back and looks at the ceiling. "I haven't exactly told her about them yet."

"You haven't? But why? She's one of your best friends. And she has a lot of pull in this neighborhood." Sarah leans in and rests her forearms on the table.

"I don't know. I guess I've been trying to build up to it. Don't get me wrong—Iris is a really good woman. She's helped me more times than I can count. It's just that, after all that she's been through, I don't want to hurt her."

"How would it hurt her?" Sarah asks.

"Well, think about it. For years before the war, she had her life slowly stripped from her by men in power. And then during the war, she watched men destroy what was left of her home, her city. She still has the scars from where their bullets hit her leg. I think it would be really hard for her to believe that a strange man roaming around in the woods isn't going to try to hurt us."

Kate folds her arms and sits up straight. "Iris helped save this neighborhood. She helped implement the new rules, helped move people in from the demolished areas. And she was one of the main proponents for the reeducation of the few men who were left. She's not going to suddenly just forget about all that she's worked on."

Sarah fiddles with the handle of her cup. "But everything you just said about Iris . . . it's all true for you, too. I mean, you went through similar things, and you did a lot to help our neighborhood. And maybe I'm wrong, but I thought you were always on board with the changes, too." Sarah glances up to Michael, who is watching Kate. His face is expressionless. His hands lie still in his lap. Turning back to Kate, she says, "I guess I always thought you agreed with the other women. That you thought the same way they do. About the men. About my husband."

Kate looks into Sarah's eyes and sees the uncertainty there. For the first time, she sees what lies behind Sarah's confident demeanor, behind her seemingly limitless kindness and compassion. For the first time, Kate sees Sarah's loneliness. For years she had just listened as other women spoke badly of Sarah and the way she treated Eric as her equal. For years she had said nothing when others accused Sarah behind her back of allowing her husband too much freedom, too much authority in their house. And she has seen the thinly veiled look of jealousy in the younger women, who wish they had been the one Eric chose.

Sitting across from her friend at the table today, Kate sees the hurt this isolation has caused. How she must have felt the silent undercurrent of these accusations, and the subtle way the women of the town have hated and feared her.

"Sarah, I think you and Eric are great together."

"But you think I give him too much freedom."

"No. That's not what I'm saying."

"Kate, I've heard what people say about me. And I know I break the rules. I know I'm not supposed to let him out walking alone. I know I'm not supposed to consult with him about neighborhood decisions."

Kate shakes her head and waves her hand in front of herself, as if brushing away trivial details. "Look, we know you aren't as concerned with the rules, but we also understand why. You're young and you grew up in a different world than we did. But you have to try to understand what we went through."

"I do understand. I was young, but I was there when the ground forces rolled through. I saw my brother dragged away from us. And I can still hear in my head the way my mother begged for his life. Kate, I know how bad it was, but I don't believe it was always bad."

"You just don't remember," Kate says, shaking her head.

"Well, my mom is older than you, and she remembers. And she says it wasn't always so bad. She says there was a time when men and women worked together, before everything got so messed up. And, even more importantly, she says that during the worst of times, during floods and fires, and even during wars, there were always enough good people to outnumber the bad. Even in the worst of times, she says there were always people around who were willing to help. And that it didn't matter if you were a man or a woman. Kate, maybe I'm naive, but I truly believe that if it all falls down around you, you need to just hold on long enough for the good people to get to you. If you can just hold on, there will eventually be a hand reaching out to lift you back up."

"Sarah, we are that hand. The women have been trying to do just that. That's what we've been working on for the past ten years. All we want to do is help," Kate says, leaning forward in her chair.

Sarah looks into Kate's eyes and asks, "Then when will you start helping the men?"

Kate feels the weight of Sarah's words fall like bricks onto her heart. All the accusations of apathy she has leveled on men throughout her lifetime, and all the times she has despised men for not standing up for justice and equality ring in her ears. Kate drops her eyes to the table, unable to look at the man sitting across from her now.

"You know," she says. "We've all worked so hard to make this neighborhood what it is, and I'm proud of what we've accomplished. We survived. And as a group, we did what we thought we had to do to bring peace back to society. But I know it's not perfect. I know it's not balanced. I know we still have a lot of work to do."

Sarah reaches across the table to touch her hand. When Kate looks up, Sarah says in a gentle voice, "Maybe this could be the start of that work."

"It's not going to be easy." She sighs. "Iris isn't going to trust him."

"You did," Sarah says.

The corner of Kate's mouth curves into a small smile, and she looks across to Michael. His right elbow is resting on the arm of the chair, and his fingertips are pressed into his temple. His jaw is clenched, and he is glaring at her from below his furrowed brow. Kate is taken aback by the anger she sees in his eyes.

Sarah doesn't seem to notice, and she continues. "And if we made changes here, it wouldn't be the first time. I've heard there are several places where the men are being allowed more freedom."

"Where?" Kate asks, pulling her eyes away from Michael.

"Some towns back east. Places where the steel mills and foundries are running again."

Kate sighs and says, "Well, those places are far from here. I'm not sure how much sway that would hold."

"Maybe not. I'm just saying it wouldn't be

unprecedented." Sarah picks up her mug and sips her tea.

Kate looks back to Michael and is surprised to see the malice gone from his face. His arms rest lightly on his lap again, and he smiles gently at her. "Um," she says opening her hand toward him. "Well, what do you think?"

"About which part?"

"I guess about the part where I talk to Iris. Sarah is right—she would be a powerful ally for us. But I'm not going to do it unless you're on board."

He slowly looks from Kate to Sarah, and then back to Kate. Then he leans forward and rests his elbows on the table. Closing his eyes, he rubs his palm across his jaw and tugs on his chin. With a sigh, his eyes open and he says, "Let me think about it for a couple days. Is that okay?"

"Of course," Kate says quickly.

Sarah drains the last of the tea from her cup. "Well, until then, Evan is welcome to join us on Fridays. I won't tell anyone. And Kate, let me know if you want any help with Iris."

"Thanks, Sarah. I think it's best for me to talk to her alone, so she doesn't feel ganged up on, but I'll let you know if I change my mind."

"Okay," Sarah says. "I'm going to go check on the kids. We'll probably wrap up our lesson back in here. Are you two going back out to work on the fence some more?"

"Yes," Kate answers. She pushes her chair back from the table as she picks up both her mug and Sarah's. "Give a shout before you leave, okay?"

"Okay," Sarah says as she puts on her coat.

Kate sets the mugs in the kitchen sink with a soft clunk. She waits for Michael to join her, but she doesn't hear any sound from the dining room. No scrape of his chair as he gets up, no gentle thuds as his feet cross the floor to the kitchen, and no trace of his soft breathing close behind her.

She knows he still sits in his chair, and she wonders which expression is on his face now that he is alone. Is it the one that startled her, so full of hostility when Sarah talked about the rules of the neighborhood? Or the easy look of kindness that so quickly replaced it? She waits there another minute, then moves to the back door, puts on her coat, and goes outside to continue working on the fence.

~

An hour later, Sarah is just finishing up the final lesson of the day. The boys are jotting down notes about what they need to work on before next week. Laura and Margaret are in the front room, sitting on each side of Michael as he plays the piano.

"Watch me this time, then we'll do it together," Michael says, and then plays a short series of notes. The girls watch attentively, then Margaret plays the tune with him as he repeats it. "Good! Now you do it alone, Margaret."

"Can I offer you some lunch before you go?" Kate asks Sarah as she helps her tidy up the books and papers strewn across the table.

"No, thank you," Sarah replies. "I'm sure my mom will have something waiting for me when I get home."

Kate walks her to the front door and holds Sarah's backpack while she tugs on her coat, hat, and gloves. When she's ready, Kate hands the pack to her and steps to the door to open it. "Have a safe walk home, Sarah. And, thanks again for coming out here."

"My pleasure. The kids did a lot of good work today."

"And thanks for allowing Evan to join the lesson. And for your advice."

Michael stands up from the piano and moves to Kate's side. "Yes," he says. "Thank you. I'm really glad Evan got to meet you today. Really, thank you."

"You're welcome. Evan is a terrific person, and I'm happy he'll be joining us." Turning to Kate, Sarah adds, "Let me know if there's anything else I can do."

"I will," Kate says. "Will I see you at the market this weekend?"

"No. I don't have much to trade, and we don't need fish this week. But I'll see you next Wednesday."

"Okay."

The women step out into the cold noon air. The sun is at its zenith, but it feels too far away to provide much warmth. It is merely a pale yellow circle in the cloudless sky, no more than a thin disk of light arcing low on the horizon. Kate watches Sarah walk briskly across the yard. As an afterthought, she shouts, "Be safe!"

When Kate goes back inside, Michael is at the piano again with the girls. He doesn't look up as she makes her way to the kitchen. Evan and Jonah are already at the stove, warming yesterday's soup for the family.

"Jonah, can you come outside with me?" Kate asks. "I need a little help picking up the tools."

"Sure, Mom."

He collects his coat and boots, then follows her out to the side yard. "Looks like you got a couple more sections of fence up," he says.

"Yes. I'll probably work on it more after lunch, so I'd like to get everything moved over to the next post."

They start by moving the hammers and box of nails the few yards over to the next section of fence. Kate bends to lift an armful of boards from the pile and asks, "So, what's been going on with you the last couple days? You seem kind of grumpy."

Jonah doesn't answer, and walks past Kate without meeting her eye. He drops the box of nails to the ground with a crash, then sets his hand on a post. She hauls the boards to the new spot.

Stepping close to her son, she says, "Honey, I think I know what's bothering you, and I feel like we should talk about it."

He kicks the post a few times before speaking. "I just think he's around too much."

"Okay, I can understand that. I suppose it's normal for you to feel a little jealous."

"I'm not jealous. I just think it's annoying sometimes. I mean, I don't mind sharing. I know it's the right thing to do, but it's every day."

Kate shifts from side to side, trying to come up with the right words. Finally, she says, "Well, you don't have to think of it like you're sharing me. I mean . . . I'm always your mom, and I guess . . . you know . . . it's just a really different sort of relationship with Michael. I don't want you to think that he's taking your place or anything."

"What are you talking about?" Jonah steps back from her. "You think I'm mad at Michael? Jeez, Mom. I'm talking about Evan!"

"I'm sorry . . . I didn't mean . . ."

"I don't care what you and Michael do."

"But why are you mad at Evan?"

"I told you! He's always here. And why do I have to share all my stuff all the time? Laura and Margaret don't have to share."

"Sweetie, Laura and Margaret share all the time. They've had to share everything since the day they were born." Kate moves around to Jonah's side., "I thought you liked Evan."

"I do like Evan. I'm just saying I don't want to have him around every second of the day."

"Well, come on, Jonah. He's not around every second. They go fishing and hunting when I'm at the market."

"But when they are here, I always have to show him how to do everything. I just want some space!" He puts his hands on his hips and kicks the post one more time.

Kate nods and takes a deep breath. "Okay, honey. I can understand how it might be tough for you. How about this— I'll make sure you get a little more space. I'll try anyway, okay?" She bends her head to catch his eye. When he looks up to her, she smiles, then reaches out her hand to rub the back of his shoulder. "Okay?"

"Okay."

After a long pause, she asks, "Does everybody know about Michael and me?"

Jonah rolls his eyes. "Well, come on, Mom. You haven't slept in your bed in, like, forever. We're not stupid."

She looks down at the ground, both embarrassed and happy to be free of the secrecy. "Okay. I suppose Evan could sleep in my bed, then, since you all know I'm not in it anyway. That way you might not feel so crowded. What do you think?"

"I guess we can give it a try."

"Now, let's go in for lunch. Afterward, you can come help me with the fence, and we'll have Evan work inside for the afternoon."

She wraps her arm around Jonah's back as they walk together toward the house. He snorts a quick laugh and leans his shoulder into her. "Did you really think I was mad about you and Michael?"

"I guess that does sound kind of silly now," Kate says, and pulls her son even closer to her.

~ Nineteen ~

A FEW NIGHTS LATER, Kate and Michael lie huddled together in his small bed. The blankets are piled on top of them to keep out the cold, and his arm is around her as her head leans against his chest. She can hear the beat of his heart, a slow and steady rhythm that is lulling her to sleep.

In a quiet voice, Michael says, "Tomorrow is Wednesday."

Kate is pulled out of the space between awake and asleep, and her eyes flit open. She sighs deeply and replies, "Uh-huh." When he doesn't say anything more, she lifts herself onto her elbow to look at him. His eyebrows are knitted together, and a far-off look clouds his eyes. "What are you thinking about?" she asks.

Without looking at her, he answers. "Evan."

For a long time she watches him silently, letting him work through his thoughts. After a while, he lifts his eyes to meet hers and a small smile flickers and fades from his lips.

"I just wish I really knew what they'd say," he tells her at last.

"You mean the other women? If I told them about you?"

"Yes."

Kate rolls onto her stomach, and Michael pulls his arm out from beneath her. "Well," she says. "I don't know exactly what they'd say, but I think I have a pretty good idea. They'd be upset at first. They'd probably yell at me for not saying anything sooner. I'll tell them about you—how kind you are, that you are a good father to Evan, that you aren't out to hurt anyone. And then I think they'd calm down a bit and want to meet you."

"Just like that?"

"More or less."

She lifts her hand and places it on his chest, gently circling through the little bit of hair there. Though she watches her own fingers, she can feel his eyes on her, trying to read her face, to see if she really believes what she's saying or if her confidence is simply an act for his sake.

"I don't know, Kate."

"Do you want me to talk to Iris?"

"I don't know."

"I could go tomorrow while the kids are in school."

He tilts his head back onto his pillow and looks up at the bare joists in the ceiling. "Maybe."

"Michael," she says. "What's holding you back? What can I do to convince you?"

"I don't think there's anything you can do. I feel like I already have all the information. It's not like there's anything more you could tell me."

"What if I brought Evan? Maybe if they meet him, it will be easier. Nobody's going to be mad at an eight-year-old." She can feel him tense up at the idea. "They'll see what a good kid he is, and that will help them believe that you're good, too. And Sarah can tell them she's met you."

"I don't know," Michael says, shaking his head.

"Plus, Evan will be a calming force for them. They're not going to get as upset if a little kid is in the room. Not that I'm trying to use him. I just think it might help."

Michael takes a deep breath.

"Michael, I know it didn't work out in your last town. And it must have been so hard for you to live out in the woods with Evan, scrounging for food and shelter. I can't imagine how scary that must have been for you." She moves closer to him and sets her hand on his shoulder. "But maybe it's time to find a new home. Maybe it's time to start over. Here."

He is quiet for a minute. Finally, he says, "I guess I just have to decide if I believe that the women in your neighborhood can accept the idea that a strange man can be trusted."

"Do you trust me?" Kate asks quietly.

Michael rolls onto his side to face her. He stares into her eyes. "I do trust you. I know you're not going to hurt Evan."

"But do you know I'm not going to hurt *you*?"

His face softens, and she sees light flicker in his eyes. He reaches up to touch her cheek and then tucks a piece of her hair behind her ear. "I know."

"Michael," she says. "I have known all of these women most of my life. I'm close friends with many of them. I already know which ones will have the hardest time with this, and I know what I need to say to win them over. I think it's going to be okay."

"Maybe."

"I don't want to keep living like this. I don't want to keep you a secret."

A smile shines in his eyes as he wraps an arm around her back, pulling her close. His fingers trace down the length of her spine, then glide over the curve of her bottom. He presses his forehead to hers and closes his eyes, then tilts his chin up and kisses her gently.

As he breathes in the scent of her, he begins to maneuver his body under hers, kissing her more passionately. His lips and tongue move from her mouth to her neck, to her ear. She feels his strong hands take hold of her hips, and he tugs and lifts her on top of him. Below the heavy blankets, she straddles his body and straightens her arms so she can see his face. Her long hair falls down over her shoulders as he tilts his pelvis up, firmly pushing her hips down onto him, sliding into her.

~

The next morning they make their way to the kitchen together through softly falling snow. He opens the garden gate and holds it for her, then follows her past the few plants that still stand brown and wilted in the frozen earth. Kate kindles the fire in the cookstove, and watches the familiar red-orange glow of the flames as they begin to swirl with the motion of the oxygenating fan. Michael readies the bowls and mugs for breakfast, stopping from time to time to pull Kate to him, quickly kissing her or rubbing the small of her back.

In the quiet time of the morning before the children wake, the house feels small and safe, enveloped in the dim light from the slowly rising sun. Each sound seems amplified by the silence around it—the little squeak of the cabinet door, the quickening hum of the motor above the stove, and the simmering water in the teakettle.

Sure the fire has caught, she clucks her tongue three times, signaling to Kiko and Ruby to follow her to the front door. Their toenails scratch across the wood floor, and they leap happily out into the yard. Kate walks back to the kitchen and accepts the steaming cup that Michael holds out to her.

When they each have a hot mug of tea in their cold hands, Michael whispers, "While you're at school with the boys today, I think I'll try to make a pizza. I can use some of that terrible cheese you brought home. Maybe with enough sauce, some chicken, and sun-dried tomatoes, it won't taste so bad."

"With the boys?" Kate wonders if she misheard him.

He smiles at her over his mug, though his eyes still reveal his uncertainty. She quickly tries to hide her surprise and says, "Sure. That would be great." She steps closer to him and reaches out her hand to touch his arm. "If anyone can make that cheese taste good, it's you."

Michael quickly downs the rest of his tea. He walks to the counter to brew another cup. With his back to her, he says, "Laura and Margaret can help me. And I think we should chop some of the ice out from behind the dam this morning. It's getting pretty blocked."

Kate had forgotten that part of the bargain. It was over a month ago that he told her she would have to leave the girls with him if she ever took Evan to town with her. Her mind races, trying to come up with a way out of it. But what can she say? Can she expect him to trust her with his son if she cannot trust him with her daughters? In his mind, she would be taking the boy into the belly of the beast. It probably seemed a small price to ask, a bit of collateral to seal the deal.

She knows he is waiting for her to answer, but she cannot speak through the lump in her throat. She stares at his back as he scoops fresh tea leaves into his cup. He is wearing the chambray shirt he wore the day his arm was cut on the roof. The one she helped peel off as he stood almost exactly where she stands now. She notices the stitching on the sleeve where Evan sewed the tear back together and thinks about the small scar Michael will wear on his arm for the rest of his life.

"That would be fine." The words come out as a small croak, and as soon as she speaks them, she wishes she could take them back.

Michael turns to look at her, a warm smile on his face. He seems about to speak when the dogs begin to bark in the front yard. Kate sets down her mug, but he quickly says, "I'll get them. You can stay."

~

Jonah and Evan walk several feet in front of Kate as they make their way through the rubble of the old campus. The snow has begun to fall heavily now, and Kate shrugs to shift the light pack on her back before reaching down to adjust her thick belt. Subconsciously, she touches the handle of the knife held there.

The boys talk freely, and she is happy to see that they are on good terms again. She can hardly blame Jonah for needing a little more space. More than once she has felt the same feeling of claustrophobia, especially during the winter months.

Evan is excited to explore their route, and stops often to examine the gaping holes left in the walls of bombed-out buildings. Kate describes the rooms and equipment—a large lecture hall with hundreds of chairs, now covered in moldy red fabric; millions of shards of glass sparkling on the cold linoleum floor of what used to be a laboratory; the charred remains of a dormitory.

As they near the center of the neighborhood, their conversation lags and the tension begins to build. When the first of the inhabited houses comes into view around the bend, Kate says, "Let's cut back to Sarah's house first. We're early. She'll still be home."

Their boots crunch in the snow as they walk behind several brick buildings, broken remnants of two- or three-story businesses that used to line the main street. Then they cut left into a residential section, and they all tread carefully over the broken blacktop of the street. Chickens cluck and goats bleat at them as they go by, but they don't see any people in the few yards they pass. Kate notices the slightest movement behind the front curtains of two houses, but no one comes outside.

Finally, they arrive at Sarah's house. They cross the road, and Kate opens the gate, ushering the boys into the yard. Sarah's mother, Helen, opens the door and smiles brightly at Kate, but her smile falters as her eyes turn to Evan.

"Come in," Helen says before closing the door behind them. "This must be Evan." She steps back and looks the boy over for few seconds, and then a kind smile reappears. "Sarah told me about you. Peace to you, and good morning, son."

"Peace to you, and good morning," Evan replies, and Kate allows herself to exhale for the first time in what feels like minutes.

Helen turns and says, "Well, looks like you are all going to have an interesting day today." She pauses, looking into Kate's eyes. "Good for you," she says at last. "I'll go get Sarah. She'll be happy to see you."

Kate bangs the snow off her boots, and motions for the boys to step deeper into the front room. They can hear the sounds of children running around upstairs, doors slamming, and the deep baritone of Eric's muffled voice singing from the kitchen. In seconds, Sarah hurries in, beaming.

"Peace to you, and good morning, Kate and Jonah!" she says. "And especially to you, Evan. I'm so glad to see you."

"Peace to you, and good morning, Sarah," they all respond. "I'm sorry to just barge in like this," Kate adds.

"No, no," Sarah says with a wave of her hand. "Don't worry about it."

"I thought it might be better for us to stop here first,

before going to school."

"That's probably a good idea. We can all walk there together." Sarah is still smiling, but Kate can see the worry in her eyes.

"I thought I'd go to Iris's house during lessons, if that's okay with you," Kate says.

"Sure. Actually, no. I saw Iris this morning when I was shoveling the front walk," Sarah says. "And she was on her way to Elle's. She said they were going to work on a quilt there today."

"Oh." Suddenly, Kate is unsure what to do. She had assumed Iris would be at home alone. She looks down at the floor, and her fingers fiddle with the strap of her backpack.

Just then, Eric peeks around the corner. When he catches Kate's eye, he smiles and steps into view. Baby Thomas is on his hip, holding tight to Eric's thick wool sweater with one hand and holding even tighter to a warm, buttery bun in his other. Kate smiles at the baby, and he lets go of his daddy to reach out to her.

"Hey, sweetie pie," she croons, scooping him into her arms. She doesn't even mind the sticky smear he leaves on the back of her coat as the bun rubs into her shoulder. "Peace to you, and good morning," Kate says to Eric.

"Peace to you, too, Kate. Where are your girls?"

"They stayed at home today. With Michael." She notices the way Sarah and Eric shoot a quick look at each other.

Eric smiles at Jonah and Evan, and asks, "Good morning, boys. Did you eat breakfast yet? Are you hungry?"

They are both perfectly happy to follow Eric into the kitchen for a second breakfast. Kate sways with Thomas on her hip, and turns to Sarah when they are alone. "Is this okay?" she asks.

"I think it's the right thing to do," Sarah responds. "But I don't envy the conversation you are going to have with Iris. Do you want to go to Elle's right now?"

"Not really. I'd like be there when Evan meets the other children at school. Maybe I'll just wait and talk to Iris another time."

Sarah pauses, then says, "I'll have Jess run down to Elle's house. She's almost ready. She can ask Iris to come meet you at the school."

"I don't want to trouble you more than—"

"No trouble. She'll be happy to do it. I'm almost ready, too." Sarah turns to leave the room and calls over her shoulder, "We'll be ready to go in about ten minutes. Make yourself at home."

~

Kate stands in front of the group of children, her hands on Evan's shoulders as Sarah introduces him. The kids stare up at them silently, many with mouths agape at the sight of a new boy. One girl raises her hand and, when Sarah calls on her, asks, "Where did you live before?"

Evan turns his head and looks up at Kate before answering. When she smiles and nods with encouragement, he answers, "We lived in the forest."

"Did you have a house there?" asks another child.

"No. Not a house. A tree fort. Me and my dad built it."

"Where did you live before that?"

"All over. We moved around a lot. And before that, I lived in a neighborhood, but we had to leave."

"What did you eat?" one of the boys asks. "In the forest, I mean."

"We hunted for food. And we borrowed some from gardens, too." He looks up at Kate and quickly adds, "But only when we had to."

She had suspected the truth about the garden since Michael fixed the squeaking gate, but she had chosen to ignore it. She never asked him about it, not wanting to embarrass him, not wanting to accuse.

"Where's your mother?" another child asks.

"She died."

There is a small knock on the door of the school, and a six-year-old girl walks in. Sarah motions for her to join the class, but instead she runs over to her and stands on her tiptoes to whisper something into her ear. "Thank you, Jess," Sarah says. "You can sit down." She moves to Kate's side and says, "Iris is outside waiting for you."

Kate takes a deep breath and walks out to the sidewalk. The snow has stopped falling, although the sky remains overcast and gray. Iris, Elle, and Patrice are in a semicircle at the edge of the street. Iris has her arms crossed in front of her.

"Kate, what's going on?" she asks. "Sarah's daughter said you brought a new boy in to school today and you needed to talk to me."

"Everything's okay," Kate starts. "I was going to come to your house, but Sarah said you were at Elle's." She looks to the other two women and forces a smile. "Peace to you both."

"Who is the boy?" Patrice asks.

"I'm sorry to bother you while you were working," Kate says to Iris. "Sarah said you're making a new quilt?"

"Kate," Iris says. "Did you bring a new boy in to school?"

Kate nods and tries to stay calm. "I did. His name is Evan, and he's eight years old. He's a really great kid. He and Jonah have become friends, and we've been trying to figure out when it would be best for him to start coming to school."

"Wait," Iris says. "Who is he? Where did he come from?"

Elle and Patrice take a step closer to her, and she feels cornered against the wall of the school. She tries to remember the script she'd prepared in her head. She tries to seem relaxed and confident. "I think I mentioned him to you once before. Don't you remember, Iris? I told you about the boy and his father. The ones who were passing through."

Patrice turns her head to look at Iris and asks, "What is she talking about?"

"But Kate, that was a couple months ago," Iris says. "Are you saying he came back?"

"We set up my shed for them to sleep in since it's gotten cold, and they've been helping out on my farm." Kate sees the fear creeping into Iris's eyes and tries to reassure her. "They've been a big help, really. And they're both very good people."

Iris lifts her eyes to the sky and looks around, as if she hopes to find the words she needs written there. At last, she lets her hands drop to her side and says, "Kate, are you actually telling me that you have a *raider* living at your house?"

"Jesus," Patrice whispers.

"No! No, Iris. No. He's not a raider. Michael and Evan don't have any place else to go. They've been living in the wild for over a year, and they came to me for help. For help, Iris. They're not trying to hurt anybody."

Iris looks like she can't decide whether to laugh or cry. "Oh my God, Kate! And you believe him? Where is he now?"

"Iris, calm down. Yes, I do believe him. I believe them. Remember, we're talking about a little boy here. He's eight. He's never hurt a soul in his life, and, if you would just get to know him a little bit, you'd see that his father has done a good job taking care of him. An excellent job raising him."

Patrice is shaking her head. "Are you really that stupid?" she spits.

Elle stands quietly next to her, her eyebrows knitted together. Iris raises her hand to her face and covers her mouth, tugging on her chin in exasperation. She asks, "How long has this man been living with you?"

Kate doesn't answer. She doesn't need to. Iris sees the truth in her eyes, and Kate is heartbroken by the look of disappointment and betrayal she sees on her friend's face.

"Aw, Kate. He's been here the whole time, hasn't he?"

"Look, can't you admit there's a chance he's a good man?" Kate asks. "Isn't it possible that he's been marginalized by our new society, hasn't had any place to go, hasn't had any opportunity to be welcomed back into a neighborhood?"

"Is that what he told you? Is that what he said?"

"Iris, you act like it's a pickup line."

"Good men aren't just wandering around in the wild."

"How can you be so sure? There are good men in this town. There are good men in every town."

"Yes!" Iris shouts. "They are *in* the neighborhoods. They are here *with us*, living peacefully *with us*. They're not roaming around the forest with little children."

"Unbelievable," Patrice mumbles.

"And what about all these good men in our towns?" Kate says. "Do you ever think maybe we've taken too much away from them? You know there are plenty of women, even in our neighborhood, who think maybe we've gone too far."

"Too far?" Patrice shouts. "The men went too far. And we're the ones who have to fix what they broke."

"Patrice," Kate says, trying to calm everyone. "You know I agree with making this world peaceful again. You all know that I do. But there are towns out there that are starting to give the men a little more freedom now. Starting to accept the fact that not all men are violent. There's light and dark in all of us."

"Hold on," Iris says, cutting her off. "This isn't about evolving social policies. We can talk about all that later. The issue right now is that there's a strange man living at your house. Maybe he is a decent man, but that's for us as a community to decide. You had no right keeping this potentially dangerous situation a secret from us. And I can't believe you didn't tell *me* about this! Why didn't you let me help you?"

Just then, the school door opens, and Sarah emerges. She leads Evan outside with her, and the women all stare.

"This is Evan," Kate says. She smiles at the boy and holds out her hand. He steps to her side, and she puts her arm around his shoulder.

"Kate," Sarah says in a voice barely above a whisper. "I think there's something you need to hear."

"What is it?"

Sarah looks at Evan and, with a curt nod, says, "Go ahead. Tell her what you told me about you father."

"Which part?" Evan asks quietly.

"The part about when your mother died."

The other women huddle closer around the boy, and Kate instinctively pulls him tighter to her side.

Evan looks confused, but he tries to comply. "I just said that my mom was really sick for a long time. And that Michael was the one who came into my room to tell me the night that she died."

"Your father?" Iris asks gently.

"Well, yeah," Evan replies. "My dad. But back then I just called him Michael."

Kate feels the hair on the back of her neck rise, and she steps away from Evan to look at him. "What do you mean?" she asks. "Why did you call him Michael before?"

"That's what we all called him," he says with a shrug.

"That's his name."

"Your mom called him that?"

"My mom and my dad."

Kate feels the blood in her veins pulse through her body. Struggling to fight off the growing panic inside her, she says, "I thought Michael was your dad."

Evan smiles a little and says, "He is. But he's my second dad. He lived in the house next to us and helped us out all the time. He and my mom were really good friends. The night my mom died, he came into my room and told me we had to leave right away. He said that my mom told him to take me camping for a while to help me so I wouldn't feel so sad."

"And what about your father?" Elle asks.

"Michael said he wanted me to go, too."

"And you never went back?" Sarah asks.

"Well, no. Michael said he was going to take care of me from now on. He said from now on, he's my real dad."

Iris is about to speak, but when she pulls her eyes away from the boy, she sees that the color has drained from Kate's face. "Kate?"

Kate raises her eyes to her friend and whispers, "Iris, I left my daughters with him."

~ Twenty ~

SHE IS RUNNING across the pitted field. The rise of the hill is before her, and she struggles to ignore the burning of the cold air in her lungs. As she begins to ascend the hill, she slips on the snowy ground and stumbles, but quickly rights herself and climbs, plowing past the stray bits of scrub brush that line the path. When she finally reaches the summit, the sight forces her to stop in her tracks.

The expanse of old bombed-out houses and yards lies before her, with dozens of toppled and rotting trees crisscrossing under the surface of the snow. Her home is in the distance, and she can see thick black smoke billowing from the front windows. Even from here, she sees the two lifeless lumps in her front yard, surrounded by a scarlet that contrasts too terribly with the white ground around them.

As she breaks into a fresh run, she can hear the wail of the siren behind her, starting low, building to a scream.

She races into her yard and flies past the dead dogs lying in the two slight depressions their warm blood has melted into the snow. Her mind registers that their throats have been slashed, ear to ear, and she thinks of the razor-sharp knife that cut them. She runs onto the front porch, but the smoke is too thick to enter the house here, and she spins around and hurries to the back.

The garden gate is hanging open. "Please, God. Please, God. Please, God," she repeats in her head as she bursts into the smoke-filled kitchen. She coughs as the acrid air fills her lungs.

The cellar door in the kitchen is wide open. "No!" she screams, falling to the floor to look inside. Jars and bags are shattered and scattered in the small cellar, but there is no sign of her girls. Kate stands again and tries to make her way to the bedroom, but the heat is too much, and she has to run back outside.

She darts around to the bedroom window and pries off the corrugated plastic that covers it. Part of it has melted—it sticks to her hands, burning the skin, but she barely notices. "Margaret! Laura!" she screams. Between waves of smoke, she sees that the room is empty.

Backing away, Kate whirls around, frantically searching for a trail in the snow that might lead her to her daughters. She finds nothing, and runs to the shed, praying for a miracle that might have her girls safe inside. No one is there.

Kate stops, frozen in the realization that he has taken her daughters. Her panic is so deep that the world spins around her, and she collapses to the ground. She stares straight ahead, bargaining with God, begging for the chance to die if they could only be safe. She doesn't know how long she sits there, her body crumpled above her bent legs in the snow.

Suddenly, a thought leaps into her mind, and she rises and bolts out of the yard. She follows the irrigation ditch to the river, and flies over the small wooden bridge to the frozen fields on the other side. Her feet sink, tangling in the long blades of wheat that are blanketed below the snow. At the edge of the field, she pauses and looks up to the spot where she first saw the man. His camp must be up there, she thinks.

Though the muscles in her legs scream, she runs again, driven by the urgency of finding him before he can get too far. In the forest, the snow is shallower, and she has an easier time. She tears through the woods, unmindful of the breaking branches and twigs that crack beneath her feet. She has only a rough idea of the direction, and as the blood rushes through her head, she prays for divine intervention.

Suddenly, she sees him. He is walking quickly in her direction, his head down, pushing aside branches with his outstretched arms. Kate reaches to her belt. She pulls the heavy knife from its sheath and, gripping the tip of the blade, pulls it back behind her head.

Michael looks up the split second before she throws the knife at him, and as it hurtles through the air, he dives to the side.

"Kate!" he yells, tripping over a snag of branches and falling to one knee.

She is running at him, and he jumps to his feet and backs away. Defenseless now, she stops ten feet in front of him.

"Give me my daughters!" she screams.

"Kate, stop!" he shouts, looking surprised at her fury.

"Where are they? What did you do to them?" Through her anger, tears begin to stream down her face.

"They're fine! They were with me!"

"Where are they?"

"Kate! They're okay. Just calm down!" He holds his hands out in front of himself, as if to show her he means no harm, but he does not step closer. "I can bring them back."

"You're lying. You've always been lying!"

"Kate, Christ. I'm telling you, they're fine! I brought them to the camp we used to stay at." Michael lowers his arms and looks around nervously into the trees behind Kate. "What did you think?"

"I saw the house and the dogs. I saw everything. Michael, please just give me my girls."

"You think *I* did that? Kate, we were working on the dam. Chopping out the ice. The dogs started barking and ran to the front yard, and we saw them coming."

"Saw who?" she asks, bewildered.

"The men. There were four of them. I grabbed Laura and Margaret, and we just started running. I didn't know if they saw us, so we didn't stop until we got to my camp. I can see your house from up there." He pauses to catch his breath and bends over to put his hands on his knees. He cranes his neck to look up at her. "A little while later, we saw them leave, carrying everything in carts. Then we saw the smoke. Are you okay?"

She stares at him, confused by his words. She wants to believe he is telling the truth, but she remembers what Evan revealed at the school.

"Why should I believe you?" she says. "Everything you've ever told me was a lie!"

"What lie? What are you talking about?"

"Evan told us everything. He told us how you took him from his real father. You stole him!"

"I am his real father!" he shouts, standing up straight again. "He just didn't know it before."

"You're lying!"

"I'm not lying! Kate, everything I told you was true. I never lied. Claire took me in when I got to Cantonis. She let me live next door to her, and I helped her."

"You said you were married."

"I never said that." He closes his eyes and shakes his head as he catches his breath. When he opens them again, he says, "She was already married to Mateo, but they needed my help. He was injured in the war. His back was broken. He couldn't walk. He couldn't do anything."

"But you said you loved her."

"I did love her. It didn't start out that way. I was just trying to help them. But after a few months, it just sort of happened. She needed me as much as I needed her."

Sobs heave up into her throat, and she lifts her hands, pressing her palms into her eyes. "What about Evan?" she asks, looking at Michael again.

"When he was born, everybody knew he was my son. And Mateo hated me for it. When Claire got really sick, she told me he was going to have me arrested as soon as she died." His shoulders slump, and he quietly continues. "I'm not proud of what I did. I would have married Claire if I could have. And I didn't want all this for Evan. Jesus, I might have even left without him if Mateo had cared at all about Evan, but he didn't. He hated him, too."

Kate shakes her head from side to side and moans, "Why didn't you tell me any of this before? Why should I believe you now?"

Anger flashes in Michael's eyes, and he hisses, "Stop acting like this is all my fault. You could have just asked about my past, but you never did. You didn't want to know." He glances around as sees the knife wedged in the ground nearby. Fear rises in Kate again as he quickly stoops to pull it from the earth.

"This isn't about me, Michael," she says, trying to calm him. "Just tell me where the girls are. Please."

"I told you! Jesus, Kate, do you really think I would do something like this?" His arm sweeps out into the forest in the direction of the burning house, the knife held tight in his hand.

"Just put down the knife and we can talk about it. Put it down so I can trust you."

"Trust? Are you kidding me?" he says. "You can't trust me?" As he says this, he gestures with the knife, pointing first at her then back at himself. "After all I've told you, and done for you!"

"I don't know!" she yells. "Please," she begs, falling to her knees before him. "Please just give me my girls. You can take anything. Please just give me my babies."

"After I let you take my son into your neighborhood?" He pauses, and then shouts, "Fuck you, Kate! I trusted you, and you come running back here like this? Fuck you and your trust!"

"Michael, stop!" she shouts. "I'm sorry! I just want to see my girls. Please just tell me where they are."

She hears the slice of the first arrow as it cuts through the cold air, but she is still surprised when she sees the shaft of it sticking out of his shoulder. Michael takes one step backward, wincing in pain. He looks down at the wood and feathers, and reaches his hand up to touch the strange thing as he begins to feel the hot ooze of the blood dribbling down his chest. A second arrow flies past him, and he raises his head to meet Kate's eyes.

"No," she whispers, and tries to stand. A third arrow lands deep in his right thigh, and he crumbles to the ground, falling onto his side. She half walks, half crawls across the ground to him, and kneels beside him in the snow. She can hear the women calling to her, and the branches breaking as they thunder through the forest.

"No," she moans, and touches the places he's been hit. "Oh, Michael, I'm sorry. I'm so sorry."

He doesn't speak but watches her face as she tries to make sense of what has happened. When she finally looks into his eyes, he holds her gaze. The depth of the sadness and betrayal has turned his face somber and gray.

"You're going to be okay. We have a good doctor here. You're going to be okay." She tries to give him an encouraging look, but her face falls as he continues to stare. He looks resolved, as if he knew this fate would find him eventually. As she watches, she feels as if she can see the very moment he gives up on her, on all of them. He shakes his head, a miniscule movement from left to right. The light in his eyes, the light that had lured her into believing in the possibility of a future together, fades away.

"I'm sorry," she repeats, but his dull blue eyes only stare at her. Then he blinks and turns his head to the side, looking away. "Michael, please," she whispers. "I'll fix it."

Kate feels a hand on her shoulder and looks up to see Iris bending behind her. She holds her bow in her left hand, and she is panting. "Kate, step away," she says.

"No. Iris, no. I was wrong. It wasn't him."

"Kate, come on. Come on, honey, stand up. We'll take care of this."

Other women are already crowding around. Their hands reach out to take the knife from him. He doesn't resist. Iris pulls Kate up and drags her away.

"He didn't do it," Kate pleads. "I was wrong. He says there were raiders. It wasn't him." She looks around for someone else who might listen to her, but sees only the women breaking down long branches, tying them into a litter that can carry the man back to the neighborhood. "Iris, you have to believe me!"

But Iris moves away from Kate. She walks to Michael and crouches beside him. For a few minutes, she quietly questions him, asking him where the girls are, then asking for directions to the camp. Michael answers all of her questions in a monotone.

When the litter is ready, they lift him onto it and begin to pull him through the snow toward town. Iris walks back to Kate and says, "I think we can find Laura and Margaret. He says they're alive."

"I should go with him," Kate says. "I should go with him to the doctor."

"Kate," Iris says calmly as she reaches out to lead her in the other direction. "Come on. We have to help the girls."

~ Twenty-One ~

THE PAIN FILLS HER so completely she cannot think. It is like a wave rolling through her, starting low in her belly, swelling and growing as it consumes her. Her body moves without her conscious control. Her mind is overwhelmed by the urgency and agony.

Kate squats on the floor next to the mattress, with her feet spread wide on the blankets laid out below her. Her hands hold tight to Jonah's hips, and her head is pressed deep into his breastbone. He is kneeling on the edge of the mattress in front of her. Straining to hold her up, he clasps his hands behind her shoulder blades, his arms tucked firmly under her armpits. Kate has no idea what time it is, has no idea how long she has been doing this. Hours, she thinks. She is in a place deep within herself, fully engulfed in her task. As the pain subsides, she opens her eyes and notices that someone has lit the small lantern in the room. In the dim light, she sees her son's legs below her. He is wearing shorts on this hot July night, and, for some reason, the detail of the hair growing on his thighs is suddenly so clear to her. She focuses on that for the few seconds before another contraction begins to grow.

"Try to relax your jaw," Margaret says, pushing firmly on the back of Kate's hips with the heel of her palms. "Try to breathe deeply."

Kate closes her eyes and inhales as the next wave of pain washes over her. Her hips slowly swivel counterclockwise, and she imagines the baby's head pushing against her cervix, the pressure of it helping to open her. Open, she thinks. Open. With a loud exhale, her lower lip flops and her teeth chatter. She moans deep and low.

"Can you see anything?" Margaret asks Laura.

Laura is kneeling down behind Kate, her head close to the floor. She holds the lantern in her hand, angling it between her mother's bare legs. "I don't think so. I don't know." She shakes her head. "I'll put the bag of towels in the oven to warm." She sets down the lantern and quickly goes to the other room.

They were able to salvage the iron housing of the cookstove, but the electrical system was melted into a formless blob. Very little survived the fire. Forced to live in town during that long winter, the family spent two-week stints at other women's homes, trying not to wear out their welcome. In the early spring, Kate moved them all back out here, and they began the process of building an addition onto the shed where she and Michael had spent their nights together.

The neighborhood women helped them with the construction and donated pieces of clothing, dishes, supplies, and food. Iris and Sarah had worked together to make a new mattress and build a wooden frame to hold it off the floor. They took the shed door off its hinges, and transferred it to the new entrance at the front of the addition. They set up this new room as the kitchen and built a small table with four sturdy chairs.

Once the addition was finished, Rhia stayed with them for a week and helped Kate rig a chimney for the stove. Everything was difficult without electricity, but at least they were able to build a small fire for cooking again. Two large pots now sit on top of the stove, full of steaming water that Jonah collected from the river earlier in the day.

A loud moan begins to rumble up from inside Kate. It grows as she drops her jaw, rocking into the pain. When the wave breaks and crashes a minute later, she opens her eyes again. "I'm so hot," she whines. Letting go of Jonah for a moment, she reaches behind her back and unhooks her bra. She pulls it off and throws it to the floor. "I hate this!" she shouts, before wrapping her arms around him again.

Kate's face contorts as the next contraction begins, and the pitch of her moan begins to rise. She can hear Margaret's voice, telling her to relax, gently telling her to take long deep breaths, but she can't respond. It feels like there is a belt wrapped around her huge belly, somehow squeezing her and tearing her apart at the same time.

There are only a few seconds between the end of this contraction and the beginning of the next. Barely time to rest. But when it starts again, the feeling has changed. She no longer feels the stretching and pulling deep inside her. Suddenly, she feels only a heavy pressure, very low. Instinctively, she knows it is time to push, and with a grunt, she bears down, squeezing her abdomen. The memory of her other babies comes to her, and she can picture their tiny faces in the first moments after they were born. "Come on, baby. Come on, sweet baby."

The kitchen door bangs closed, and an out-of-breath woman rounds the corner to the bedroom. Her white hair is pulled into a tight bun. She unbuckles her backpack and swings it to the floor. Laura runs in and stands nearby, taking the equipment from her as she pulls it from the bag. A stethoscope, a pair of scissors tightly wrapped and tied in cloth, an oxygen mask with a thick leather bag attached, a large pouch of herbs, a ball of string. She sets each piece on a clean towel stretched out flat on the second mattress.

"How is she?" Dr. Preston asks, wiping her forehead with the back of her arm.

"Doing okay, I think," Margaret replies.

"How close are the contractions?"

"Right on top of each other."

Dr. Preston quickly moves to Kate and kneels behind her. She sets her hand on Kate's back and says, "Kate, it's Dr. Preston. I'm here now." Laura holds the lantern in position to help her see.

Through a low moan, Kate grunts one word. "Pushing."

"Okay." Standing up, she hurries out of the room, calling over her shoulder as she goes, "I'm going to wash my hands. I'll be right back."

Kate's moans have turned into long, deep roars, a primal and powerful sound. Between pushes, she whispers, "Come on, sweet baby." Her body moves on its own, rocking and bending. Her arms pull so hard on Jonah he has to brace himself to keep from being knocked over. In her mind, she can see the baby's head, hard and round, trying to squeeze through the space. She hardly notices Laura wipe the sweat from her brow.

Suddenly, she feels the head drop down inside her. "The baby's coming," she whispers in the tiny space between the nearly constant contractions. With the next deep roar, she pushes hard and feels the head slowly move, inch by excruciating inch, forcing her to open and stretch in its path.

Everything in the world ceases to exist beyond her body.

The only thing she knows is this pain and this pressure. The only thing she knows is that she must push this baby out. Three minutes later, when the head crowns, her eyes squeeze tightly shut. The ring of pain feels like she is on fire. A sound comes out of her, low at first, growing and rising through the octaves as it builds to a loud and mournful scream, splitting the night. And with a popping sound and a gush of fluid, the baby's head comes out.

"Oh!" Kate flings her head up, and her eyes open wide with the rush of adrenaline that flies through her veins. She feels like every light in the world has been turned on at once, and for the first time in hours, she sees the room around her with perfect clarity. Jonah is leaning back, straining to support her. Margaret and Laura kneel on both sides of her, their hands on her arms and her back.

Evan runs into the room, panting and sweating. Kate turns her head and looks at him. She gives him a weak smile, grateful that he ran to town to get the doctor.

Jonah sees him, too, and says, "Evan, get the towels out of the oven."

"One more push to get the shoulders out, Kate," Dr. Preston quietly says. She is behind Kate, her hands on the baby's head, gently holding it as it rotates.

"I can't do it," Kate breathes.

"You are doing it. One more."

One more push and the baby slides out into Dr. Preston's hands. She expertly catches it and lays the baby on the blankets below Kate. "These are all wet. Give me one of the warm ones."

Evan runs back in, opens the cloth bag, and pulls out a towel. He gives it to Dr. Preston and watches as she loosely wraps the baby, rubbing her hands over its body.

"Kate, can you move up to the bed?"

"I'm so tired."

"Kids, help her up. Come on."

The four children do their best to guide Kate onto the mattress. Crawling carefully, she maneuvers her body back to the corner and turns around, leaning against the pillows wedged there. She has to lift her leg over the umbilical cord as Dr. Preston dips the baby under her foot.

Dr. Preston sets the motionless baby on her chest, then reaches a hand out to Evan. He hands her another warm towel, and she begins to vigorously rub the baby's head, arms, legs, and torso, being careful of the thick, ropy cord that pulses rich oxygenated blood from the placenta.

"Hi, sweet baby," Kate croons. "Come on, sweetie."

"That's good," Dr. Preston says. "Just keep talking."

Finally, the tiny baby begins to squirm. Kate watches the little head lift, and sees its chest expand as air rushes into its lungs. Its mouth wriggles open, and a loud cry fills the room. Kate smiles down at the new baby in her arms. The children look around at each other, laughing at the sound.

The ten fingers are curled into tight fists, and Kate gently pries them open, examining each hand, slowly going over the baby's body, inspecting the arms, belly, legs, and tiny toes. Everything looks perfect. She looks back at the baby's beautiful face, and watches as its eyes open, blinking at the new world. They are a brilliant blue, shining just like Michael's.

Dr. Preston busies herself, checking Kate's pulse, monitoring mother and baby for any signs of trouble. Kate snuggles the baby to her breast, and marvels at the way the little head instinctively knows to turn toward her. She gently passes her knuckle over the baby's mouth, flipping the lower lip down as she expertly guides the latch. Margaret and Laura are huddled around Kate, cooing and doting on the baby. Jonah and Evan are right behind them, reaching their hands to touch the tiny feet poking out of the bottom of the warm towel. They are so enthralled by the funny wiggles and grunts, that no one hears the kitchen door gently close.

Michael hobbles around the corner of the bedroom. He is out of breath, and leans over to rub his right thigh where the arrow had been. He winces in pain and takes two limping steps into the room as he looks up. Kate lifts her eyes to meet his, and a huge smile beams from her face. He doesn't smile, doesn't speak, but slowly moves to the side of the bed.

Kate watches him lean closer, trying to see, and she tugs the towel away from the baby's head a bit. She watches Michael's eyes, waiting for his reaction. She has worked so hard to win back his trust over the last seven months. She has argued with the women of the neighborhood for his sake, traded everything she could to pay for Dr. Preston's help in nursing his wounds, and suffered through the months of his silence and anger. Once he could walk, her children helped him build the small hut in the woods where he and Evan chose to stay, and she made the trip to his home every day to leave food outside his always-closed door.

Now, here she lies, with his baby on her breast, hoping for some sign of forgiveness. Michael silently watches the newborn nurse for several minutes, then with a trembling sigh, eases himself down onto the mattress near Kate. She pokes her pinkie into the corner of the baby's mouth, breaking the latch. Turning the warm bundle in her arms, she angles herself so Michael can see the child more clearly.

"It's a boy," she whispers and looks up to meet Michael's eyes. He blinks, and she sees a tear spill down over his cheek. He holds her gaze, and she thinks she can see a small smile begin to curve the corners of his mouth. The baby moves his head from side to side, and he opens his eyes.

Acknowledgments

Thank you to Leslie Wells and Elizabeth Johnson, whose gentle and wise editing helped this book evolve into something much more concise and interesting than I could have come up with alone. To CJ Casson, for the author photograph.

Thanks also go to Tristan Uecker and Maggie Czajkiewicz, for letting me ramble on about this idea long before it was a real story, and for finding the time to read my drafts between raising all their own wonderful children. To Lori Bennett, for all her technical help and moral support. And to David Thibodeau, for his decades of *Tales from an Old Timer*.

Finally, thank you to Alex, Marin, Rowan, and Skylar, for being patient with me and allowing me time to sit at the computer when you would have much rather been snuggling.

About the Author

Kari Aguila has lived in Wisconsin, Massachusetts, Maine, Idaho, New York, Texas, and Washington. She was a geologist for many years before taking on the challenge of raising her three wonderful children. Although she has numerous scientific publications, this is her first novel. She currently lives in Seattle with her husband, two beautiful daughters, and one seriously handsome son.

68205255R00179

Made in the USA
Lexington, KY
04 October 2017